PRETEND WE'RE OVER

A Fake Marriage Romance

ELLA MILES

PROLOGUE

MILLIE

I open my eyes, and I'm staring at the hottest man I've ever seen in real life. And he's in my bed! Well, technically not *my* bed—we are in the honeymoon suite of the Paris Hotel. So not my bed, but it doesn't matter because he's naked and adorable, and any minute now I'm going to wake up and realize that this is all a dream.

I pinch myself.

But Sebastian King is still in my bed. I'm still staring at his muscled chest. A chest I could reach out and touch and—

A blaring alarm goes off, and I squeeze my eyes shut. I'm not ready for Sebastian to realize I'm awake yet. I need time to process—to put everything in order in my head.

Everything is fuzzy at best. I remember coming to this hotel room with Sebastian to wait for our friends—Oaklee and Boden. This is their room. *So how did we end up using it?*

I don't know.

But here we are. Two people, who are basically

strangers, in bed together—strangers who turned quickly into enemies.

We don't belong in bed together. We don't belong together period. Yet, here we are.

I open my eyes, letting him know that I'm awake. And that's when the accusations begin. I blame him, tell him it's all his fault, even though I know it's not.

I just wish I remembered what happened. *We couldn't have fucked each other?* I don't do one night stands. I don't do men in general. I've sworn them off for the time being.

And yet, all the evidence points to us fucking.

Us waking up in the same bed.

Him completely naked.

Me wearing his shirt and boxers.

The opened condom wrapper.

There is no denying that we fucked.

I grip the shirt I'm wearing tighter. Of course, the first man I've fucked in forever, I can't even remember.

I sigh—*this is just my life.*

I won't let it get me down, though. The fucking isn't the part I have a problem with.

"I think you should put some clothes on," I say.

"Why? Are you hoping for a round two? Because I don't—"

"No, that's not it."

"Then what? Does my naked body make you uncomfortable?"

He hasn't figured it out yet. There is one clue that he hasn't found yet.

I hold up my left hand, flashing the pretty rock that wasn't there yesterday.

He shakes his head, not understanding.

God, he's such an idiot.

I point to the ring, pointing out the obvious.

"Fuck, Millie, you're engaged?"

I roll my eyes. He thinks he fucked an engaged woman. I would never, ever cheat.

"No. At least, I don't think I'm just engaged." I think a lot more than just getting engaged happened last night.

"Is that Oaklee's ring? Are you safeguarding it?"

I shake my head. Oaklee's ring is pink; this one is gold.

"Okay...what am I missing?" he asks.

I nod my head in the direction of his left hand, unable to find the words.

His eyes follow my gaze.

"No way," he says, staring at the gold ring he's sporting on his left ring finger.

"No!" he says again.

I wince but force myself to say the words. "I think we got married last night."

1 SEBASTIAN

"I'm getting married tomorrow!" Boden yells through the heavy beat of the bass in the bar's too-loud sound system. He slams down his shot glass before throwing it back.

We all follow suit—all twenty of us. Ten males, ten females all gathered in one section of a strip club on the Las Vegas strip.

This would be most men's heaven. Half-naked women are dancing all around and over us. We have unlimited alcohol, and the only thing that will stop us is the night ending, which by the look of the happy couple, should have already ended. But it's just past eleven at night—the night is still young.

Boden, the groom, is getting handsier and handsier with the woman dancing all over him as he tucks dollar bills into her thong. While Oaklee, the bride, keeps getting more and more sloshed, pretending she's completely okay with what her soon to be husband is doing. She's not, but she won't start her marriage by nagging.

"Can I get you another drink?" A waiter wearing tight black shorts and a shirt that barely covers her double D boobs asks me. She picks up the shot glasses littering the table in front of me.

Before I can answer, I feel all surrounding eyes on me. My brother, Kade, looks at me with suspicion. My sister-in-law, Larkyn, looks at me with pride in her eyes like she knows I'm going to say the right thing. My friend, Shepherd, looks at me nervously, like he's going to be the one to pick up the pieces if I fall off the wagon.

It's been over ten years—over a decade of sobriety. And still, everyone thinks that I'm one mistake from falling back into my old ways. I'm not a twenty-something alcoholic anymore. I'm not addicted to drugs. I'm sober. I'm clean.

I haven't put one toe out of step this entire time, but the way all of my friends and family are acting, it's clear they think I am one wrong choice away from turning into the old Sebastian—the fuck up. The boy who was hell-bent on destroying my own life by drinking away the pain.

They're right. That's the life of an addict. I'm always one wrong choice away from throwing away all the work I've done, but that's why I live the way I do. I don't put myself into these situations often. I don't go to bars, strip clubs, or anywhere with temptation.

The only reason I'm in the most tempting place of all is because my best friend is getting married—the last of my friend group to do so. I wouldn't miss it, even though he chose the worst place in the world for a recovering addict like me.

When Boden told me, he was the only one not concerned that I might slip into old habits. He doesn't understand that for an addict like me, I'm either drinking or recovering, there is no middle ground. It's something I've learned running a healing and recovery center with Larkyn

—you are either doing the program, or you're an addict. Once you stop, it's all over.

"Just a club soda with lime, thanks," I say.

The waitress smiles at me before getting Shepherd's order.

"See, told you he wouldn't slip up," Larkyn says, giving me a wink as she snuggles into Kades's shoulder.

He looks at me with a tightness in his jaw and a squint to his eyes like he doesn't believe me. But then, he never does. He's my older brother, he's married, has three children, and an empire to run. He still looks at me as the screwup. I'm single and work for my sister-in-law, not exactly grown-up in his eyes. He thinks the only way I can be happy and show that I'm an adult is if I live my life like him—married with kids.

He doesn't realize that's exactly what would cause me to fall back into old habits.

The waitress returns with our drinks, and I take my drink that looks like a mixed vodka drink. I don't usually care to order drinks that make me feel like I'm drinking, but here in this club, I just want to fit in with as few questions as possible.

Oaklee stumbles over onto the couch I'm sitting on. We all turn our attention to her. She's wearing a white dress complete with a sash that reads 'bride' and a sparkly tiara. Her outfit is screaming for attention, but her eyes keep cutting over to Boden, whose buttoned-down shirt is now open as a woman dances over him with her tits in his face.

"So, are you ready to get married tomorrow?" Larkyn asks her.

"Of course, I've never been more excited," Oaklee answers, pretending to look at Larkyn, but still staring at her fiancé.

"What about you, Sebastian? When are you getting married?" Val, one of the bridesmaids, asks, as she sits on Shepherd's, her husband's, lap.

I frown at her but notice that her question has even gained the attention of Oaklee. So I guess it's worth it to make Oaklee feel better while, Boden, my best friend, makes an ass of himself. Oaklee seems cool, but she's not that cool. She may not bring this up for years to come, but someday, she will. When they are fighting about whose turn it is to cook dinner, or why he bought another bottle of fancy liquor when they can barely afford to pay for little Oaklee's dance classes, this will come back up. And on that day, Boden will wish he had listened to me when I told him having strippers at a joint bachelor and bachelorette party was a bad idea. There is one male stripper, but other than one obligatory striptease, Oaklee hasn't let him anywhere near her. While Boden has been attached to one stripper or another all night.

"Not anytime soon," I chuckle and give her a wicked grin making it seem like I like playing the field. Really, it's just self-preservation keeping me from getting married. Every person here is married, or is about to be married, except me. We are in our mid-thirties. That's what happens. I'm the only lone wolf left, and it's going to stay that way.

Val rolls her eyes at me as she strokes her husband's face. "You just don't realize what you're missing. Still such a boy."

I take a deep breath to stop from bulldozing over her and telling her that I'm not a boy. I'm all man. Choosing not to get married doesn't make me a boy. She thinks I spend my nights plowing into any girl I can get into my bed. Sure,

I fuck often, but I treat every woman I'm with well. I'm not a playboy. I just don't want to get married.

"What about Simone? I thought you two were getting serious?" Oaklee asks, looking at me with big red-shot eyes, slurring her words. I stare at the drink in her hand. She's had more than enough to drink tonight, but she has no intention of stopping anytime soon. This is her last night of freedom. Her last night to party before marriage, and she's not going to let her soon to be husband outdo her, even though we all know he can drink her under the table.

"Nah, we weren't serious. We only dated two months," I answer.

"For you, that's a long time."

I stiffen. *Don't let her comment bother you. She doesn't mean anything by it.*

"I think Simone's already engaged to Reece," Larkyn says, trying to cover for me, but she's only going to make it worse.

Simone and I stopped 'dating' last month. The fact that she's already engaged makes me look worse, not better.

"When did you and Simone break up?" Oaklee asks.

I give Larkyn an annoyed glare before turning sweetly to Oaklee. "We were never really together."

She smirks. "So, you just fucked?"

"If that's what you want to call it, yes. We fucked. We weren't ever in an emotionally committed relationship. We were always free to see other people." In fact, we only fucked once. That's my rule. One night of fun and then move on. It just took me a while to get to the one night with Simone. She kept holding out hope that if we dated a while first, by the time we had our one night together, I would want more.

"You're such a slut, Sebastian. You're thirty now. When are you going to stop sleeping with other people's wives?"

My lips fall. "Simone wasn't married. She wasn't engaged. She—"

"She was clearly dating this man if she's already engaged while you two were fucking. You could have ruined something special. Maybe Simone thought she had a chance to change you, to get you to propose."

I run my hand through my hair and then sip on my bubbly water. For the first time all night, I wish it was spiked with something so I could deal with these women.

Simone knew what she was getting when it came to me —amazing sex. That's it. That's all I ever offered her.

"Actually, I think Simone rekindled an old relationship right after she and Sebastian stopped...well, whatever they were doing. They realized they weren't getting any younger, and wanted to get married right away," Larkyn says, once again trying to save me, and once again, putting her foot in her mouth.

"Exactly, at our age, you should want to get married and get settled down. That's the mature, proper thing to do," Oaklee says smugly before looking dreamily over at her almost-husband who had his hands down a lady's thong.

"Charming," I say under my breath.

"What did you say?" Oaklee asks, turning back to me.

"You heard me. Not everyone is cut out for marriage. I just happen to think that it's mature to realize you shouldn't get married before you pop the question."

Oaklee pouts, full lip out, and I swear there are tears behind her eyes.

Shit.

I was too harsh. I shouldn't have said that to a woman who is clearly having doubts about getting married tomorrow. I know my best friend. He's a good guy, just an idiot when it comes to reading other people.

I lean over and pull her into a hug before I whisper into her ear, "Boden's a good guy. You two are great together. You found one of the good ones; I'm just not like Boden. I'd make a terrible husband."

I hear her sniffle into my shoulder. *Fuck, is she really crying?*

I try to glance down without pulling her away and exposing her tears, but I can't. All I hear are her gentle sobs.

Larkyn and Kade stand up and walk over to us. "The sitter called. We have to go," Larkyn says.

"Oaklee, did you hear that?" I ask.

More soft sobbing.

"Um...okay. I'll get a ride back to the hotel soon. And um...Oaklee, we'll see you tomorrow," I say.

Kade just shakes his head at me, and I can read his silent words. *You're the asshole who made the bride cry the night before her wedding. You figure out how to get out of this mess.*

Larkyn squeezes my shoulder as if to say good luck. *Get her a drink*, Larkyn mouths at me.

I raise my eyebrows. *Really?* This woman doesn't need more alcohol. She needs a bed and to sleep it off.

Larkyn smiles sweetly. "Have a goodnight, Oaklee. I can't wait until tomorrow." She strokes Oaklee's hair and then is gone.

The rest of the bridal party gets back to doing shots, sloppy dancing, and lap dances. Leaving me alone with Oaklee, who I swear has turned from sobbing to snoring.

"Oaklee?" I ask, trying to unglue her from my shoulder.

"Hmm." She rocks back.

"What are you drinking? I should get you another

drink. Why don't you go pull that fiancé of yours onto the dance floor?"

Her eyes light up. "I want another one of those fizzy drinks that light up."

I smile. "Can do."

Then I turn to her fiancé, who thankfully is done with the lap dances. "Dance with your fiancé!"

He grins, and I push Oaklee into his arms, while I carry my own drink toward the bar to go buy Oaklee another drink. Not that she needs it, but it gives me something to do until I can leave. I don't have the excuse of kids like Larkyn and Kade do. As everyone pointed out, I'm single. I'll be expected to close down the club with the rest of them.

I'm walking toward the bar when I'm ambushed from the side, a swish of hair, makeup, and freckled skin knocks into me, jarring my glass from my hand. Some of it splatters onto my dark jeans, but that's the thing about not drinking, it's just water.

I look up, expecting to see a drunk woman wearing nine-inch heels, a heavy cast of makeup, and a tight skirt. What I get is jeans, a black tee with the name of some band I've never heard of, and off-white sneakers. Her makeup is tame compared to all the other women here. The only thing I got right was her mane of strawberry blonde hair in thick waves around her face. Her hair isn't highlighted or cut in professional layers; her hair is as wild as the twinkle in her green eyes. The only thing that tells me she's part of our party is the sash she's wearing across her body with the word 'bridesmaid' on it.

"Oh my god! I'm so sorry," the woman says. She starts trying to brush off the liquid on my pants with her hand, like that is somehow going to magically soak up the splotches of club soda on my pants.

"What are you doing?" I ask.

She blushes. It's an adorable shade of pink below her pale, freckled covered cheeks that make her look likes she's about fifteen. But one glance below her adorable cheeks tells me she's all woman. Even though she's wearing an oversized T-shirt and jeans, it doesn't hide the swell of her breasts and the curve of her hips, leaving me watering. She may not be my normal type, but I can appreciate a beautiful woman's body when I see it.

"Sorry." She immediately stops trying to dry up the water on my pants and realizes her hand had slipped dangerously close to copping a feel.

Her gaze drops to the shattered glass on the floor. "I'm so sorry. Let me buy you a new drink to make it up to you. I'm not usually a stumbling drunk like this."

She's rambling. It's enchanting, but she's in the bridal party. Everyone is married in the bridal party, except me, and I don't flirt with other men's women.

"No," I say.

"No? Please, I insist...What's your name?"

"Sebastian. And you don't need to buy me a drink. All the drinks are free, courtesy of the bride and groom."

"Oh, I know, I just meant that I should at least order you another drink and get it for you so that you can keep enjoying whatever you were doing. Another lap dance or whatever or..." Her cheeks blush again as she blinks rapidly like she's batting her eyes, but I don't think she realizes she's doing it. "I'm Millie, by the way. Amelia, actually, but everyone calls me Millie. I'm getting you a drink. I—"

"Millie," I say, putting my hands on her shoulders, trying to get her to stop rambling. "You really don't need to get me a drink."

"No, but I insist. I don't want you to think of me as the

drunk who spilled your drink all over you. What were you drinking?" She looks me up and down and then to the drink on the floor.

"Vodka?" she asks.

"No."

She scrunches her nose up as she tries again. "Gin?"

"No."

"What were you drinking then?"

I sigh. I don't like telling people that I'm not drinking. They never understand why, especially in a setting like this. It's not that I'm embarrassed to be a recovering alcoholic, but I don't usually broadcast it.

"Club soda with lime," I finally answer.

"Oh." Just one syllable, but I know more is about to spill out of her. "Well, I don't feel so bad now because club soda shouldn't stain." She holds up her own drink. "I should switch to club soda; it's more fun than what I'm drinking."

I study her clear drink in her hand for the first time. "Which is?"

"Water." Her cheeks burn red again. "I'm on a diet. Alcohol is one of the biggest culprits of weight gain."

I blink rapidly, taking in her words. *Diet?* What beautiful woman like her needs to be on a diet? But I don't ask more. If it's just an excuse to not explain why she's not drinking, who am I to judge? She could be an addict like me, or pregnant and not ready to tell yet. There could be a million reasons why and none of them matter to me. After this weekend, I doubt I'll ever see Millie again. She must be one of Oaklee's friends. And as much as I like Boden, I don't plan on hanging out with his wife's friends after this weekend.

I realize that she's stopped talking and is staring at me,

waiting for something, but I was more fascinated with the way her lips moved than what was coming out of them.

I'm an ass.

"I don't want a hangover tomorrow."

She nods. "I'll go get you that drink."

I shake my head as I put my hands in my pocket to keep from touching the curves in front of me hidden beneath layers of clothes. There is something about her that intrigues me. But whatever mystery she's hiding, it will stay hidden.

I didn't spot a ring on her finger, but if my pregnant theory is correct, her hands may be too swollen to wear her ring. I remember when it happened to Larkyn. I don't know which of the lucky bastards here gets to call her his wife, but he's definitely lucky. She seems more real than any of the other chicks here, even if she is a little strange.

She and I would never work, though. A woman like Millie is looking for forever. She expects a good man who flatters her and brings her romantic gifts—I'm not that man. I'm focused, disciplined. I work out two times a day, eat three perfect meals, meditate, journal, and crunch numbers to keep the business afloat. That's my day. I don't have room for a woman like Millie. A woman who is wild and untamed and seems to dance to her own drum. I have room for an occasional fuck, nothing more.

"Don't bother with the drink, I've had enough anyway." And with that, I start toward the group of guys chatting with Boden. I need to get away from her before I make a mistake. A man like me can't make a single mistake. For me, a single mistake leads to a lifetime of fuck ups, and I've worked too hard to mess it all up now.

2 MILLIE

I watch Sebastian walk away toward the groom. *God, his ass looks great in those jeans.* It's tight and firm, and damn do I want to run my tongue all over it...

"Earth to Millie," Oaklee says, snapping me out of my haze.

"What?" I say, taking a seat next to Oaklee and across from Cynthia.

"What are you staring at?" Oaklee asks, sitting up in her chair to get a better look.

"Nothing," I mumble into my water.

"That's not nothing. That's Sebastian King," Oaklee says, her voice rising higher as she speaks.

"Sebastian, who?" Of course, his last name has to be King—figures. He looks like royalty in his deep blue shirt, dark jeans, and muscles for days.

"Sebastian King," Oaklee says again before pulling the straw of her fruity drink into her mouth and staring at me with a knowing smile.

I lean back in my chair. "Am I supposed to know the name or something?"

"No, but you should definitely get to know the man. He's cute."

"So? There are a lot of cute men here."

"He's single. He's like the only man here who is our age and still single."

I huff. "So because he's the only single man here, that means I should go after him? Sorry, but I'll pass."

Oaklee and Cynthia trade glances. "No, you should go after him because he's hot."

I still, trying not to react because my friends mean well. Really, they do, but they don't understand my life. They don't understand that a man like Sebastian King would never go after a woman like me. Even if he did, I'm not interested. My life is too complicated to get involved with a guy right now.

"Please. There are plenty of hot, single men here."

"Where?" Oaklee asks, batting her eyelashes at me.

We scour the room, but every man my eyes turn to seems to be coupled off.

"What about him?" I point to a man in tight jeans, tattoos, and long hair. He's not really my type, he's kind of got a biker vibe going on, but I'm trying to prove a point, not actually date the guy.

"Gay," Cynthia answers.

"No, he's—" I start, but then a skinny man in leather walks over and kisses him firmly on the lips. "Fine, he's gay. That doesn't mean..."

"Honey, you're thirty-two and at the last of your single friends' weddings. I'm not saying there aren't single men out there. There are plenty, but not here. Even if there were plenty of single men in this bar, Sebastian King would still top them all. I mean, look at the guy," Cynthia says.

We all turn to Sebastian. He's talking with two of the

groomsmen, who are both married. He really is the only single guy in this room. *How could that be?* We are only in our early thirties. Plenty of people don't get married until later in life. *How did I end up with friends who all took the plunge by thirty?*

Sebastian cocks his head toward us. He must have felt the three pairs of eyes staring, and at least one woman drooling in his direction. He frowns when he spots me staring and then quickly turns back to his conversation.

I exhale a breath. If he hadn't already made it clear he wasn't interested, that one look did it.

"He's so dreamy," Oaklee says.

"Down girl, you're getting married tomorrow, remember?"

"It doesn't mean that I can't look at attractive men. Sebastian has always been good looking, but in the last couple of years, he's somehow grown more muscle, more chiseled, more refined. And that dimple just above his jaw is swoon-worthy," Oaklee says.

I let my eyes drift. I haven't seen said dimple yet, because he has yet to smile in my direction. Shepherd makes him laugh and what do you know, he does have the sexiest dimple. I want to put my tongue in it and...

"What?" I ask when I notice Oaklee and Cynthia staring at me again.

"We all agree Sebastian is cute. You already bumped into him."

I moan. "Don't remind me. I literally bumped into him and made him spill his drink."

"So? That's a classic meet-cute moment—an adorable story to tell your kids someday."

"We won't be telling our kids anything because there

won't be any kids. There won't be anything. Sebastian isn't interested."

"Are you kidding me? You're hot as hell, Millie. Why wouldn't he want to go out with you?" Oaklee asks.

I stare down at my clothes. I had every intention of wearing a dress and heels tonight like all the other girls here, but I don't usually wear dresses. So when I packed the single dress I own, I didn't think to try it on first. I didn't expect the zipper to snap when I put it on tonight, only moments before we were supposed to leave—the consequences of the ice cream and wine I've been consuming to drown out my feelings lately.

And it wasn't like I could borrow a dress from my abnormally skinny friends. They are a size zero, while I'm a twelve. The dress was a size ten. It was a struggle to fit my thick thighs and large breasts into the dress on a good day, let alone with the ten-pound weight gain I'm currently carrying around.

I look back up at Oaklee. I'm not going to spell out for her why a sculpted man like Sebastian wouldn't go for a soft curvy woman like me. Even in the best shape of my life, I never looked skinny or fit. I've always been curvy. I don't have a problem with that, but Sebastian King is too arrogant to be knocked off his high throne to consider dating a woman like me.

"Trust me, after basically plowing him over and spilling his drink all over him, he's not attracted to me."

Oaklee frowns. "I'm sure he's just wasted like all the other guys here. He didn't realize you were flirting with him."

"He wasn't drunk." *He didn't even have a single drink, just like me.*

"Well, he isn't dating anyone. He's a single guy. And it's

19

not like he has a lot of choices here," Oaklee says absent-mindedly. "Oh my god!" She looks at me. "I didn't mean... I'm sorry, Millie."

I down the rest of my water, but it does nothing for me. *Screw my diet. I need a drink.*

A waitress passes, and I jerk two shot glasses off her tray. She tries to stop me as the shots aren't for me, but I don't give a damn. I have some catching up to do. I throw both shots down, while Oaklee and Cynthia stare me.

"Millie, I'm really sorry. I didn't mean to imply that you were Sebastian's only choice. You're hot as hell and the smartest, funniest chick here. You are..." Oaklee keeps talking, but I ignore her. She's a bitch, but we've been friends for years. It's not the first time she's said something like this to me. We are always honest with each other, and she means well.

"I just don't want you to be alone forever, Millie. It's time you get back out there," Oaklee says, squeezing my hand with pity in her eyes.

Dammit. I thought we had gotten past the pity.

"I'm fine, Oak."

"I know you are. I just worry about you, now that I'm getting married. You'll be alone, again."

I sigh. We've been through this before. Oaklee and I have technically been roommates for the last six months, not that she's spent much time at our place. She's been practically living with Boden the whole time.

"Go talk to Sebastian," she says.

"I will, but not so that I can date him. I don't think he's dating material."

"Then what?"

I wink at her, and she smiles. "As long as you get back

out there. It's been too long. And for what it's worth, you and Sebastian would make a cute couple."

I roll my eyes. She thinks everyone would make a cute couple. She's in love and just wants that for everyone else.

I start to walk toward Sebastian.

"Wait!" Oaklee says.

I stop and turn toward her. She studies me a second, then runs her hand through my hair, giving me a deep side part, before she pulls out some red lipstick from her purse and applies it to my lips.

"You finished?" I ask. I'm used to Oaklee using me like a dress-up doll. This isn't the first time she's put makeup on me or fixed my hair.

"One more thing." She grabs the hem of my shirt and rips it.

"What are you doing?" I screech as she rips my favorite Lumineers T-shirt.

She looks down at my shirt that now ends just below my boobs. She knows that I'm not wearing a bra, I hate the things—so constricting.

"I can't go over to him like this. He's already seen me normal. This is..."

"Sexy?"

I look down as I cross my arms over my now bare stomach. Oaklee quickly knocks my hands down and attempts to give me a confidence-inducing look.

I take a deep breath. I look sexy. I have curves—curves men find attractive, even if I'm not as thin as Oaklee and Cynthia.

"Perfect, go get him." She slaps my ass as I walk toward Sebastian. I'm not his usual type, but as I walk toward Sebastian, I feel men's eyes on me. Oaklee did good work. I stand taller, feeling sexy as I let my hips sway back and forth. My boobs are playing peek a boo with the bottom of my shirt, and my red lips and overdone hair scream fuck me. And that's exactly what I want—to fuck Sebastian. I'm not looking for a date. I'm definitely not looking for a husband—just one night of passion.

Sebastian doesn't notice me approach. That's okay. I like it better this way. It gives me a moment to study him and decide my opening line. I don't want to make a fool of myself again and do something stupid like spill his drink all over him again.

"I think she might be pregnant," Shepherd says.

"Who? You mean Millie?" Sebastian asks.

Just then, Shepherd notices me approaching the group. "Um...hi, Millie."

But it's not Shepherd I'm pissed at. I turn my anger at Sebastian, who is now eyeing me up and down, obviously noticing the changes Oaklee made. He doesn't drag his eyes up and down slowly like I had hoped. His eyes race like he's trying to find the next bumble I made—assuming I did something stupid or clumsy, not like this look is sexy and intentional.

"Millie, uh..." Sebastian grips his neck as he stares at me.

"Why do you think I'm pregnant?" I ask.

Sebastian doesn't hide his glance. He stares straight at my bare stomach. A stomach that protrudes just a little over my jeans, but apparently enough to make me look pregnant.

"You're unbelievable. You know what, I thought...never mind. You are a disgusting pig who only finds women who are model thin attractive. You wouldn't know what to do with a real woman like me anyway!"

He blinks at me rapidly, like he doesn't understand a

word I'm saying, which is fine by me. I'm glad I found out what kind of ass Sebastian is before I slept with him. I've sworn off assholes, even hot assholes. I've been down that road before, and it almost killed me. I've done too much work on myself to let a jerk like him call me fat. I'm out of here.

3 SEBASTIAN

I fucked up. I'm an asshole, but I'm not usually so cruel.

I adjust my tie as I stand uncomfortably in my suit, leaning against the door of the groom's room where we are getting ready in the small chapel, hoping that Millie walks by and I can talk to her before the wedding.

"Shut the door, Sebastian. Oaklee will kill me if I get a glance of her before the wedding," Boden says.

I sigh and wait one more second before closing the door and leaving any hopes of talking to Millie before the wedding. I should have tracked her down last night after she stormed off with tears in her eyes; tears I caused because I was stupid. I thought she was pregnant because she wasn't drinking, nothing else. I thought she was trying to hide her stomach beneath her baggy clothes. A statement she made abundantly false when she walked back over to me with her T-shirt ripped so high that I could see the undersides of her breasts.

I always thought women in tight dresses were sexy, but I'm beginning to think the cut off T-shirt look is hotter. It was clear that she wasn't pregnant, but by then, I'd already opened my big mouth and effectively called her fat.

"Shots!" Boden says, as Shepherd begins passing out shot glasses.

Ugh, really? I can't even avoid alcohol during the wedding.

I stand next to Kade, who reluctantly hands me a shot glass. A bottle of tequila is passed around, and everyone pours a shot into their glass, everyone but me.

"To Boden," Shepherd shouts.

We all clink our glasses, and then everyone but me drinks their shot.

I look at my best friend, who pours himself a second shot and takes it quickly. A man shouldn't need to do two shots before walking down the aisle. *But what would I know about it?* I'm the only man here not married or about to be.

Kade looks at me looking at Boden. He doesn't have to speak for me to know that he agrees with me, but there is no sense in jinxing their marriage right now. *Who am I to judge?* If they are happy, that's all that matters.

Brittany, the wedding coordinator, pokes her head in the door. "It's time! If I could have you all line up, we will get you walking down the aisle."

We line up in order. I'm the last, just before Boden, as I'm his best man.

"Who am I walking with?" I ask Boden. I flew in late last night and didn't make the rehearsal, so I never found out.

"Millie. She's Oaklee's maid of honor," Boden answers.

Fuck me. Now I really wish I had found her and talked to her before the wedding.

One by one, each of us are led out of the small room

and into the hallway where we meet up with the brides-maid we are to walk down the aisle. In everyone's case but me, their bridesmaid is also their significant other.

My heart thumps, trying to come up with a way to fix this. The church is small and quaint. It's pretty enough, but I don't know why we had to fly to Vegas when they were just going to get married in a church just like they could back in Santa Barbara.

The door opens again, and I walk out into the hallway where Millie is already waiting at the double doors that lead into the chapel.

I hold out my arm, and she reluctantly puts her arm through.

"I'm sorry," I say, leaning over to Millie.

"Shh," Brittany gives me a look, and then the doors are opened. A crowd of a hundred and fifty stares at us.

I put on my best fake smile, and Millie does the same next to me. She's wearing the same lavender dress that all the other bridesmaids are wearing, except Millies has an extra sash that's darker to mark that she's the maid of honor. It matches my boutonniere.

We start walking forward, away from Brittany, who can no longer call us out for talking while we walk.

"I'm sorry," I try again.

"Now's not the time," Millie says through a clenched smile. I notice that her hand is barely touching my arm, trying to pretend I don't exist at all.

"Please, we need to talk. I'm so sorry."

"Little late for that."

"I'm sorry. Let me buy you a drink and apologize for real." We are close to the end of the short aisle. We are about to run out of time together, and I can't have her glaring at me the entire ceremony.

"I don't need a pity date right now."

"It's not a pity date. It's—"

And then it's too late. She's walking away from me toward her spot near the altar, and I'm left standing in front of my brother.

"Why is Millie glaring at you like that?" Kade asks.

I glance over, and I feel the full fury of her. Fortunately, it gives me an excuse to really take her in, instead of trying to come up with words to apologize. Her strawberry blonde hair is curled and pulled back on one side with a sparkly clip. Her face is painted, but it's tame compared to what it was last night with the red lipstick. The dress falls straight on the women behind her, but hers curves in at her waist before swelling out over her ass. *Did she walk in heels?* I glance down at her feet and smile. She's wearing white Adidas tennis shoes.

Millie notices that I'm smiling at her, which only deepens her glare. I fucked up, but making it up to her is going to be fun.

"No reason," I answer Kade, feeling happier than I have in a long time. I just found someone who is going to make this weekend bearable. Tomorrow I can go back to my normal life.

The music changes, and we all turn as Boden leads Oaklee down the aisle. Oaklee's parents died a few years ago. She doesn't have a brother, so Boden decided to walk her down the aisle himself. Just another thing that feels off about this wedding.

I turn my sights back on Millie when the happy couple reaches us. She's no longer looking at me. In fact, she seems to be trying to look anywhere but me.

I smile wider. *Why didn't I notice it before?* I know Millie and I had a rough start, and we don't belong together, but that won't stop us from enjoying tonight. I let my tongue run around my mouth like a warm-up for what I plan on doing to her body later.

"Do you take this man to be your husband?" The minster has been talking for a while, but I haven't been paying attention. I've been too busy undressing Millie in my head and imagining all the sounds she's going to make tonight when I get her back to my hotel room.

"Ah," Oaklee grabs her stomach.

That breaks me from my daydreams as I stare at her. I may not have been to rehearsal, but I know the appropriate response to that question is, 'I do.' And from what I can tell, Oaklee hasn't said the magic words yet.

The room is silent as everyone stares at Oaklee.

Boden's head tilts slightly, but otherwise, he doesn't move. He doesn't so much as mutter a single syllable to ask her what's wrong.

Oh god, oh god, oh god. This moment drags forever. I hate uncomfortable silence. I want to speak, do something to fix it. That's what I would do at work: jump in and save everyone. But I'm not at work. This isn't my life. And I don't get involved in fixing relationships, just people.

My eyes flick from the back of Boden's head to Oaklee. She swallows hard, as she releases Boden's hands and grabs at her neck like she can't breathe. Her face turns green. She's about to be sick...

And then she runs. She takes off like a sprinter back down the aisle. Her dress is hiked up, and her heels are clanking loudly with each step against the hard floor.

"Fuck," Boden mutters under his breath, before running after her.

And then twenty groomsmen and bridesmaids are left

standing in front of a congregation of almost two hundred without a clue what to do.

Millie steps forward. "The flu has been going around, and—"

In June? Not believable, Millie.

"And this morning, Oaklee woke up with a small fever."

I chuckle, *yea, she was hungover from last night.*

"But she was so excited to get married today, that she fought through it. It seems like the illness finally caught up with her."

The crowd stares at her bewildered, not having a clue what to say or do. It's not like they are used to witnessing a bride running out on her own wedding. We've all seen the *Runaway Bride* plenty of times, we all know our role is to sit back and laugh and be cynical while the groom chases after the bride to no avail.

"If you could just give us a moment, I'll go check on the bride, and then hopefully we can continue the festivities," Millie finishes, and then she is walking hurriedly out of the chapel. She's on a mission, but won't let anyone see her frazzled, adding to the chaos that is this wedding.

I doubt a single thing Millie said was true, but I do know that even if it is true, there is no way Oaklee will be stepping foot back in this chapel anytime soon. You don't come back from this level of embarrassment.

The minister looks at me, and I realize now that Millie is gone, I'm the one expected to hold everyone's attention.

I glance at the pianist. "Play until I get back."

She hurriedly returns to the piano and begins playing a soft song.

"Where are you going?" Kade hisses behind me, knowing he will be the next expected to entertain the crowd if I leave.

"Getting the groom back," I say. I start walking towards the exit and see my nieces and nephew sitting in the front row. I turn my head to Kade just as I leave and mouth, *Get Hazel to sing.* That adorable little girl could entertain a crowd for hours.

I get back to the small entryway that leads in two directions—to the bathrooms and to the two dressing rooms. I don't know which way everyone went. I listen carefully for voices coming from either direction. Instead, I hear the start of an engine from outside.

Fuck. Why did I agree to be Boden's best man? From now on, I'm not just swearing off getting married myself, but being in other people's weddings. It's too much responsibility for someone who doesn't believe in the constitution of marriage.

I push the doors open and go outside, hoping like hell the bride hasn't actually taken off, and that this is all a big misunderstanding.

4   MILLIE

I thought Oaklee was sick—I truly did. I saw the way her face turned green. I heard the heavy breathing and saw the glisten of sweat on her neck. All the signs pointed to her being sick.

So when I gave my little speech, I thought I was speaking the truth. *Well, okay, maybe I thought she was hungover, but that still classifies as sick.* I knew they should have had the bachelor and bachelorette parties earlier instead of the night before the wedding, but it wasn't up to me.

I thought Oaklee was sick, until I watched her run out the front door instead of turning toward the bathroom.

She turned to see who was chasing her, and I saw the fear in her eyes.

Oaklee isn't sick—she's running, I just don't know why.

I watch as Oaklee speaks to the limo driver before rounding the limo and heading to the backseat. Boden stands nearby, shouting at her for running out. She stops at the last second before climbing in and begins yelling back.

I stand back a second, but when I see the tears flowing

down Oaklee's cheeks, and watch as Boden doesn't do a damn thing to stop it, I lose my cool and run up to Oaklee. I take her hand and squeeze hard, just letting her know I'm here but won't interfere unless she wants me to.

She squeezes back like she always does. Other than holding her hand, I don't have a clue what to do next.

The church door opens, and I'm afraid the entire congregation is going to run out and witness, well, whatever this is...

Instead, Sebastian King runs down the three steps and then over to us.

"What are you doing?" I snap at him while Oaklee and Boden continue to shout at each other. They don't even realize that Sebastian is here, or seem to care that I'm here, other than I'm holding onto Oaklee's hand for support.

"Same as you. I'm the best man. I'm trying to fix this mess." Sebastian looks at the arguing couple for the first time. "Not that I think this is fixable."

I frown and turn back to the couple, listening for the first time to the words they are saying.

"Oh, you're going to fix this, huh?" Oaklee turns her attention to Sebastian.

"I can't fix this, but I can help. Only you two can fix this," Sebastian answers. It's surprisingly mature and rational sounding coming from him.

"Where were *you* last night when Boden had his tongue down some slut's throat?" Oaklee releases my hand and storms toward Sebastian; her anger deflected off Boden for a moment. "Where were *you*?" She pushes a finger against Sebastian's hard chest. He doesn't move an inch; he doesn't seem bothered by the red hot female unleashing all her rage on him.

"I'm not your fiancé's keeper," Sebastian says.

She laughs. "Of course not. You're just his bad influence. Because, to answer my question, *you* were right next to him, sticking your tongue down another woman's throat instead of telling him to do the right thing. *You're* no better than *he* is."

My mouth falls open as I watch Oaklee storm towards the limo and climb in without looking back at the two idiots. *Well, one is an idiot, the other is a cheating asshole.*

I can't believe Boden cheated on Oaklee. She had to have gotten that part wrong. Or he had to have been manipulated in some way. Boden and Oaklee are perfect together —both so strong and fierce. He rocks the business world; she rules the courtroom. They have the perfect life. There is no way I'm watching it fall apart.

Both of the men are still staring at the door to the limo, like Oaklee might come back any second. Like this is all one big lie, and any second she's going to just walk back out, laugh this off, kiss Boden, and then they are going to go back into the church and get married.

But I know Oaklee—she's as stubborn as she is smart. And whatever Boden did, she won't forgive him easily. As much as she loves him, she won't marry him until she's forgiven him.

I climb into the back of the limo and find Oaklee has made her way to the midsection, where the bar is stocked with a chilled bottle of champagne and two flute glasses. She's working on getting the cork off, but each time she tries, she just ends up breaking off another piece of cork with the cheap knife she's using.

"Here, let me—"

She snarls at me, and I snap my mouth shut. *Okay then.*

I sit next to her while I wait to see if the guys are going

to get their acts together and climb in before Oaklee orders the driver to leave.

"Get your ass in there," I hear Sebastian shout.

Interesting—I would have thought for sure he'd abandon his friend by now. Or at least told him to give up on fixing his marriage. He was there when Boden was sucking face with a woman who wasn't his fiancée. Sebastian was probably kissing a married woman—ruining two marriages in one night.

I feel my chest constrict as I imagine Sebastian kissing another woman after our fight. I spent my night tossing and turning, replaying our conversation over and over, while he was out kissing some floozy, not giving me a second thought.

"Get out!" Oaklee and I shout at the same time.

"No," Sebastian says, shoving Boden in the car. Boden just slumps in the back, staring out the window. Sebastian closes the door, and then I hear the driver start the limo.

"I'll just drive around the neighborhood until you give me more clear directions," the driver says before rolling the divider up.

We start moving, and all of us fall silent for a second, not sure what to do next.

Oaklee is still fussing with the champagne bottle, trying to get it open.

Boden is staring out the window, but I don't think any thoughts are playing in his head.

And Sebastian is staring at me with intense eyes.

Sebastian takes a deep breath before breaking his gaze from mine and looking back and forth between the unhappy couple. He breaks the silence first.

"Now, I've been to a lot of counseling sessions. Not a ton of marriage sessions, but enough to know that nothing will get better if you two don't talk to each other. No matter if you decide to get married today or not, you won't be able to move on with your lives until you talk to each other. So who wants to go first?"

He's been in a lot of counseling sessions? For what?

Sebastian looks between Oaklee and Boden, waiting for one of them to speak, but it's clear they don't want to talk.

"Oaklee, you seemed to have plenty to say before, would you like to start? Tell Boden why you are upset with him," Sebastian tries in a surprisingly calm voice. *Is he a therapist? No, there is no way. I've never seen a therapist in as good of shape as him, or one as cruel as him.*

Oaklee hisses at him.

"Okay, Boden, why don't you start? Tell Oaklee why you're upset? Or maybe apologize for what you did?" Sebastian tries again.

Nothing.

"Good job, Dr. King. It doesn't look like your little therapy session is going to work," I say.

Sebastian leans back, "Then, by all means, you give it a try if you think you know what's best."

Dammit. I didn't think before I gave my smart-aleck comment, which is why I don't usually say hurtful things. I don't like dealing with trouble.

"Oaklee, it sounds like you are upset that Boden kissed another woman. Is that true?"

She laughs deviously. "You think I'm upset about a little *kiss*? Are you serious? I'm not upset that the asshat kissed another woman. I'm upset he *fucked* her!"

My mouth drops. I thought it was an innocent kiss—a drunken mistake. But there is no way you can mistakingly slip your dick into a woman who isn't your fiancée. That's not a mistake, that's a choice.

I stare at Boden wide-eyed, and then I glance at Sebastian, who doesn't look at all surprised by what Oaklee is saying.

"You knew?" I ask, looking at Sebastian.

He doesn't answer me with his words, but I don't need his words. His silence proves his guilt. He helped break up a relationship, one destined for marriage, for forever.

Oaklee continues to fumble with the bottle. Boden stares out the window like he's in a daze, and Sebastian smirks like he's enjoying ruining other people's lives.

I'm the helpless optimist stuck in the middle of all these fucked up people. I grab the bottle and knife from Oaklee's hands and slice the cork off in one pop.

Champagne spills onto my lap, but I don't care. I just need the fucking champagne.

"Flutes," I say calmly to Oaklee, who grabs one and holds it out to me. I pour, expecting her to drink from one and I the other. Instead, when I fill both glasses, she crawls over to Boden and hands him one, sloshing some of the liquid onto his pants.

He takes it wordlessly. Then she hands the other to Sebastian, who stares at it like it's a foreign object to him.

Oaklee sits back next to me and rips the bottle from my hand before finding a wine glass. She pours champagne into the glass before handing it to me.

And then she holds the bottle out.

"To realizing what an ass Boden was before I married him," Oaklee says.

"To kicking said asshole to the curb," I say, holding my glass out.

Boden's eyes flicker to us, and then he gives Oaklee an angry smile. "To finding out how much of a prude you were before I gave you half of everything I own."

Boden looks to Sebastian, who is watching us all like we are crazy.

"Your turn, buddy," Boden says.

We are all holding our glasses out, or in Oaklee's case, the entire bottle. We are all waiting on Sebastian before taking a drink.

Sebastian sits up in his seat, reluctantly, and holds his champagne flute out gingerly, only in his fingertips. His eyes scan to the three of us. "To not losing myself while I save all of you."

I frown. Of course, his was selfish; he didn't even back his friend like I did for Oaklee. And as for saving us, Sebastian is as far from a knight in shining armor as you can get. He won't be saving anyone.

"Happy wedding day," Oaklee says, and then she lifts the bottle to her lips.

I do the same.

As does Boden.

Sebastian just stares at his glass like it's piss we are asking him to drink.

Boden and I finish our glasses in one chug. Oaklee stops halfway through drinking what's left in the bottle and stares at Sebastian. "Drink!"

He startles, coming out of his daze. He opens his mouth like he's going to say something but then thinks better of it.

Boden even opens his mouth and is about to snatch the drink from his friend when Sebastian tosses his champagne back in one gulp.

Oaklee smiles like she just got Sebastian to drink poison, before finishing her bottle.

I can't help but feel like I've been left out of something very important, as Oaklee lowers the partition and tells the driver to head to the hotel.

5 SEBASTIAN

I broke my sobriety.

I had a drink.

Champagne.

God, I can't believe that champagne is what I broke my sobriety with. That stuff was disgustingly sweet. I swipe my tongue around my mouth, trying to dispel the liquid there, but there is no use. I'm going to taste the disgusting sweetness judging me forever.

I should have said something, but I didn't feel like I had a choice. The way Oaklee was looking at me with a vengeance. She knows why I don't drink; I'm a recovering alcoholic. She knows I run a freaking recovery center for goodness sakes. But she blames me for Boden's actions.

Maybe she has a right to—I'm Boden's best friend after all. I should have said something. Put a stop to his idiocy, or told him to call off the wedding.

But I didn't.

Although, I didn't do what she's accusing me of either. Last night, I left shortly after Millie did—close to midnight. The party went on until three or four in the morning. I don't know what Boden did, but I wasn't there. I wasn't by his side, but I sure didn't have another woman's tongue down my mouth. The only tongue I want is currently sitting a few feet away from me, fuming.

Millie seems sweet and kind, but the glares she's shooting my direction tell me not to ignore what she would do for her friend. I'm the enemy, and she will toss a grenade my way if I'm not careful.

So I took my punishment. I drank the alcohol. I ended over a decade of perfect control. I've seen addicts fall off the wagon before—when the pain got to be too much, when the cravings became too strong, when the peer pressure got to them, and they thought one drink wouldn't cause them to backtrack. I've never seen any of them be able to take one drink and not go all in. That's why they call it an addiction. We can't stop after just one.

I'll have to deal with the consequences for myself later, whatever they are. However big the setback, this is just a setback. I won't let it become anything more.

Oaklee finishes her bottle, satisfied that I served my punishment. *Thank God there was only one bottle of champagne in the limo.* She'd have me chug a bottle to get back at me if she could. It's not a mystery why she's taking her anger out on me instead of Boden. She may hate what he did, but she still loves him. Being mad at me doesn't hurt her. Being mad at Boden changes her entire life. Once they talk, they will realize there is nothing to fix. Boden doesn't love her the way she deserves.

Fuck marriage.

Marriage is an antiquated institution in today's age. We don't need to be legally tied to another person to raise kids or show our love. Love rarely lasts a lifetime anyway.

Marriage is something we do to make ourselves feel

better. To pretend that our significant other will never leave us, no matter how big of an ass we act like. They are trapped, stuck with us forever. It's all a lie. People have no problem getting divorced; the only hold up is the paper-work. But that isn't enough to keep people together.

Marriage doesn't work—Oaklee just figured that out before it was too late. No amount of pretty dresses, fancy gifts, or playing princess for a day was enough for her to go through with it in the end.

After some rude directions from Oaklee, the limo pulls up in front of the Paris hotel. I didn't know where the happy couple was staying tonight, but I guess it makes sense that the Paris hotel seemed like the most romantic choice to them.

I step out of the limo, and Boden follows me. He looks straight ahead as he walks inside and up to the front desk to check-in without a word.

Oaklee and Millie enter next. Oaklee rips her veil from her head as she enters the lobby and looks around at all the people staring at her. Even in Vegas, people still stare at a woman in a big fluffy white dress.

"I'm going to get a drink," Oaklee says, marching toward the bar.

Millie nods but doesn't follow her. Instead, she stomps over to me.

"This is all your fault," Mille says, pushing a finger into my chest. One little touch sends zings through my body, firing me up, making me want her more. She's so bossy and determined and...

"Did you just growl at me?" Millie folds her arms and takes a step back. I can see the heat in her eyes. I may not have noticed the sound I made involuntarily, but her body sure did. I let my eyes glide down her. Her nipples have pebbled, her eyes heated, and she's biting on her lip aggressively like she's angry at herself for finding me attractive.

I smile wide. "I most definitely did. Want to hear me do it again?" I make a bold move, swiping my hand through her hair and gripping her neck to pull her closer.

For a moment, her body takes control instead of her mind. She lets me hold her. Lets me pull her until our bodies are flush against each other.

We fit perfectly. Most women are too short, too skinny. But Millie's body curves into mine, filling every hard inch of me with her softness.

It's unnerving how well our bodies fit, when it's so clear that we don't belong together.

"No, focus." Millie swipes at my arm, forcing me to let go of my hold on her.

I put my hands in my pockets as I stare at Oaklee with a fruity drink sitting at the bar. She's mindlessly drinking through the straw as she stares off into space.

I glance behind me, where Boden is taking his damn time getting a room.

It's clear to me what needs to happen next, but I want to know what Millie thinks.

"Do you think they belong together?" I ask.

"Yes, of course."

God, she's a romantic.

I roll my eyes.

"Do you?" She pushes back.

"No. I thought this marriage was destined to fail after six months. I'm glad they figured it out before signing the damn papers."

Her head snaps back like I just crushed all her little romantic dreams. "But they've been together five years. They met in grad school and started dating their final year.

They moved to Santa Barbra together. Traveled the world together. They belong together."

"Doesn't matter." I shake my head.

"So you don't believe in love?"

I sigh. Now she wants to get all philosophical on me. And the more I talk, the more I show how different we are, the more likely it is that we will be spending the night apart. I'll be with Boden trying to keep him from blowing all his money gambling or on strippers. She'll be holding Oaklee's hair back after she drinks too much and keeping her from drunk dialing all her exes.

Either way I slice it, tonight is not going to go well so I might as well tell Millie exactly what I think.

"I believe love between two adults doesn't last. Oaklee and Boden were in love at one point. But people grow, they change, their annoying habits set in and they realize that whatever love they felt has a limit. Fairytale romance doesn't exist. The only love that is real and everlasting is between a parent and child."

Millie glares at me. "You're so cynical. Just because you haven't found love, doesn't mean it doesn't exist. What about your brother? Isn't he happily married?"

"Kade and Larkyn are the exception to the rule. And they only truly work because they have kids and work hard to make it work. They don't stay together because of how in love they are."

Millie raises an eyebrow. "Who is the woman, and what did she do to hurt you?"

I chuckle. "Why do you think I was hurt by a woman to feel this way?"

"Just a hunch."

"Well, you're wrong."

"So what do we do with Oaklee and Boden? Get Boden

a stripper while I hope there is enough alcohol for Oaklee to drown out her pain?" Millie asks with plenty of snark.

"No, we lock them in their suite together and force them to hash things out."

Millie blinks rapidly at me.

"What?" I say.

"You just surprise me, that's all. I assumed you thought their relationship was a lost cause."

"Oh, I think it is. But I'm not the one who gets to decide. They have to decide if the relationship is over or not. They have to be the ones to decide if we call the limo and drive back to the wedding or if I call Kade and tell him to send everyone home."

"Are you a counselor or psychologist or something? Because I think you would make a terrible counselor if you don't believe in love or marriage."

"Good thing I'm not a counselor then." And with that, I turn and walk away before Millie starts digging any more into my past. She doesn't need to know my history in order to decide if she wants to sleep with me or not. That's the only decision she needs to make, because that is all I can ever offer her.

I snag the room keys from Boden and then whistle to Oaklee. "Let's go." To my surprise, all four of us end up in the same elevator together. I stare at the buttons as the lift starts ascending to the top floor.

Please, mother of god, don't let us get stuck on this elevator.

6 MILLIE

I watch the numbers rise higher and higher as we head to the top floor. Boden sprung for the Napoleon Suite at the Paris hotel, and Oaklee showed me the pictures. It's one of the most romantic rooms I've ever seen.

Sebastian can be heartless all he wants, but all we have to do is get them into that room, and they will fall in love all over again. With the pretty decor, the champagne, the chocolate-covered strawberries, and the heavenly looking bed—there is no way they don't fall head over heels in love again. They may not make it back to the chapel today, but they will salvage their relationship and get married in the courthouse or with one of those Elvis impersonators that are so famous around here.

Everyone saw Oaklee almost get sick. We will just tell them she got sick, and they had a quick wedding before heading out on their honeymoon after Oaklee felt better. Everyone will understand that. There will be nothing for Oaklee and Boden to be embarrassed about. This was just cold feet. Just a big misunderstanding when it came to

Boden kissing another woman. He was just drunk and trying to sabotage his wedding because he was scared.

I smile to myself. This will all be fixed, just as soon as we get them to their honeymoon suite.

The elevator stops suddenly on the 17th floor instead of the top floor, but the doors don't open.

"What's happening?" Oaklee asks, her voice high-pitched and worried.

Boden stares at her like she's an alien.

Sebastian closes his eyes; this is his nightmare. He then steps to the panel and hits the call button.

"Hello?" a bright woman's voice says through the speaker.

"Hi, uh, we are in the elevator on the North side. And we are stuck," Sebastian says.

Oaklee sucks her pink liquid through the straw quickly now.

Boden cringes.

I stare wide-eyed. *Good job, universe. You couldn't just let us get to the room first before you started playing matchmaker.*

"I'll send for emergency services immediately. Everyone remain calm. This does happen from time to time, and almost always, the elevator starts moving again before the emergency response team arrives," the happy lady says like we aren't stuck in an elevator.

Sebastian releases the button and then turns, staring us all down individually like he's assessing each of our ability to get this elevator moving again ourselves.

"Don't look at me like that, this isn't my fault," I say, snarkily.

Sebastian ignores me and walks between Boden and Oaklee, who are standing about as far apart as humanly possible in the small space. I stand in the middle at the back, and Sebastian stands in the middle at the front, now facing all of us.

"Well, since we now have nothing but time on our hands, I think it's time you two talked to each other," Sebastian says.

My eyebrows shoot up. *He's going to get them to talk? Here? Really?* Wait until we get to the fancy, romantic room where they will have no hope but to fall in love again.

Apparently, Sebastian either can't read my frustration or disagrees with my strategy.

"I have nothing else to say," Oaklee says, slurping on her drink until the last of the pink liquid is gone from the cup.

Sebastian takes the cup from her hands.

"Hey!" she says.

"It's empty." Sebastian holds it up so she can see it's empty. She folds her arms, no longer having something to hold onto.

"Boden, I think you should start. Look at Oaklee and tell her how you feel."

Nothing.

Sebastian takes a deep breath, and if possible, his voice gets quieter, calmer. All the muscles in his body relax as he speaks. "Tell Oaklee how it hurt to have her walk out on your wedding day."

Boden glares at Sebastian. "It hurt like hell. I don't know what has gotten into her. She can't just walk out on me on my wedding day! I thought we were in this together, forever."

"And I thought we had agreed to be monogamous," Oaklee yells back.

They look at each other finally, and they're definitely about to kill each other.

Good job, idiot, I mouth to Sebastian.

He ignores me.

"Thank you for looking at each other. Conversation works better when you are watching and listening to the other person's feelings."

Both of them bare their teeth to each other like vampires about to suck all the blood out of the other. I don't think this is what Sebastian had in mind when he said that.

"Now, Oaklee, tell Boden how upset you were to hear that he kissed another woman last night."

"I didn't—" Boden starts but shuts up when Sebastian gives him a look.

"I felt like he's a lying cheating bastard! Like he never loved me at all," Oaklee's voice breaks as she says it.

I reach over and take her hand in mine and squeeze three times, our secret signal to tell each other we love each other and are here for each other. We got the idea from a Taylor Swift song and have been doing it ever since.

She squeezes back, sucking the sobs back down as she stands strong in front of Boden.

"You think I never loved you? Really, Oaklee? I loved you with all of my heart." Boden steps forward toward her.

What is happening?

"Loved?" Oaklee asks through a terrified hiccup.

"Love—I still love you, Oaklee. I will never stop loving you. I fucked up. I thought you cared more about our wedding than me. I was stupid, and I made a drunken mistake. It doesn't mean that I ever stopped loving you."

I blink as I look between the two of them.

And then, before I realize what is happening, Oaklee releases my hand, and she jumps on Boden. His hands grab her ass. Hers go around his neck. Their lips hungrily devour each other in between *I love you*'s and *I'm so sorry*'s.

And then past it all, I see Sebastian. He's leaning against the doors with a smug smile and cocked head as if to say, *I gave you what you wanted. I got them back together, now what are you going to do for me?*

I suck in a breath, but I can't tear my eyes from him. I'm hot and bothered. My panties are wet. My nipples hard. I want him.

No, it's just because I'm going through a dry spell. That's all. Sebastian King is hot, and he knows it. But I have to be attracted to the man underneath in order to sleep with a man, not just find him physically attractive. He's cynical and has a cruel streak, not the type of man I want in my bed even for one night. I bet he's a selfish lover, making it all about him, not even caring if his partner comes or not.

He strokes his stubbled chin with his hand. I know he shaved, but the stubble has started to grow back already. I can imagine it against my thigh, his tongue at my slit, his fingers in—

"Millie," Sebastian says, breaking my trance.

"Yes?"

"The doors are opened."

"Oh." I look behind him and see that the doors are, in fact, open. Oaklee and Boden are long gone.

I step off the elevator with Sebastian right behind me.

"Where did they go?" I ask.

"Not sure, we are only on the 17th floor, not their suite floor. They couldn't have gone far. Let's go to the room and hope that's where they're headed," Sebastian says.

"Just not on the elevator," we both say at the same time.

I smile and follow Sebastian to the stairs. We head up to the top floor and make our way to the corner suite. Sebastian puts the keycard in and waits for it to turn green before entering. I follow after him.

There is no Oaklee or Boden. For one, Sebastian has both keys. And they weren't waiting outside the door.

I pull my phone from my bra.

Sebastian stares at my chest.

"Really?" I say, and he smiles before turning his attention on the beautiful suite I haven't let myself enjoy yet. I've always wanted a fairy tale wedding. I've wanted a romantic honeymoon. *What girl doesn't?* But I know it's not in the cards for me.

Once Sebastian has adverted his eyes from my chest, I dial Oaklee's number. She doesn't answer. I leave her a voicemail telling her we are waiting in the suite, reminding her of the room number, and to meet us here when they are ready.

"No luck?" Sebastian asks.

"Nope."

I look past Sebastian into the room for the first time, but it's not just a room. It's a whole series of rooms.

I'm speechless. I know my mouth is hanging open, but I don't care.

Sebastian opens his mouth to say something, but I just hold a finger up, silencing him.

He's quiet while I take in the suite of rooms. Everything is decorated in red and gold accents, making me feel like I just stepped into a royal palace. Every room has its own chandelier perfectly designed to fit each of the three bedrooms. There is a baby grand piano, a wet bar, and a room that holds a jacuzzi tub as big as a kingsized bed.

But that isn't what takes my breath away. It's the roses scattered on the bed—the chocolates. The romantic note lying on the bed from Boden to Oaklee, that I promise to myself I won't read no matter how much I want my heart to swoon at his beautiful words.

And then I see the most romantic part of all—the Eiffel Tower view out the window.

"Wow," I say, taking in the beautiful view right out the bedroom window.

Sebastian, who has been following behind me wordlessly, finally speaks.

"You know it's fake, right? The real Eiffel Tower is in Paris. Does that squash your fairy tale?"

"Of course I know it's not the real Eiffel Tower. But it is a real structure, and it's still beautiful." I flip him off.

"Did sweet Millie just flip me off?"

"I did. And I'm not sweet."

Sebastian leans forward until his lips are right over my ear, and I can feel his hot breath on my sensitive flesh.

"How about I kiss you and find out just how sweet you are?"

If my mouth hadn't already fallen open, it did with his words. I clear my throat and step away before I do something dangerous to my health like fuck him in this bed—a bed that Oaklee and Boden are supposed to be fucking in.

"Maybe you should try calling Boden; see if he answers you."

Sebastian pulls out his phone and starts texting.

"I said call."

"I'm aware, Bossypants. But since the last time I called Boden was after his grandmother died, I think it's better that I text. He might respond to a text; he won't answer if I call."

I nod, he's got a point. I quickly pull out my phone and send Oaklee a text as I walk back to the living room, realizing that the bedroom is dangerous.

"So what should we do while we wait? Someone should call and let the minister know what's happening," I say.

"I already called Kade and told him to tell everyone that Oaklee is sick, so there won't be a wedding today. They should enjoy the food and drink if they want, though."

"Good, that's good. Even if they reconcile, they probably won't want to get married at the chapel still. We should look into places they can get married around here." I pull out my phone again.

"Or, we could use one of the dozen bedrooms in this place while we wait." Sebastian winks at me.

"First, there are only three bedrooms, not a dozen."

"You got me there."

"Second, unless you plan on napping in one of them until they get back, the bedrooms will not be getting used."

"Yes, Bossypants."

"Will you stop calling me that? I'm not bossy."

He chuckles. "Yes, you are. You are also adorable and beautiful and so damn sexy."

"Just stop. You've already apologized for calling me fat. No need to continue trying to flatter me."

"I never called you fat."

"No, you just assumed I was pregnant."

He frowns at his loss for words. *Hurry back, Oaklee. I can't stand to be here much longer.*

I spot the wet bar and walk over to it. I'm going to need a drink to get through this wait with Sebastian. And because I'm nice, I decide to make a drink for Sebastian too.

"What are you drinking while we wait?" I ask.

He looks at me with a stern expression I don't understand. My mouth goes dry. *How is serious Sebastian sexier than flirty Sebastian?*

I'm in trouble.

7 SEBASTIAN

An alarm blares in my ear. I don't remember setting an alarm, but I don't remember falling asleep either. I don't even remember what I'm supposed to be doing this morning.

I reach over to my nightstand to hit it off like I always do. But when I wack the alarm, it keeps blaring.

Dammit.

I force my eyes open, even though I don't want to wake up. My body is begging me to go back to sleep. When I open my eyes, I realize I'm not in my bedroom.

I'm somewhere far fancier.

I blink rapidly, assuming this is a dream. I would never stay in a hotel this foo-fooie, but every time I look around, red and gold accents are staring back at me.

I grab the still-blaring alarm and find the switch to turn the bastard off. Then I flop back and look up at a bright chandelier staring down at me.

Where the hell am I?

I glance down at myself—I'm naked, which is normal. I always sleep in the nude. When I shift in the bed, my back creaks. This mattress is far too soft for me, and I know when I stand up, I'm going to have a massive crick in my neck and back.

But that won't be the only thing hurting. I turn my head just slightly, and the pounding headache I'm rewarded with terrifies me.

Not because of the pain. I can handle a little pain. But because what the clues all lead to—the headache, the tiredness, the loss of memory. They all point to one thing—I drank last night.

That's not who I am anymore. I thought I was past this part of my life.

I turn my head, and the culprit of my drinking snores next to me—Millie Raine.

I always knew a woman would be my downfall. I just didn't expect sweet Millie Raine to be the one to take me down. But apparently, she did.

I smile, looking at her drooling on her pillow as she sleeps soundly, most likely sleeping off her own hangover. For a moment, she looks peaceful and happy. And falling off the wagon almost seems worth it since I get to wake up next to her this morning.

I got Millie Raine in my bed. *What could be better?* The only problem is I don't remember what happened last night. I don't remember our first kiss. I don't remember how her body felt in my hands. I don't remember what thrusting inside of her felt like. I don't remember my one night with Millie. And as badly as I want it, there won't be a second night. That's my rule, and it's kept me safe thus far.

Millie is the reason I'm drunk; I remember her offering me a drink. I remember Oaklee pushing me to drink in the limo. Women are my downfall. And as much as I want Millie, I need to get as far away from here as possible. I can't have a second night where I get to remember. Hopefully, with time my memory of tonight will come back, and I can relive last night over and over. But for now, Millie is off-limits.

Suddenly, Millie's eyes fly open as if she knew I was staring at her.

She smiles at me at first, like she's happy that I'm here in bed with her, but it won't last. The rational side of her brain will return soon, and the happy memories will disappear.

Her smile drops suddenly, and she sits up quickly before realizing that might not be a good idea. She grips her pounding head.

I sit up slowly next to her.

"How are you feeling?" I ask.

"Like I got run over by an elephant. My head is pounding. My body aches everywhere. I'm afraid if I breathe too hard, whatever poison is in my stomach is going to explode everywhere."

I laugh. "Same."

Her eyes turn to me as she takes in my naked chest. Her eyes run over every ridge, every hard line, every muscle.

I hold my breath as she examines me, but I can feel the heat bouncing from her eyes. Her fingers are itching to touch me, and if I let myself breathe, I know I'm going to let her. That is the absolute last thing I should be doing.

Finally, her gaze meets my eyes, and she blushes.

"Sorry, I didn't mean to stare."

"Yes, you did."

She clears her throat, but it does nothing to reduce the blush to her face. "So, uh, what happened?"

"What happened?" I cock my head, making her spell it out.

"Did we...?"

"Did we, what?"

"Did we have sex?" She finally gets the words out.

I smirk. "I'm completely naked. And you are wearing my shirt and boxers."

She stares down at herself for the first time, taking in my clothes she's wearing.

"What do you think?" I ask smugly. I got Millie into my bed. *Except you can't remember fucking her, you asshole.*

Semantics.

"Oh god," she flies out of bed and then starts running her hands up and down her body and then grips her head. "Why can't I remember last night?"

"Because we got drunk."

She frowns. "I've never blacked out drunk before." She grips her body like she's trying to hug herself.

I understand the feeling. It doesn't feel good to not remember. Unfortunately, I've had too many of those days myself. It's a scary thought, not remembering moments of your own life.

*"You—*did you put something in my drink?" She accuses me with a glare.

"What? You really think I put something in your drink?"

"Yes. I've been drunk plenty of times before, and this has never happened to me. It has to be because of you."

I jump out of bed, ready to fight back.

Her eyes drop, and I remember I'm naked. *Well, I'm not going to back down now.*

"I didn't drug you!"

"Yes, you did. You drugged me and raped me!"

I chuckle. "Oh, sweetheart, I wouldn't need to drug you to have my way with you. From the way you are staring at my cock, it wouldn't take much to convince you to ride me."

This time her face turns bright red as she rages at me. "I would never fuck you!"

I shrug. "Too late to make that statement, sweetheart. Seems like you already did."

She huffs, flipping her hair off her face as she does. "I don't believe you. What happened last night?"

I sigh and cross my arms to mimic hers. "I don't remember either."

"What?"

"I. Don't. Remember."

She narrows her eyes.

"You don't remember what happened?" she persists.

"Nope, just like you don't."

She grips my shirt she's wearing tighter. "So we...?"

"Fucked? Most likely. Unless you usually allow men to sleep naked next to you who you haven't fucked?"

She shakes her head, her big green eyes staring at me all innocent-like. *Damn, I wish I remembered.* I have a feeling it was a night to remember.

"And I'm guessing you are sore. Most women are after I fuck them." I wink.

She rolls her eyes before she collects her thoughts.

"Did we use protection? Are you clean?"

"I'm clean." And I search the floor for evidence. Our clothes are scattered haphazardly around, and then I see the glint of foil that I'm looking for. I pick up the ripped square and hold it up to her.

She gasps like this is a mystery novel, and I just found the murder weapon.

"I'd say we fucked. Unless you can think of another use for a condom."

She looks away, like she's embarrassed.

"It wasn't..." Now I'm the one at a loss of words.

"It wasn't?" She smiles at me because she knows what I'm afraid to ask.

"It wasn't your first time, was it?" It's another one of my rules. I don't fuck women more than once, and I don't do virgins. Sure, it makes me sound like an asshole, but it's all about self-preservation.

She bats her eyelashes at me, eyelashes that still have a thin layer of smudged mascara on them from last night.

"No," she finally puts me out of my misery.

I let out a long breath. "Good. We can move on then. We had our one night together; now we can go back to Santa Barbara and continue on with our lives."

Millie stills as if my words hurt her.

Jesus, is she one of those women who will date a man no matter how clearly wrong he is for her just because she slept with him? Instead of admitting that sometimes she likes to fuck men just to fuck them?

I rub my neck, and her eyes fall to my dick again. "Can we just admit the sex was great, but that we don't belong together? That we shouldn't waste each other's time dating?"

"I think you should put clothes on."

"Why? Are you hoping for a round two? Because I don't—"

"No, that's not it."

"Then what? Does my naked body make you uncomfortable?"

She holds up her left hand like that's supposed to mean something to me.

I shake my head, not understanding.

She points to her ring finger, where a large diamond sits.

"Fuck, Millie. You're engaged?" I don't fuck engaged women. Or married women. That's where I draw my line. Except apparently, I do fuck taken women. I need to know who she's engaged to so I can apologize and let him punch me, which I clearly deserve for fucking his fiancée.

"No, at least, I don't think I'm *just* engaged."

She's talking gibberish. "Is that Oaklee's ring? Are you safeguarding it?"

She shakes her head; that isn't true either. Oaklee's ring is pink; this one is gold. I was with Boden when he picked it out.

"Okay...what am I missing?" I ask.

Her head nods in my direction. I follow her gaze to my left hand, where a gold band sits.

"No way," I say, staring at my ring that wasn't there last night. My gaze lifts to Millie's ring, that now that I think of it, also wasn't on her hand last time I checked.

"No!" I say again.

Millie winces but forces herself to say the words. "I think we got married last night."

8 MILLIE

"What do you mean we got married? Why would we do that?" Sebastian asks, finally picking up his suit pants and putting them on.

I'm happy not to have the distraction anymore, but Jesus, do I wish I could remember getting fucked by that cock. I've been soaking wet and ready the entire time he's been standing naked in front of me.

"I don't know. But we are both wearing rings that weren't there last night, so it's just a guess."

He frowns as he stares at his ring, trying to remember last night. I try to remember last night too, but it's all a fog. We must have really hit the alcohol to not remember anything after we stepped foot inside this suite.

We hear buzzing, and we both kneel down to search through our clothes for our phones. We both find ours at the same time, both ringing.

Oaklee.

Kade.

"Fuck, do you think they know?" I ask.

"No, we don't even know what happened. I'm sure they don't." Sebastian answers his phone.

So I hit accept and put my phone to my ear, not having a clue what I'm going to hear when I answer. "Hello?"

"Millie! Oh my god! How was the wedding night sex?" Oaklee shouts at me.

I gulp. *This doesn't sound good.* "Um...wedding sex?"

"Oh, don't even act like you two didn't do it."

"Umm..." *How do I respond to her? How do I make this go away?*

"Eek, I just can't believe it! I want to hear all the details when you come meet everyone for brunch! You are not missing brunch. I don't care how good the sex was last night, get your ass down here in the next twenty minutes before everyone arrives and quizzes me about why Boden and I didn't get married last night."

"But you're going to get married today, right?"

Now it's Oaklee who has gone silent.

What am I missing?

"Just get your cute butt down here. You saved my ass. You're all anyone can talk about."

Shit.

Oaklee ends the call before I can ask anything more. I stare at my phone a second in a gaze, and then I see Sebastian standing in the entry to the living room in the same way.

"So everyone thinks we're married," Sebastian says, looking from the phone to his ring.

"No, we can't be. There would be a marriage license. I'm sure these rings are fake, worthless. We must have gotten them in a vending machine or something."

Sebastian walks over to me and grabs my left hand with his calloused fingers. Fingers that have touched my body, but I can't remember what they felt like. If the electricity in my hand is any indication, the sex last night was like fire racing through my body.

"The rings don't look fake to me," Sebastian says, running his thumb over my diamond.

I pull my hand out of his grasp so I can think clearly. "Then we can get it annulled. It will be like it never happened."

He nods. "That's a good idea."

We are both silent as our minds go somewhere else.

"What about brunch?" Sebastian asks. "We could hide up here until our flight this afternoon."

As much as I want to, I won't do that to Oaklee. I don't know what's going on between her and Boden, but I need to see her. And our friends might have some insight into what happened last night. Surely, we didn't actually get married. It was probably some act to distract from the pain Oaklee is feeling if she isn't married.

"No, we have to go," I say.

"And say what? We don't know what happened last night."

Sebastian follows me back to the bedroom—the scene of the crime.

"What are you doing?" he asks, as I walk into the closet.

I pull out one of Oaklee's dresses and khakis and a button-down from Boden's suitcase—luggage they had brought up when the room was ready yesterday. "Here, put this on."

"I'm not wearing Boden's clothes."

"Well, there is no time to go back to your hotel room to get dressed. So yes, you are."

I hold up the dress that I know is going to show off my

every curve. Sebastian stares at it, his eyes imagining it on my body.

"Fine, if you're going to wear that, I can manage wearing Boden's preppy clothes."

"Good." I walk into the bathroom and shut the door in Sebastian's face.

"If we are husband and wife, I should really get to see you undress!" he yells through the door.

"We aren't, so you don't get to look!" I shout back as I change out of Sebastian's clothes. Oaklee wants us downstairs in twenty minutes, so I don't have time to shower and get ready.

I stare at the shower. I should shower. I should remove all evidence of Sebastian from my body, get his scent off of me.

I take a deep breath, breathing in his shirt. It smells like pine and fresh grass and man. It smells like Sebastian. I fold the shirt up neatly along with his boxers and put them on the edge of the counter.

Then I flip the shower on and step under the cool spray. I can't get sentimental when it comes to Sebastian. He's not mine. It doesn't matter if we are technically married or not. It doesn't matter if we slept together or not. We aren't together.

I step out, quickly blow dry my hair, and slip into one of Oaklee's dresses. I don't have time for makeup. I don't have time to search through Oaklee's bag to find hers. So instead, I pinch my cheeks. I don't wear makeup that often anyway, I'm more a tomboy than a girlie girl.

I open the door and find Sebastian. He turns when I step out, staring at me with his intense smolder that would have me jumping back into bed with him.

"That won't work," I say.

"What won't?"

"That look you are giving me won't convince me to fuck you again."

He leans in close.

I hold my breath, so I can't breathe him in. I'm strong enough to fight his good looks, but there is something about his smell that makes me weak in the knees and ready to do something stupid for him.

"Good thing I wasn't asking then. Because I only fuck women once."

I roll my eyes and start walking toward the door. "Of course you do. You're one of those man-whores who thinks his dick is so special that it can only grace a woman's pussy once. When in reality, no woman would make the mistake of fucking your disgusting dick twice."

I reach the door and grab the handle, but Sebastian slams his hand on the door, preventing me from opening it.

"Oh, sweet Millie, by the time I'm done with you, you'll be begging to ride my cock again."

"No way in hell."

And then he runs the back of fingers softy down my cheek. I melt on the inside at how gentle and warm his touch is.

This is the man I want.

The kind of man who puts my needs above his own.

But this is just pretend for Sebastian. In reality, he's selfish. I don't even know if he made me come last night.

I grab his hand forcefully, letting him know I won't deal with his crap.

"Want to make a bet?" I ask.

He grins. "My sweet Millie, I never thought you'd gamble on something as dirty as this."

"We are in Vegas," I say.

"I bet that you will be begging to be back in my bed by the end of our time together."

"And when I resist?"

"I'll get down on my knees and worship your body at your feet. I'm a king; I never kneel." He winks at me.

We both exit the room and enter the elevator to take us to brunch. *Please, don't get stuck.*

I look at Sebastian watching the elevator with the same trepidation.

When the doors open on the bottom floor, we both let out a breath. But I'm not sure if I'm relieved or disappointed. Being stuck on the elevator sounds better than dealing with this brunch.

"I resist, you become my servant for one day, Mr. King."

"Deal," he says.

"What about you? What do you get if I give in and beg for you?"

He smirks as he steps between the open doors.

"You—I get you."

9 SEBASTIAN

"Congratulations!" The room breaks out in one big cheer as Millie and I step into the room of the restaurant that has been reserved for us. It was supposed to be Oaklee and Boden's send-off brunch before their honeymoon with the wedding party and a few other special guests, but it appears the news has spread that Millie and I got married instead.

Millie freezes in shock as she stares at all our friends hooping and hollering for us.

I'm just as shocked as she is, even though we both should have known this is what was going to go down. There was no hope that news like this hadn't spread. For all we know, they were all at our wedding.

I go through the options in my head of surviving this.

One—say we were drunk and did it for fun to distract everyone and that we are getting it annulled immediately.

Two—deny, deny, deny. No one has proof that we are married. We don't have a marriage license. No one can prove shit.

Three—it was a one-night stand turned insta-love. We

fell hard and instantly and just had to get married immediately.

I look at Millie, whose cheeks are redder than I've ever
seen them as people start throwing questions our way.

Option one is the most honest, but also embarrassing
and reckless.

Option two isn't feasible. Everyone already thinks we
are married.

And option three isn't believable.

But there is another option...

I take Millie's hand in mine, marveling at how perfect
her small hand fits my larger one.

"What are you doing?" Millie hisses through a fake
smile.

"I'm getting us through this with the least bit of embarrassment possible."

"How?"

"Trust me."

She snickers. "I don't even know you."

"Well, then it wasn't very smart for you to marry me,
was it?"

She frowns, but at least she doesn't look embarrassed
anymore, which is an improvement.

"Thanks! I'm so lucky to have found the love of my life.
Millie is the most incredible woman I've ever met. Only she
could get me to settle down," I say, gripping Millie's hand as
we walk into the banquet room covered in flowers.
Everyone is either holding a mimosa or bloody mary.

There is a table at the far end that says bride and groom
on each of the seats. I notice that Oaklee is sitting to the left
of the table, which means we are expected to sit in the
chairs.

"We can't sit there. That's for—" Millie starts.

"Oaklee isn't sitting in the chair, and I don't know where Boden is. Come on, just follow along, and we will get out of here unscathed."

Millie reluctantly follows me to the chairs labeled Bride and Groom and takes a seat next to me.

"How did you meet?" Val asks. "Tell us your love story!" She practically squeaks.

"Umm," Millie is expected to answer, but I take over.

"Millie got a job in my marketing department. We've been dating secretly for months. Millie didn't think it was appropriate to let it be known that she was dating her boss."

Everyone laughs. "No way, Millie is wild. She wouldn't care that she's dating the boss," Val teases.

Millie's eyes cut to mine, and I raise a brow. *Apparently, Millie is wilder than I thought.*

"Just how wild we talking?" I ask Millie at the same time Millie asks me, "You work at a marketing firm?"

"Not really," but I don't say more about my job.

"My wild ways are overblown."

I smile and throw an arm around the back of a chair as a waitress places two mimosas in front of us.

I look up and find Larkyn looking at me curiously. If my story checked out, there would be no way she wouldn't know that Millie and I were dating. She knows everything that happens in the center. And she's one of my best friends. I tell her everything. I'll tell her the truth later. Kade is looking at me with a surprising amount of pride on his face, not usual coming from my brother. So I'm going to enjoy this ride for as long as I can.

I reach forward, grabbing my glass before realizing I picked up the damn mimosa instead of the water glass. I set it down abruptly and pick up the water glass.

"You okay?" Millie asks, noticing my move.

"Yes, just still hungover and don't want to drink."

"I know what you mean. I'd be happy never drinking again."

I nod and stare at the mimosa. I'm surprised the cravings haven't kicked in. But so far, I don't crave alcohol any more than usual. It's going to be damn embarrassing when I go back to the center and have to start my sober countdown all over again.

"So it was an opposites attract situation?" Shepherd asks.

I frown. "What do you mean?"

"I just mean that Millie is fun, outgoing, adventurous, and kind. And you're serious, responsible, and well...a bit boring." Shepherd smiles when he calls me boring, knowing that I'm going to punch him for that later.

"I just mean your life is so routined, and hers isn't. How does that work?"

I realize that I know practically nothing about Millie's life. I don't know what she does for a living. I don't know even know if she lives in Santa Barbara with me so that my meet-cute story could be true or not. And I sure didn't take Millie for adventurous and spontaneous. To me, she's just sweet, kind, adorably sexy, Millie.

"Ooh, show us the ring!" Oaklee squeals.

Millie holds out her hand, and all the bridesmaids swarm. Oohing and awing over the ring I must have bought her. I don't know how much it cost me, but it doesn't matter. I have more money than I know what to do with.

"When did you propose?" Oaklee asks.

"Weeks ago. We just didn't want to overshadow your big day."

"That's so romantic."

"Why'd you get married so fast?" Val asks.

"Well, we were in Vegas and thought, what the heck? All our friends were here to celebrate with. And we just knew now was the time. We didn't want to wait," I say.

One of the bridesmaids rubs her tummy as if to ask if Millie is pregnant.

I glare at her. "No, that's not what this is. We are in love. We didn't want to wait," I say to her sternly through a tightened jaw.

She drops it.

Just then, brunch arrives. Everyone turns their attention to the food, so the conversation turns away from us.

Oaklee takes this moment to move to our table, though, leaving us no room for alone time.

Just a little bit longer, I think. Once this meal is over, everyone will go their separate ways, leaving Millie and I time to get our marriage annulled quietly and spread rumors that we decided to be just friends. And more importantly, give me time to win our bet. I may not fuck women more than once, but with Millie, I'd like to make an exception since neither of us can remember our first time.

"Where's Boden?" Millie asks Oaklee.

I frown at Millie. It's not really the most important question to be asking Oaklee when we have her all alone to ourselves right now. The questions we should be asking are what happened last night and how in the world did we end up married.

Oaklee sighs. "He's gone."

"Gone? How could that be? Last we saw you two you were making out and—" Millie says.

"And then we had an epic fight and decided to break up for good." A tear escapes Oaklee's eyes, and Millie grabs her and pulls her into a tight hug.

"Oh, Oaklee, I'm so sorry. What do you need? What

can I do to make this better for you? Do we need to go up to the room and order gallons of ice cream?"

"No, nothing like that. Just keep being the center of attention. No one asks about Boden when they are focused on the surprise wedding of the century."

"Oaklee, about that..."

"We will keep all the focus on us, don't worry," I wink at Oaklee, and she smiles back.

"I knew you two would make the perfect match for each other. I just didn't realize you were dating. You were so mean to each other," Oaklee says, giving Millie a sly smile.

Millie exchanges a glance with me. "Yea, well, we were trying to keep our relationship on the down-low."

"I'm glad you aren't doing that anymore. I told everyone Boden is in our room sick with the same bug that I had and that we will reschedule or have a smaller wedding later. But it isn't true. He's probably at a strip club and already found another woman he's fucking by now."

Millie takes Oaklee's hand and squeezes three times. She squeezes three times back.

"I know," Oaklee says. And for a moment, she and Millie share a secret conversation without me.

I know Oaklee will be one of the few people who eventually learns the truth about Millie and I's relationship, but for some reason, the thought of the two of us being together makes her happy, so I guess we will pretend around everyone, at least for today. Tomorrow we return to our own lives.

"Ooh!" Oaklee starts jumping up and down excitedly.

Millie grins, seeing her friend so happy, but I know better. I cock my head suspiciously in her direction as I cut my eyes around the room. Thankfully, no one is paying us much attention.

"You have to stop jumping up and down so you can tell us what you're thinking," Millie laughs at her obnoxious friend.

Oaklee stops jumping and grabs both of our hands. "You should go on our honeymoon."

"Oh no, we couldn't do that," I say, terrified. I have a life to get back to. And if I know Boden's dumb ass, their honeymoon was probably planned for Florida. *No, thank you.*

Millie shakes her head. "I think you should go, Oaklee. Maybe take a close friend to go with you. It could be healing."

Oaklee shakes her head. "Nope, I don't want to go and sulk. I want someone who is actually going to enjoy it to use it. It will be my thank you for taking the attention off of me."

"Oaklee, I really don't think—" Millie starts.

"I'm not taking no for an answer. You are going. You deserve a honeymoon after that crappy Elvis impersonator wedding you had and getting married in lavender instead of white. I'm going to do this for you. I just need to get the names changed on the flight and reservations."

Oaklee pulls out her phone and starts making calls.

"Shit, well, how are we going to get out of this?"

Millie bites her lip. "I think we should go."

"What? We can't go. I have a life to get back to!"

Millie takes my hand and strokes the back of it. I instantly feel calm. *How did she do that?*

I stare at her holding my hand so casually, like we've been doing it for months.

"I know, I have a life to get back to as well. But surely

since you're the boss, you can take a week off from work. I can get time off. And it will give us time away from everyone to figure out what to do about our situation."

"I'm not spending a week in some crappy motel in Florida. If we are going on a 'honeymoon,' we are going somewhere nice at least."

Millie laughs. "They weren't going to Florida for their honeymoon. Oaklee booked the most expensive hotel in Maui."

"Hawaii?"

She nods.

I frown. "I guess I could spend a week in Hawaii."

She laughs harder. "So accommodating of you to spend a free week in Hawaii. It's very noble of you, King."

Apparently, that's my new nickname. I've been called that plenty of times before, but somehow, hearing it fall from Millie's lips gets my heart beating a little faster in my chest.

Clinking of silverware against glass gets our attention.

"What are they doing?" I ask as everyone taps their forks, spoons, and knives against their champagne flutes.

Millie sighs. "They want us to kiss."

The corner of my lip curls up. "Oh, do they? *They* aren't the only ones."

"I'm not kissing you. I'd lose the bet."

"No, the bet was that you'd be begging me to fuck you by the end of our time together. Which apparently, just extended to a week in romantic Hawaii. A show kiss isn't you begging."

"Fine." She plasters a fake smile and is about to lean over to give me a chicken peck on the lips. That's not going to fly—with me or them.

So instead, I grab her hips and jerk her up. The room erupts in hoops and hollers and yelling for us to kiss.

Her eyes light with fire as if to say, *you wouldn't dare.*

Oh, honey, you have no idea how far I would dare.

I dip her back away from the room. And then I lower my head over hers. My hand is running up the side of her smooth black dress that clings to her full hips and breasts. She should be wearing white, not black, but no one argues when it's Millie we are talking about. She's my sweet, bossypants.

She licks her lips, waiting for the kiss, but she doesn't close her eyes, which excites me even more. She doesn't play by the rules. She likes to watch.

"Are you going to kiss me or not?" she dares me.

I lower my lips, and she parts hers, preparing for more than a chicken peck.

I stop just short. Our lips are so close that if I'm not careful, they'll collide. But I'm very careful. I don't want the first kiss I remember with this woman to be in front of a crowd. I want our first kiss to be because she's begging for it.

Instead of kissing her, I breathe my hot breath into her mouth.

"I won't kiss you, sweetheart, until you beg me to. Which based on how fast you're breathing and how hard your heart is thumping, is going to be very soon. And once I kiss you, you'll be begging for more."

I run my hand through her hair, messing up her hair just enough for everyone to believe that we've kissed, and then I pull her up.

Millie bites on her bottom lip and blushes as the crowd cheers. *Oh, my dear sweet Millie, I'm going to enjoy getting you back into my bed.*

10 MILLIE

The brunch was hell. Going on a honeymoon is going to be like burning in an inferno. Resisting Sebastian to win a bet and keep my pride is going to be unbearable.

The hotel had our bags brought to this room, so Sebastian and I have been spending the last hour getting ready before our flight and avoiding each other. Well, I've been avoiding him. He's been as obnoxious as possible, trying to get me to fuck him in this bed before we leave.

Not going to happen.

And as beautiful as this hotel is, if I was going to use my one night in the sack with Sebastian, I wouldn't use it now, I'd wait until I get to Hawaii.

Nope—get those thoughts right out of my head. Sebastian and I are not happening. I'm not fucking him again. The first time was a mistake. If I fucked him again, it would mean I'm a screwup. And I finally have my life together. I'm not going to let a man take me down a dark path again.

I pull the zipper on my backpack after changing into my own clothes of shorts and a tank top.

My phone buzzes in my pocket. I pull it out, expecting

Oaklee to be calling with more details about my honey-moon. She's my closest friend. She lived with me. I don't know how she thinks Sebastian and I have been having a secret relationship for months now. She's delusional if she thinks Sebastian and I belong in the same room, let alone married to each other.

I freeze when I see the text isn't from Oaklee.

An unknown number flashes on the screen.

No.

No.

NO.

This can't be happening. I was free. I was...

I click on the text message and open it, even though I know better. I should just delete it.

UNKNOWN NUMBER: Where R U?

MY BODY REACTS immediately to the threat. It may not seem like a threatening text message, but I know better.

Chills worse than I would feel in an old mansion filled with ghosts dance down my spine.

My ribs constrict around my lungs, rocking them with fear.

Sweat drips down my neck as anxiety spreads.

Not again.

I swipe the message, deleting it before I toss the phone on the bed. If I stop touching it, it can no longer have an effect on me.

I close my eyes and take several deep breaths as I wash the images out of my head, scrubbing my brain clean like

I'm Cloroxing a bathroom, that's how hard I force the dangerous thoughts out of my head.

Sebastian opens the door from the bathroom as he sings a Justin Bieber song about how yummy I am and then switches to how his only intentions are to get me into his bed.

"You know you are combining his songs, right? And when Bieber sings those lyrics, he's being sweet, not an asshole," I ask, keeping my eyes closed.

"I'm just improving his lyrics."

I open my eyes and see his crooked grin as he dries his wet hair. And then I make the mistake of glancing down and see that once again, Sebastian is completely naked.

"Goddammit, what is it with you and not wearing clothes?" I cover my eyes with my hands.

He chuckles. "Don't pretend that you don't like what you see. And we are married after all. If I can't prance around naked, what benefit is there to being married?"

"Can't you wait to dance around naked with your next wife?"

"This will be my only marriage, so I have to take full advantage."

I lower my hands to look at him. He can't be serious. Yet, the playful gleam in his eyes is gone. I may not know Sebastian King very well, but I doubt his statement was anything but honest.

"Just get dressed and packed. The car will be here in ten minutes to take us to the airport."

His lazy eyes run down my body until they land on the bottom of my short shorts that barely cover my ass. Shorts that I think are a little too short, but Oaklee says I look smoking in. I just wear them because they are comfortable, but now that Sebastian sees me in them, I regret packing them. I can't read him. I don't know if he finds my ass attractive or if he thinks it's too large.

His pregnant comment still stings. Even though he defended me in the room during brunch. He thought I was pregnant. He basically called me fat. And now he's staring at my ass in the same way.

He tilts his head. "What are you thinking?"

"That you now have eight minutes to get dressed and packed before the car arrives for us."

He shakes his head slowly as he walks to me. "Liar. What are you thinking?" His voice is soft and dreamy, like melted chocolate. He's trying to caress me with his words to pull the truth from me.

And why not tell him? We are going to be stuck together for the next week.

"I'm thinking that you think my ass is too big."

His brow furrows, his jaw tenses, and his eyes darken. "Look at me, Millie."

I do.

"No." He cups my chin, dragging my eyes down his naked body to his rock hard cock.

I bite my lip to keep from saying something stupid.

"I'm hard because of you. I'm extremely attracted to you, Millie. All of you. Your natural beauty. Your freckles. Your sparkling green eyes. Your full breasts. Your curvy hips. And your ass—god, your ass might be my favorite part of you. I wish I could remember how it felt in my hands."

My mouth falls open.

And he takes a step back, his hand falling away from my chin. I don't know if he's stepping back because he wants me to get a better look at his body or because he needs to put distance between us, so he doesn't jump me.

Silently, he turns and gets dressed. I do my best not to stare. Not to crave him. Not to want him.

"Moron," I whisper under my breath.

"What was that?"

"I said, moron."

He buttons his jeans. "You called me a moron, why?"

"Just ensuring that I win our little bet."

He laughs hard. The muscles in his belly contract, drawing my attention to them, until I see his smile that reaches up to his crystal blue eyes.

He takes my breath away; that's how good looking he is.

"Jerk," I say.

And it makes him laugh again.

"You are something else, Millie Raine."

I blush but don't respond.

He grabs a T-shirt and finally puts it on. Then he finishes his look with a worn-out baseball cap. He zips his bag and then turns to me.

"Where is your bag?"

I pick up my backpack. "Right here." I sling it over my shoulder.

He frowns. "That's your suitcase? How are you going to survive a week in Hawaii?"

"I only packed enough for two overnights, so I didn't need much."

He holds up his rolling suitcase on wheels. "This is a normal size suitcase for a weekend trip."

I shrug. "I travel light. And all I need when we get to Hawaii is a swimsuit anyway."

"Hopefully one of those red thong bikinis that cover practically nothing?"

I laugh. "Nope, a full wetsuit that covers every bit of me."

His smile drops before he recovers. "That's okay, I like the catsuit look as well."

He rolls his suitcase out while I carry my backpack. We take the elevator down, both of us staring intently at the numbers as we descend. The doors finally open on the bottom floor, and we both exhale a deep breath at the same time and then laugh at how ridiculous we are being. We were trapped in an elevator for all of two minutes. It wasn't a big deal.

As we walk to the lobby, cheering starts in along with bubbles floating all around us. Apparently, the wedding party has decided to wish us well on our way.

Before I realize what's happening, Sebastian takes my hand in his. Just like the last time he touched my hand, there's a spark followed by a warmth spreading through my body.

It's just because our hands fit together so well, that's all. There is nothing else to read into.

Sebastian leads me through the weave of people as we make our way through the lobby. We get outside to the waiting car that says 'Just married' on the back.

Just married.

I still can't believe those words.

"Kiss, kiss, kiss," the crowd starts chanting again.

Sebastian hands our bags to the driver, and then he flashes his signature grin showing off his white teeth. This smile is fake, unlike the other ones I've seen from him. He's putting on a show for the crowd, and I prepare myself for an untimely kiss.

But maybe if he finally kisses me, I'll get over him. I'll realize he's just a man, and I'm just horny. It's nothing some quality time with my vibrator can't fix.

He flicks his baseball cap off and then leans in. I part

my lips waiting for his kiss. At the last second, he puts the cap over our faces, hiding them from the world as he leans in as close as he can get without kissing me.

"Are you begging yet?"

"Are you done being a prick yet?"

He smirks. "Keep calling me names, Millie. It only means I'm getting under your skin and getting closer to winning."

I exhale my breath—a mistake because it means I have to inhale, and all I breathe in is him.

The hollers grow louder, and eventually, Sebastian lets go of me. He opens the door to the car, and I slide in. He follows after, and then we are driving toward the airport.

There will be no more people to put on a show for. We are all alone. We don't have to pretend anymore. We could even change our flights and head home early, and no one could stop us.

We are silent as we both get lost in our phones. Until the texts start in again...

WHERE R U?

CALL ME.

I NEED YOU.

YOU CAN'T HIDE from me.

. . .

I'LL FIND YOU.

DELETE ALL.

"Shoot," I breathe.

Sebastian looks at me. "We don't have to go to Hawaii, you know. No one would know."

I nod. "I know."

"But maybe we should. We could both use a break."

"And the trip is already paid for, nonrefundable. It seems silly not to go."

"So, we're going."

"We're going."

"I, uh, talked to my lawyer," he says while I fidget with my phone, thinking about the deleted messages.

"He said that he could get our marriage annulled before we get back. I'll cover the costs of the legal fees."

My mind is racing with so many thoughts. *Could being married to Sebastian save me from my past?*

I glance up at Sebastian, who is oblivious to the thoughts in my head. I have to tread carefully, to get him to agree to my plan.

"About that..."

11 SEBASTIAN

"What do you mean you don't want me to use my lawyer?" I ask as we stand in line to board our plane.

She runs her hand through her hair, making it look even more wild and untamed. If I didn't know better, I'd think she had a quick fuck in the bathroom before boarding. But the look is just Millie—a little wild, a little messy, and probably an animal in the bedroom. *Too bad I can't remember.*

We are headed to Hawaii for an all-paid, week-long vacation. I'm going to win our little bet. I'll get my one night yet. One that this time, I'll make sure I don't forget.

Millie mumbles something under her breath that I don't catch.

"What was that?" I ask.

"Sir, your ticket," the flight person says. I hold out my phone, and she scans it, then scans Millie's.

"Have a nice flight," she says.

We walk down the ramp. Me pulling my carry on, Millie still sporting her backpack that somehow fits a weekend's worth of clothes. I'm okay with her not having many clothes. It means she can spend more time naked around me.

"Window or aisle?" Millie asks when we get to our seats in first class. Boden really went all out for this honeymoon. I texted him in the limo, but he never responded to me. I don't know where he is. I just hope he's taking the breakup as well as Oaklee is.

"Aisle," I say.

Millie smiles. "Good, I prefer the window."

We both take our seats after I put my bag in the overhead compartment, and Millie squeezes her bag under the seat in front of us. We look like a happily married couple, which is why you should never believe appearances. They can be faked.

"Welcome, Mr. and Mrs. King. Can I get you some champagne before we take off?" our flight attendant asks.

"No!" Millie and I both answer at the same time, equally emphatically that we don't want any champagne.

"Hungover?" he asks us.

We both nod.

He chuckles. "How about some coffee then?"

"Yes, please," I answer.

Millie nods as well.

"I'll be right back with your drinks, Mr. and Mrs. King." And then he leaves us.

"Do you know that you do this blinking and wincing thing every time someone calls us Mr. and Mrs. King?" Millie asks.

I turn my head toward her. "I don't think I do."

"You do."

"Is that a problem? We aren't really married."

"Actually, we are."

I roll my eyes. "Fine, we're married, but not by choice.

And we won't be for much longer. As I said, I spoke with my lawyer—"

"Why do you have a lawyer? I don't have a lawyer who I can call when I get into trouble. Why do you?"

I sigh and look down the aisle to where our flight attendant is preparing our coffee. *Hurry up, man, I'm going to need it to survive this flight.*

My legs start bouncing up and down, and my heart races—all the familiar signs of a craving starting. Now, I really want that coffee.

"Here you go, Mr. and Mrs. King." We are both handed our coffees, and I grip mine like it's the only thing keeping me from raiding the liquor cabinet for bourbon, my liquor of choice.

"Thank you," Millie says brightly when I don't say anything. Our flight attendant returns my smile and leaves us.

"Are you rude to everyone like that?" she asks.

"I wasn't rude." I grip my cup tighter.

"Yes, you were. And now the vein in your forehead is popping out. The one that pops out when you're mad."

I shake my head. "Can you stop overanalyzing me so we can talk about our situation, and then I can put my headphones on and spend the rest of my flight watching the latest Fast and Furious movie?"

She makes a disgusted face.

"Really? You don't like Fast and Furious? It's like we weren't meant to spend the rest of our lives together."

She chews on her bottom lip.

"What? Spit it out."

"Um...I just don't want to get lawyers involved."

I sip on my coffee again.

Millie puts her hand on my forearm like she's trying to

calm me, which only makes my breath fly. I glance at the couple sitting next to us, sipping mimosas and enjoying life. And suddenly, I want a mimosa.

No, it's just the addiction talking. I don't want a damn mimosa.

I turn back to Millie.

"You can't be serious?"

Millie looks at me nervously—she's serious.

"I told you I'd pay for legal fees. That includes *your* legal fees." There is no way I can get this annulled or even divorced without a lawyer. Kade would kill me. I don't know if I should trust Millie or not yet, but if she finds out how big my bank account is before the annulment or divorce goes through, I'm going to be out a lot of money. Not that I care, but I'm not going to let a complete stranger take half my money.

"It's not that..." Millie looks out the window like she's lost in thought as she once again mumbles under her breath, talking to herself. If I didn't work with mentally ill people all day, if I wasn't mentally unstable myself, I might think Millie is losing it.

I let her be for a moment, even though I want to quiz her about what's going on in her head. The flight attendant collects our mugs, and then we are asked to turn off our cell phones before takeoff.

Millie turns hers off like she can't turn it off fast enough and then practically throws it into her backpack. I assume that Oaklee or our friends have been texting her with a million questions about our relationship the same way my friends have been.

Then we are taking off, my fingers now dancing on the armrest.

Millie stares at them. And I think she's going to ask

another question about why I'm behaving this way. I'm sure she'll find out I'm a recovering alcoholic at some point, but I'm not in the mood to share my life story right now.

Instead of asking a question, though, Millie simply takes my hand and holds it. I stare at our interlocked fingers that just fit together, and I feel calmer and electric at the same time. Like I've just been plugged into an outlet, and I'm charged, ready to fire but also grounded at the same time.

The plane begins to take off, and Millie squeezes my hand three times like she did with Oaklee. I realize that she must assume I'm a nervous flyer.

"What does that mean when you squeeze my hand three times? I saw you do it with Oaklee."

She smiles at me softly but doesn't answer. Which is okay because I don't want to talk too much either. She would just force me to talk too.

"I think we should stay married," Millie hits me with words I never expected to hear. From her. From anyone.

I blink over and over, making sure this isn't a dream. And then I remove my hand from her grasp because maybe she thinks there is something between us that isn't there.

She glances down at our now separated hands.

"Millie, I like you, but I don't want to be married to you. I'm sorry if you think there is something going on between us but—"

"No, I don't think there is anything between us. I think you are an arrogant jerk. Trust me, I don't think we fit well together."

I narrow my eyes. "Okay, then I don't follow your logic. If you are afraid of what everyone is going to say when we go home, I think we can just play it low for a few months and then announce that we quietly separated. Our only shared friends are Oaklee and Boden, who we can tell the truth to if you want. And then we can just bury ourselves in our work and tell Oaklee in a few months to say we rushed into marriage too fast and just decided to remain friends. It can't be more embarrassing than Oaklee running out at her own wedding."

"I'm not worried about being embarrassed. Trust me, having people find out the truth is one of the least embarrassing moments of my life."

"Okay..." I rub the back of my head, not understanding.

Her eyes go to my shirt that has risen up, and her eyes sink into my abs, getting lost in my body for a moment. I welcome her heated stare, except I'm worried that my body is why she wants to stay married.

"Do you think staying married is the only way I'll bend my rule and fuck you again, because I already told you, I'd gladly wave my rule and fuck you again. I think we both deserve a do-over," I ask after I put my arms down.

She shakes her head. "You're so full of yourself. I'm not fucking you again."

"Are you trying to get me to fall in love with you?" trying to figure out her reason.

"No."

"Only believe in sex after marriage?"

"No."

"Need to be married to get a promotion?"

"No."

"Need to be married to inherit?"

She sighs. "This isn't about money."

Good, because baby, you aren't getting any of mine.

I pull out a piece of gum and start smacking it, knowing it will help my antsy body.

I rub my chin, trying to figure her out. Millie Raine isn't

like any woman I've ever met, though, so I don't know how to figure her out.

"Why?"

She looks out the window again, all joking gone. There's a reason. She just doesn't want to tell me.

Well, too bad, if she wants me to stay married to her, she better damn well tell me why.

"Don't you want your first marriage to be with someone you love?" I ask.

She snaps her head with a soft chuckle, but it's hiding pain. Her green eyes dilate; her eyelashes blink faster, trying to keep the pain inside.

"Don't you?" She throws my question back at me.

"Since this will be the only time I'm married, that's not an option for me."

"A good looking guy like you only thinks he's going to be fake married to me for however long I convince you to stay married to me, and doesn't expect to be taken by some Miss America, living in the dream house with the two-point-five kids and golden retriever? I'd bet that you'll be married to the woman of your dreams in the next two years."

"I'd say I'm way more likely to win my bet than you are yours." I lean closer to her and watch her squirm away in her seat, knowing that if I so much as breathe on her, she's going to be begging me to help her join the mile high club.

I nod at her with heated eyes. "My point taken. Now, you didn't answer my question, you deflected. Don't you want your first marriage to be with someone you love?"

She looks down at her nails. I notice they have little flecks of black nail polish still on them that she's obviously picked off instead of removing with nail polish remover.

Finally, she looks back up at me with determination in

her eyes, like how she answers this one question is going to persuade me to stay married to her.

"I won't marry again after this, either."

I freeze. No way is this woman planning on not getting married. She's not conventional. I expect her to tell me that she's a musician or a travel blogger instead of a school teacher or medical professional or lawyer like most of the women I know. But every woman I know wants to get married. Hell, every man I know does too. Except, maybe Boden.

"What do you mean?"

Her chest rises as she takes a deep breath and looks me dead in the eye, like she's trying to talk to my soul.

"I mean—I'm just like you. I don't want to get married. This, whatever this is, will be my last marriage. I'm not a romantic. I don't believe in happily ever after. I believe marriage only works between two people who want it to work, usually because of their children. I don't want a house. I don't want children. I've gotten by pretty well on my own. I'm happy. I don't want to get married. You and I may differ on a lot of things, but we don't differ on this."

"Then why did you think Oaklee and Boden should get married? You wanted them to get back together."

"Because despite what I believe, I thought that's what they wanted. I thought they might be the exception to my rule that everlasting love doesn't exist. I was wrong about their marriage, but not about this. Love isn't real. Love is just lust well hidden."

Her words hit me like a bullet. I've said those exact words to Larkyn before when she asked why I didn't want to get married. Larkyn and Kade are my exception just like Oaklee and Boden were hers.

"So why do you want to stay married to me if you don't

believe in marriage?" I ask, sitting on the edge of my seat, entranced that no matter how different we are, I may have just found the one woman on the planet who feels the same way as me.

"Maybe I just want to pretend that love exists for a little while longer before I return to being cynical." Her words are a lie. I know it, she knows I know it. But her words strike me. Like a blow from a sword, they weaken me. They may not be true for her, but they are true for me. For once, it would be nice to not live in my perfect bubble with my perfect routine and life all planned out. It would be nice to pretend that I could be like everyone else. That I could believe in love even if that love isn't real.

I stare at Millie. She stares back and lets me see a flicker of her pain behind her green eyes.

The reason Millie wants to stay married to me is serious. It's hiding her pain. I want to know why. And someday, I'll know why, but not today.

Today, I just have to decide if I'll go along with her plan even though all I'll get out of it is spending more time with her in hopes of winning my bet and getting to fuck her again. I get to get everyone off my back about getting married. When this is all over, I can say if a marriage couldn't work between me and Millie, a woman who is lovable in every way, then how could a marriage between me and anyone work?

I don't know all the details. I don't know what is expected of me.

All I know is that with a single look, my entire world just changed. I will do whatever this woman wants, something I thought was only reserved for Larkyn and Kade and their kids. But for some unexplainable reason, I want to help Millie.

"I know it's a lot to ask. I think we should stay married —" Millie starts rambling, but I've already made my decision. I don't need any more persuading.

I lean over and press Millie's lips together to get her to stop talking. And then I give her my answer, letting her know that I'm all in.

"How long?"

12 MILLIE

"Are you seriously considering doing this?" I ask.

"I'm not considering; I'm doing this."

I lean in close, too shocked to remember that it's a mistake getting near this man. His scent is like honey to a bee, except he's the honey and the bee. If I fall for him, I'm going to get stung.

"You are?"

He chuckles. "I want details, Millie. Not more questions. How long?"

He's agreed. I don't know why. *What does he get out of this?* Not much. At least, not much that he's making clear. Maybe he thinks I'm going to fuck him every night that we're married. I'm going to have to put that in the rules—no fucking. That's the only way our '*marriage*' is going to survive.

"One year?" I ask.

He cocks his head with a sly look. He can sense my fear. I know he's dying to know the truth, why I want to stay married to him, but I'm not revealing anything.

"Six months," he counters.

"Deal." I'll take him for as long as I can get. Six months gives me plenty of time to figure out a solution.

"Where do you live?" he asks.

"I share an apartment with Oaklee."

"Then I guess you are moving in with me. There is no way in hell I'm living with Oaklee. She's a diva."

I laugh, thinking about all the makeup and hair products everywhere in our apartment. Her needing her sparkling water and special protein shakes every morning. And how she complains about me being messy.

"She's definitely a diva. Where do you live?"

"I have my own apartment downtown. On 9th street. Does that work for you?"

"Shouldn't be a problem."

"Good, I have plenty of furniture. So you can either keep your stuff at Oaklee's or put it in storage. I'll make sure there is closet space for you."

"How generous of you."

"Own any pets?"

"No, you?"

"Nope. I don't have a spare parking space."

"I don't have a car, so I won't be needing one."

"Night owl or early riser?"

"Night owl."

He frowns.

"Let me guess; you're an early riser?"

He nods.

"What is your rent?" I ask.

"You don't need to worry about paying rent."

"I want to. Oaklee can easily cover the rent on the old place. And after our marriage is dissolved, I won't be moving back anyway. So I can cover my fair share. It's the least I can do since you are agreeing to this."

"Really, it's not a problem," he tries to assure me.

"Will you just tell me what your rent is?"

"Two thousand."

"See, that wasn't so hard. I can easily cover that." The old rent was fifteen hundred between Oaklee & I, so it won't be much of an increase.

Sebastian grips the armrests, his jaw set tightly, and his eyes flicking to the flight attendant who is now going through the first-class cabin pouring wine. He must really be a nervous flyer by the way he keeps tensing and glaring at the flight attendant. I know he has a monster of a hangover like me.

"You know I've heard that sometimes if you drink a little in the morning, it can cure a hangover," I say.

"I'm good," he practically growls at me.

Okay—I won't make the mistake of trying to be nice again.

He runs his hand through his unruly hair and then looks at me as he lets out a sigh. "I'm sorry. I'm just..."

"A nervous flyer? A crabby hungover monster? Or just naturally a jerk?"

He smiles. "Hungover. Do you want some wine?"

I shake my head.

"More coffee?"

I nod.

We wait until we get more coffee in our systems before we finish our conversation.

"So we agreed to six months and that we will live at my place, what else do we need to discuss?" he asks after he drinks half of his new cup of coffee.

"Sex," I blurt out without thinking. The older woman sitting next to us gives me a scowl around her husband, who is smiling at me.

Sebastian grins. "My favorite conversation."

I roll my eyes. "I just meant that you need to know I won't be fucking you just because we are staying married. Nothing has changed."

"I think *everything's* changed. But I will definitely fuck you again before our time is over. Not because we are married but because I have every intention of winning our little wager." He leans in again, in what is quickly becoming his signature move. He likes watching me squirm. He knows how badly my body craves his. If I let my guard down for a single second, I'll be fucking him, which is a horrible idea.

Why is it a bad idea again?

It just is, I tell my inner conscious. *It just is, for so many reasons.*

"I'll fuck you, because you want me to. You can fight it. Actually, I prefer it that way. I always enjoy a good chase. But no matter how much you tell yourself that we shouldn't, in the end, it will happen because it's the best damn idea either of us have ever had."

My entire body flushes, not just my cheeks. My nipples pebble. My panties flood. My breath catches. My heart races.

Damn him. He knows exactly how to push my buttons. He thinks he's going to win, and maybe he's right. But if he wants a chase, a chase he'll get. He'll be begging for me long before I'm begging for him.

I purse my lips and let out a long slow breath to try and calm my raging hormones. And then I throw it back at him.

I lean over in his seat, pushing him back with the air between us. Neither of us touches each other, but it doesn't matter. We know the game we're playing. The first to beg, the first to touch, loses.

I run my tongue over my bottom lip and watch his eyes watch my lips. I let my thumb pull down on my bottom lip and then let it fall down my body, my neck, stopping just above the curve of my breasts.

He's practically panting as he watches me.

"Game on, Mr. King."

When I say his name, I know I just won this battle. The large bulge in his pants confirms it.

I laugh and fall back into my seat.

"I'm going to enjoy being married to you, Mrs. King," he finally says, when he's caught his breath again.

"You are going to have the worse case of blue balls ever."

"Oh, I doubt that."

Which makes me frown. "Um...that leads me to my next term."

His eyebrows shoot up. "Which is?"

"We can't fuck other people while we are married. I know we won't be fucking each other. I have no right to ask, but I just..." I can't handle being married to a cheater. I can't handle anyone finding out that Sebastian fucked other women while being married to me, even if our marriage isn't real.

"I don't want to fuck anyone else. Just you. If I have to be celibate for six months in order to get you once, it will be worth it, sweetheart."

I swoon at his words. *How is a guy like him not taken?* I know he's cocky, and he sometimes says the wrong thing, but when he says the right thing—oh my god, he's the perfect man.

"How does this end?" I ask, knowing this is the last major point we need to figure out.

"How do you want it to end?"

"I want it to be believable, but I don't want either of us to be at fault."

He nods. "Well, everyone seemed to believe that we were together easily enough. It should be easy enough to convince everyone that it just didn't work out, that we decided we are better off just friends. That I wasn't suitable for marriage."

We both aren't suitable for marriage, but I don't tell him that.

"We need an event. Something where we can stage a fight or show off how well we don't work together," I say.

"Larkyn's birthday is just shy of six months away. We can stage a fight. We can pretend we're over, that we didn't work. Then when we announce we're getting divorced a few weeks later, it won't come as a shock."

I nod. *Six months*—I have six months of protection. Six months to pretend that my life isn't what it really is. Six months to escape my own reality.

I glance over at the sexy god sitting next to me. Maybe I should enjoy my time with him, enjoy the escape. If I'm smart, I'll start pretending it's over now, before my heart does something stupid, like fall for him. A charming man like Sebastian King is easy to fall for—that's the real reason I can't have sex with him. If I fuck him, I'll want to keep him forever, and he's not mine to keep.

13 SEBASTIAN

"Here is your suite, Mr. and Mrs. King," the manager says as he holds the door open to us.

"Holy shit," Millie and I both say at the same time when we enter top floor suite that Boden and Oaklee reserved. Boden has money like me; I'm just surprised he sprung for this nice of a suite and didn't cancel, or at least try to get his money back. If I was a better man, I'd offer to pay him back, but I'm not going to.

"Your luggage is already in the closet. There are champagne and chocolates for you by the minibar. Do you need anything else, Mr. and Mrs. King?"

"No, thank you." I tip him as he leaves, and then we are alone in a beautiful suite with an incredible view.

"Can you believe this? Have you ever stayed anywhere so nice before?" Millie runs out onto our private balcony, complete with a jacuzzi tub.

I'm silent. I don't want to ruin the moment.

But Millie's big eyes don't miss a beat. "Oh my god. You have, haven't you?"

I nod but don't elaborate.

"Well, don't ruin this for me. I may never stay anywhere this nice again."

I walk over and lean against the railing next to her. "I won't ruin anything. And even though I've stayed in hotels this nice before, I've never been to Hawaii."

"You're going to love it! It's one of my favorite places I've ever been to."

"You travel a lot?"

She nods but doesn't elaborate either.

We both stand next to each other in silence, enjoying the ocean breeze and sun on our faces. I may not have realized it before we came, but this is exactly what I need. It's been a long time since I've gone on a vacation or been out of my normal routine. One week here with Millie might finally prove to myself that my life is perfect and that I can handle a week vacation a year.

"We should go snorkeling! And hiking to the volcano. Oh, and surfing! You know how to surf, right? If not, I can teach you. And dancing! I love dancing."

I chuckle, a grin slipping back onto my face as I listen to all the things Millie is excited to do. I haven't smiled this much in years, but find myself grinning all the time when I'm around Millie.

"You're laughing at me. You think this is all a bad idea. Well, what do you want to do, Mr. Boring?"

I laugh again. "Actually, it all sounds great, Millie. I'm up for whatever you want to do this week."

Her eyes narrow as she tries to figure out if I'm lying or telling the truth. "You sure Mr. Stick-Up-His-Ass is up for an adventure?"

"I am. I'll say yes to anything this week."

"Anything?" Her eyes light up.

"Anything." My eyes sear with all the dirty thoughts I'm thinking.

She notices, and her eyes turn fiery.

She grabs my hand and pulls me back inside. I'm hoping her first choice of activity will involve us both getting naked and using the ginormous bed or jacuzzi, but when she drops my hand and picks up a brochure, I know that's not where her head is.

Too bad. My cock twitches in my pants. I've never been this hard without a release. Six months and only one night of sex with this woman is going to be a nightmare.

Something catches Millie's attention, and I follow her gaze to the bottle of champagne chilling.

Do I tell her that I won't be drinking? Do I tell her why? It will be such a buzz kill. I've been sober for ten years.

No, I've been sober one day. I don't care if it was just one night. It was a slip-up. A major slip up that led me to getting fucking married. Although, I might take the fresh start with my sobriety if it means I get to spend a week in this hotel with Millie.

"I don't think we should drink this trip," Millie says, which sounds like music to my ears.

"Oh? Why do you say that?" I ask as casually as I can.

"Last time we got drunk, we ended up married to complete strangers. Who knows what we would do if we did it again."

I nod, agreeing.

"And besides, I'm on a diet. This should be a healthy vacation. We'll spend our time doing fun, adventurous things instead of gorging on gluttonous food and alcohol that is only going to mean I leave fifteen pounds heavier."

I frown. I don't know why Millie insists she needs to

lose weight. She looks fucking incredible—perfect curves in all the right places.

It's because you basically called her fat, you jackass.

I sigh. I need to fix this.

"I agree that this should be a healthy vacation. One where we do things that are good for us instead of indulging in drinking, but not because we might gain fifteen pounds. Even if you gained fifteen pounds, you'd still look smoking hot."

"But you—"

"I know what I said. I was an idiot. I should have never assumed you were pregnant just because you were the only one not drinking that night. I'm sorry. I thought everyone in the bridal party was married except me. I knew you weren't drinking and just jumped to conclusions. I don't think you are fat; far from it. You're beautiful."

Millie gives me a relaxed smile, one where she keeps her lips pressed together instead of letting her smile reach her eyes. She doesn't fully believe me, which means I'm going to have to prove it to her.

"Can we start over? We didn't get off on the best of foot, but I really think we could have fun together this week."

Millie nods. "Yes, let's start over." She grabs two champagne flutes. *Dammit, I thought we were past the drinking thing.* She digs through the mini-fridge and pulls out some sparkling water and fills our glasses.

"To starting over," she says, as she hands me a glass.

"To being Mr. and Mrs. King."

She smiles bigger now. "I'm still not fucking you, Mr. King."

"Oh, we will see about that. There is only one bed, after all, I don't think you'll be able to resist having me sleep next to you every night and not fuck me."

"This suite is huge. I'm sure you can sleep on the couch, or the hotel can bring up a cot for you to sleep on."

I step closer to her, into her space. She doesn't step back. She's too determined to not let me affect her.

"I don't think the hotel would know what to do if the couple in the honeymoon suite asked for a cot."

"You're full of shit, Mr. King. You don't give a fuck what the hotel staff thinks of us."

"But *you* do."

She cocks her head and folds her arms. "Actually, I don't. But the bed is huge. I think we can manage to sleep next to each other like adults and not fuck like bunnies. Unlike you, I don't have sex with someone just because they share a bed with me."

"I don't either, Mrs. King. But I'm very much going to enjoy fucking *my wife*."

Her breath catches. I got the reaction I wanted. Now it's time for the real fun.

14 MILLIE

The entire day has been one activity after the other. We've been going non-stop since we left the room early in the afternoon.

We've explored the city, went zip-lining, and then finished the day off with a jet ski tour. We haven't had time to stop, even to enjoy a romantic meal together all day, which was intentional.

I don't want to give Sebastian any opportunity to say sweet things that makes my heart go pitter-patter. Staying in a honeymoon suite in Hawaii with a hot man like Sebastian is just asking for trouble, so I need to keep us out of that hotel room as much as possible. We will only return when we are both seconds away from crashing.

Sebastian, to his credit, has been a good sport. He hasn't complained once about the crazy schedule I've made us keep. His only attempt at romance was when we were renting jet skis, suggesting that we share one. I quickly said I wanted my own, and he didn't protest too hard. And when I looked back at him, he seemed to be having a good time driving his own jet ski.

But now it's getting dark. The day is ending, and I'm running out of excuses for us not to go back to our hotel room.

"Let's go for a walk on the beach," I say.

"Lead the way," Sebastian says, just like he has all day. He's gone along with every activity. I wonder if he will truly let me decide every activity of this vacation. So far, he has.

I kick off my flip flops. Sebastian does the same as we walk along the hotel's beach in the moonlight. We pass a few couples holding hands. If we were really here on our honeymoon, we would be doing the same. Although, if we were really here on our honeymoon, I doubt I would be making an excuse to not go back to our hotel room right now. In fact, we'd probably spend our entire time in the hotel room.

"So we haven't had time to talk much. What do you do for a living?" I ask.

"Nope, we aren't going to go there."

I frown. "How are we going to pretend to be married to each other if we don't know anything about each other when we return?"

"First of all, we will know all the important things, like you hate pineapple, and I hate sushi."

"Which is absolutely ridiculous, by the way. Who hates sushi?"

He ignores me. "I'll know that you snore and how long it takes you to do your makeup."

"I don't snore and five minutes."

He chuckles. "I guess we'll find out tonight."

"But what about our jobs, our mothers' names, where we grew up? We should know the answers to those questions."

He nods. "We will. We can talk about all of that on the flight home. But I don't want this to feel like a first date. First dates suck. I want this to be fun, an adventure. We can learn the important things about each other after we leave. Agreed?"

"You know for a man who claims he isn't adventurous; you sure got this adventure thing down pretty fast," I say.

"I'm adventurous when I want to be."

"Good, because I've decided our next activity."

He looks around in the dark. Only the moonlight and the lights from the hotel in the distance pierce the darkness.

"I assume you mean go back to the hotel to sit in the jacuzzi? I don't think there is anything else to do at midnight."

"You are such an old man." I grab the hem of my tank top and pull it over my head.

He blinks his surprise as I stand in my sports bra. I should have had us wear our swimsuits under our clothes, but I only brought one, and it's not the most comfortable thing to wear all day.

"What are you doing?" he asks.

"What are *we* doing, you mean." I shimmy out of my jean shorts until I'm standing in front of him in just my sports bra and thong. Even in the darkness, I can see his eyes heat at the sight of my body. He wasn't lying when he said he found me attractive.

"Strip," I say.

I don't have to tell him twice. He removes his shirt and khaki shorts in record time, not even asking why we are stripping in the middle of a public beach. The darkness makes it hard to see every groove of muscle on his body, but I don't have to take in every wave of his muscles to know how ripped he is. I already have the memory of his shirtless body to fill in any gaps.

I turn around before I lose my nerve, and then I pull my sports bra off.

"Millie, what are you doing?"

I slip my panties down, and then I'm running into the waves. "Skinny dipping!"

I don't wait for Sebastian. If I do, I'm going to catch sight of his naked body again. I'm going to see what lies beneath the bulge in his boxers, and this isn't about that. It's about doing something crazy and adventurous.

Sebastian seems plenty of adventurous to me. We're married for goodness sakes; if that isn't fearless, I don't know what is. But I get the feeling that other than his hookups, he usually isn't too adventurous. He must have a boring desk job or something.

I hear Sebastian splashing in the waves behind me, and I dive under. Chills immediately set in as soon as my head dunks under the water. It's springtime in Hawaii at night. There is a reason no one else is in the water—it's fricking cold.

My head rises out of the water and comes face to face with a soaking and very naked Sebastian.

"You're crazy! This water is so cold," he says.

"You said you were up for anything. I wanted to see how far I could push you. Ever skinny-dipped before?"

He shakes his head. His eyes go to my bare shoulders and chest that bob up and down with the waves, threatening to reveal more of my body to him.

I shiver. We need to head back before we freeze to death and ruin our vacation on the first day.

"Come here," he says. His voice is calm and trusting. He holds out his arms and waits.

I move closer, suspecting it's a trap. When his arms go around me, I realize he's just being a gentleman. He's warming my body against his—it's sweet.

"We should head back before my cock falls off from hypothermia."

I laugh, and we start swimming back. We get close to where the water will no longer hide my nakedness from him.

"Go on, I'll turn around until you're dressed."

"Nope, we go together. It's too cold to wait in the water." I grab his hand and pull him toward our clothes. Neither of us looks below the other's eyes, no matter how badly we both want to, as we slip our clothes back onto our soaking bodies.

"You're shivering," Sebastian says.

I look up at him. He's put his shorts back on but not his shirt. Water drips down his chest in beads, bouncing over his rock hard muscles.

When my gaze meets his, there is a familiar grin. "Put your arms up."

I frown, not understanding, but I do what he says. He slips his T-shirt down over my body.

"Better?" he asks.

I tremble again, but I'm not sure if it's from being cold or his touch.

He frowns. "Let's get you inside and warmed up." He takes my hand, our fingers melding together like all the other couples on the beach. But they don't stay together for long and then Sebastian has me pulled against his side. His arm is draped over my shoulders, and his hand runs up and down my bicep, trying to keep me warm as we race back to the hotel.

All I can focus on is his touch against my skin. His arm over my shoulders. His smell is filling my nostrils.

"Still cold?" Sebastian asks as we enter the lobby.

"Nope." In fact, I'm burning hot from his touch. An unfamiliar ache grows in my belly—want, desire, lust. Things I haven't felt in such a long time.

We enter the elevator—our nemesis. Sebastian hits the button for the top floor and then holds me tighter to his side.

"You don't have to keep doing that. I'm warm."

"I know." His answer is confusing; I have no idea what that means.

I stare ahead as the numbers climb, his arm feeling surprisingly perfect around me, even if he's turning my hormones upside down with need. The numbers jump from ten to the eleventh floor, and I panic. I don't want to be stuck in an elevator alone with Sebastian. Not when we are soaked. Not when both of our minds are on the reckless thing we just did. Reckless because we were naked, and it spurred our desire, not because I was afraid we'd get caught.

"I think for once I'm hoping it will get stuck," Sebastian whispers in my ear, his voice somehow dropping an octave.

"Oh yea, why's that?" My voice grows raspy as I speak.

"I'm pretty sure I'll win our bet if we get stuck."

Just then, the doors open on the top floor. "Maybe you'll have better luck next time."

We step out. Sebastian's arm is no longer around me as I strut to the door and pull the room key out of my pocket. It flashes green, and then I step inside, feeling burning hot even though I'm dripping wet.

"What are we doing now?" Sebastian asks, making me jump.

I turn around to face him. "What do you mean?"

"You're in charge of all our activities. What are we doing now?"

I'm staring at his chest again. Damn, he has a nice chest. *Why does he have to have such a nice chest?*

"Millie, does the next activity involve us ogling each other? If so, you need to remove a layer of clothing to make it fair." He winks at me.

I breathe again. The shiver returns.

"I think I should be the one to decide the evening's activities, or at least tonight's activity," Sebastian says.

And just like that, my breath is gone again. I nod.

He laughs.

"Let's warm-up in the jacuzzi. Your nipples are rock hard; you must be freezing."

I look down and, for the first time, I realize that you can see straight through the two layers of shirts I'm wearing. I should be embarrassed, but Sebastian's heated gaze keeps me from feeling anything but want.

I want him.

You shouldn't.

Maybe I should?

Just get a redo on the one time. Something to remember this time.

No, Millie.

Sebastian's eyes flicker back and forth over my forehead like he can read my mind.

"Where's your suit? I can get it for you," Sebastian says.

He's just as affected as I am. If we are going to fuck, it's going to be because he begged for it, not because I did. I don't usually strut around naked; it's not my style. But I want to with Sebastian.

He thinks I'm wild, and I am, but not in this way.

I grab the bottom of both of the shirts I'm wearing and lift them over my head, still facing Sebastian. He's frozen as he stares at me, not hiding where his gaze is this time—on my breasts.

I let him take in my body. I let the memory burn into his brain. My next move is even bolder—I undo the button on my jean shorts and slide them down my body until I'm naked in front of him.

His hand balls into a fist, and he bites his knuckles to keep from begging for me. I can see how close he is to breaking.

Give in, Sebastian. I want you, too.

But he doesn't.

Soon, one of us is going to break. It's only a matter of time.

"My first wife is hot."

I blush.

He steps closer and drops his shorts.

Fuck me.

He's gorgeous.

His cock is hard, just like every other part of him.

"So is my husband."

"You ready to put our last activity on the table?"

"Are you?" My eyes cut down to his cock, which is very ready.

"Just say the word, Mrs. King."

"Not until you beg, Mr. King."

And then I turn and strut toward the jacuzzi on our private balcony.

"Fuck, you're good, Millie," I hear Sebastian curse under his breath.

I know. And if I'm lucky, I'll get to fuck him and win

the bet at the same time. I'll get the fantasy husband for one day. I just have to remember it's a fantasy. In real life, I'll never get the perfect husband.

15 SEBASTIAN

Watching Millie's naked body walk away from me and not at least trying to get her into bed was one of the hardest things I've ever done. It takes all of my restraint to not beg her, to not literally get down on my knees to let me fuck her.

Millie Raine is the hottest woman I've ever seen. She's got more confidence than Taylor Swift does when she struts around on stage. Her body is fit and curvy, and I want to grab onto every one of those curves.

Why the hell did I make a bet saying that she would be begging me? I'll be the one begging. She's a predator. When she removed her clothes, she knew exactly what she was doing—winning.

I don't care that she's winning. I want her to win. I just hope she decides to collect on her prize. I hope she lets me worship her body, taste between her legs. I want it all, and if she won't let my cock enter her body, I at least want to touch and taste every part she'll let me.

"You coming?" she yells as she hits the buttons on the jacuzzi, turning it on and leaning over the tub in plain view.

My mouth is dry. I'm at a loss for words. So I don't answer with my words, I just head out onto the balcony.

She climbs the two stairs leading up to the hot tub.

"Here, let me," I say, holding my hand out like a gentleman. I've been acting nice all day, even though my thoughts have been anything but gentlemanly. They have been dirty, debasing, and needy.

She takes my hand, her eyes practically glowing with victory as she sinks beneath the bubbles. I follow after her. She scoots over; I assume to give me room to sit by her, but I sit opposite her in the tub.

We've both teased each other enough. We're both single. Technically we're married. We should fuck. There is no reason not to.

"You win," I say, hoping if I let her win that we can both stop this charade pretending we don't want to fuck each other and just do it already.

She laughs. "I win, huh? I thought I was going to be begging you for sex?"

"Your body is, your mouth just hasn't gotten there yet, and I'm an impatient man."

"If you want to fuck me, why are you sitting way over there?"

"I'm not going to touch you until you tell me to. I'm not asking you to beg. I'm just asking you to tell me it's what you want."

She shakes her head. "Nope. Not going to do that. Just because you are ready to beg me for sex doesn't mean I'm going to fuck you."

"You can't deny that you want me. I can see your desire in your eyes."

She bats her eyelashes but doesn't deny it. She doesn't

confirm she wants me either. The nibble of her teeth on her bottom lip lets me know how twisted up inside she is.

"It doesn't matter what I want. It matters what's good for me. And fucking you isn't good for me."

"It will be very good for you."

"We're friends. We are going to be living together for months. I don't want sex to get in the way."

"Sex doesn't have to get in the way."

"It will, though. It always does." She looks off in the distance, and I realize she says that because sex has gotten in the way for her in the past. That's why she's so hesitant to fuck me now.

"If we don't fuck, we are always going to wonder. We've fucked before, but neither of us remember. We need to fuck so we can remember. So we don't always wonder what happened between us, we'll know."

"We could remember still."

"Do you remember?"

"No."

"I don't think the memory is coming back, unless we fuck."

She chuckles. "Is sex your answer for everything?"

"Yes." I wiggle my ears, and my dimple drives into my cheek. She laughs at both.

"I had a good day with you, Sebastian."

I sigh. It seems she's done talking about sex.

"You don't fight fair," I say, looking down at her naked body covered in bubbles.

"Neither do you."

I sink lower into the bubbles, up to my chin. "I had a good day too, Millie." *A really good day.* I can't recall a day where I laughed more than I did today with Millie. No matter what happens between us, I shouldn't ruin it. Millie would make a great friend.

She would also make someone a good wife someday. That's a topic I need to dig deeper on. A woman like Millie should definitely get married, not because she needs a guy, but because she's so fucking incredible.

"What crazy things do you have planned for us tomorrow?"

"Who says I have a plan? I didn't today."

I smile at that, before yawning.

"It's past someone's bedtime," she laughs, as I yawn two more times.

"I told you, I'm an early bird, not a night owl."

She yawns too. "I think it's time for bed."

I climb out of the tub, feeling her gaze on me as I dry off and then wrap the towel around my waist before waiting to see what she's going to do. *Is she going to be as brave leaving the tub as she was going in?* All she has to do to get me to leave is say the words.

But when she stands, water dripping down her naked body, it's too much for me. I grab one of the towels and hold it up, blocking my view of her body.

She smirks and then wraps the towel around her.

I turn and walk inside. "You can have the bathroom first."

"Thanks."

She grabs her clothes; I assume to go to the bathroom to change. Instead, she drops her towel and then pulls an over-sized T-shirt over her body.

"You're sleeping like that?" I gape.

"Do you have a problem with that?"

I moan. My cock is throbbing. My body is aching for her. She's not even wearing any underwear.

"Nope. I uh…" I run my hand through my wet hair. "I think I'll sleep on the couch after all."

"The bed is plenty big enough."

"Um…fuck."

She laughs at my words. "I'll put on panties if it will help."

I don't think it will help. I don't think anything will help.

There is a buzzing coming from her bag that draws her attention—giving me time to compose myself. She may not need to go to the bathroom, but I need to go jack off if I'm going to have any hope of falling asleep.

I grab my toiletry bag and head toward the bathroom. Once I'm done in the bathroom, I exit and glance over at Millie sitting on the bed. The phone is pressed to her ear, she must be listening to a voicemail, but her face is as white as a ghost.

"Everything okay, Millie?" I ask.

She stops breathing, her body growing paler.

Fuck. Whatever is in that voicemail isn't good. *Did something happen to Oaklee? To some of her other friends? Is it her parents? A sibling? Is someone in the hospital? Did someone die?*

A million scenarios go through my head. I'm actually really good in a crisis. I know all the steps you should take. I know how to stop someone from having a panic attack. I know the stages of grief. I know how to help her get through a five-hour flight back home while dealing with the news that someone died, if that's what I have to do.

I just don't want to. I don't want our time here to end. It barely got started. Once we return home, our lives will change. The flirting will end. The possibilities will close. We will go through the motions of pretending for a few months, and then this will end, it will all be over. I'm not ready to go back to my old life.

I kneel down in front of her, putting my counselor hat on, hoping that in a few minutes, I can take it back off again and go back to being the asshole who's trying to get in her pants. I'm still just wearing a towel around my waist. Kneeling practically naked in front of her should draw a smart comment from her.

Instead, she acts like I'm not here.

She's in shock. I've seen it before.

Slowly, I reach up and place my hand around the phone pressed to her ear. She doesn't flinch. She still doesn't acknowledge I'm here.

Carefully, I take the phone from her hand. When I do, her gaze finally meets mine.

"It's okay. Whatever happened, it will be okay. I just need you to focus on your breathing. In and out..."

Her breathing is shallow. She's not focused on her breathing. Her head is still wherever the phone call took her.

I stare at the phone a second. It's unlocked. I could listen to the voicemail myself and understand what I'm dealing with, but even though technically I'm her husband, I won't breach her confidentiality like that.

"Millie, breathe with me." I take her hand and press it to my bare chest.

I stifle down my own moan at the touch of her hand on my skin. My cock is throbbing beneath my towel as I kneel between her spread, bare legs.

"In," I take a deep breath, and Millie does the same.

"Out." She exhales with me.

"Good, one more time." We breathe together in and out in long, slow breaths. Our eyes lock, and slowly, I see the

117

light return to her eyes. She's coming back to me. When she realizes that she's touching me and I'm between her naked legs, she jumps back.

"It's okay, nothing is going to happen."

She nods.

"Do you want to tell me what happened?" I don't know if I want to know, or I want to pretend that everything is okay more. I just want more time without the baggage that is our lives. I want more pretend, even if I'm curious about her life.

She shakes her head.

I nod.

"You don't have to tell me anything, but do we need to head back home early?"

She shakes her head, emphatically. "No, I don't want to go anywhere."

Her words are music to me. Her voice is soft and sweet, and it's practically begging me to be the one to lose—the one to beg for more, for sex, for her.

God, do I want to. I want her more than I've ever wanted anything.

But I won't have her when she's so vulnerable. When we fuck again, it will be because we both want it, not because she's scared and wants to use me to forget whatever was on the other end of that voicemail.

"We should try to sleep. We have a big day ahead of us tomorrow."

She smiles at that.

I stand up to give her space, but she grabs my hand, seeming to know that if I leave, I'll come to my senses and sleep on the couch.

"Stay," she says.

Fuck, I curse under my breath.

Stay.

I can't deny her what she wants, not when she's this emotional. *But Jesus, this is going to test me.*

I nod.

Then I watch as she scoots up in the bed and starts pulling the covers back. I'm still just wearing a towel; I should at least find my boxers to put on, but then she's patting the spot in the bed next to her.

Fuck it.

We are both adults. It doesn't matter what we are wearing. We are just going to sleep.

I remove my towel, climb into the bed, and pull the covers up over us, doing my best to tuck her in. She seems unsettled next to me. I turn off the lamp, and then we are lying in darkness.

She sits up suddenly. "Can I?"

I know what's she asking even though she doesn't say the word. I can feel her fear. And right now, I'm the only person in her world who can take away the fear.

No matter what happens tonight—*I will not fuck her tonight. I will not fuck Millie.* I repeat my mantra over and over in my head.

Then I pull her to my chest. Her head rests perfectly on my shoulder, her body fitting like a glove to mine. She takes a deep breath, relaxing into me. Minutes later, she's snoring.

I smile. I knew she was a snorer. I won't be able to sleep. I've slept for years alone in my bed, but I could listen to the soft sounds she makes all night. It will be worth the lack of sleep.

I kiss her forehead, breathing in the salty ocean water and sand still stuck to her hair. Something stirs deep inside me, a feeling I've never felt before. A feeling I didn't know I could feel.

Want.

I want her. Not just to fuck her. I want more with her. I want to feel everything with her, even if our time together is limited. I want to protect her.

What are you doing to me, Millie?

And then I close my eyes, and the strangest thing happens. I fall into a deep, content sleep.

16 MILLIE

I'm warm, too warm, but also so damn comfortable that I don't want to move. Maybe if I just kick the covers off, I can sleep some more without being so hot.

I kick, knocking the comforter and sheet to the floor. Not what I intended, but I feel so much better. The sun is warming my skin through the large window. Quickly, I realize that the main source of heat isn't the sun or the covers, it's the very hot, naked man that I'm practically groping.

"Oh my god!" I squeal when I realize he's naked—completely naked. My thigh is draped over his waist, and his cock is straining against my leg. My hand is gripping his pec, and his hand is gripping my ass.

Sebastian stirs awake from my outburst. I might have been a little too dramatic.

"You're naked," I exclaim in horror. Right now, my memory of last night is a little foggy. In fact, I don't think I've ever slept harder or better, except maybe the night that got us in this mess in the first place.

He chuckles. "You're observant."

I pull my body back, ripping myself from him even though what I really want to do is snuggle deeper into his shoulder, grip his cock, and then climb on top of him and fuck him awake.

Instead, I do the right thing, which is to act like he's a hot stovetop I can't touch.

"Did we? We didn't fuck again, did we?" I ask in horror. If I fucked this man again, and have no memory of it, I'm going to kill my brain for having such shitty memory. It's not fair that my body gets to experience such pleasure, and I can't relive the moments over and over again. I remember every embarrassing comment I've made, but I don't remember Sebastian King fucking me.

He stretches his arms over his head, and his cock rests back against his hard stomach. "No, we didn't have sex."

I let out a long breath.

"But we can change that." He winks at me.

The memories start coming back. The voicemail that ruined our perfect day. Sebastian being kind and holding me while I fell asleep. He kept my demons away last night. He was so sweet. He was the kind of guy women could fall for.

Thank god he's back to his playful, joking, sex-focused self this morning.

"Are you ready to beg?"

"Are you?"

I smile. We don't have to talk about what happened last night. I just need a few more days without thinking about the voicemail—about him. I need this. I need to be carefree and fun Millie again. I haven't been her in years. Sebastian lets me be her. He wants me to be her.

I pull on the hem of my shirt. Last night it seemed like a good idea to sleep in just this T-shirt. Now, in the bright daylight, I feel vulnerable. I feel naked, even though Sebastian is the one who is naked. I'm covered, but all my old insecurities come flying back.

"Don't," he says.

I narrow my eyes as I bring my knees up to my chest.

"Don't think you're less than. I don't know who made you feel that way but don't let them win. You are incredible, Millie. My cock thinks so, and so do I."

I stare down at his dick—hard, long, and thick.

"It's just because it's morning. That happens to all guys in the morning."

"No, it's because it's you."

He rolls over and grabs my hands pulling them away from my legs so he can look at me. "I'm not the man who can give you the happily ever after that you deserve, but I am the man who can remind you of how beautiful and incredible you are. If I could choose any other woman to be fake married to, I wouldn't. You're the only person I would want to be fake married to."

I shake my head.

"And before you go thinking that was just a line I tell women to get into my bed, know that you're truly the only woman I've ever been fake married to."

I laugh. "I'm still not fucking you."

"I didn't say that so that you would fuck me. I said it because it's true. I've never met a woman like you, Millie. Don't let anyone stifle you."

My stomach growls. "I think it's time for breakfast."

"More like lunch."

"What?" I frown, looking over at the clock on the nightstand. "Oh my god! It's twelve-thirty. I haven't slept in this long since college."

I look at Sebastian. "Me neither."

We stare at each other. Both of us know that we should leave this bed before we do something stupid. *Although, maybe it isn't stupid?* We have chemistry. We're adults. In six months, we are going to be nothing but a bad memory. Maybe we should fuck and get each other out of our systems.

"Can I plan today?" Sebastian says suddenly.

"I thought I got to decide all our activities this week?"

"Please?"

"What do you have in mind?"

He shakes his head. "Nope, if I'm in charge, it's a surprise, just like when you choose the activities."

I sigh. "Fine, but whatever activities you have planned, we have to keep our clothes on."

"That wasn't the deal when *you* did it."

I fold my arms over my chest. "That's my condition. Take it or leave it." I know it's hypocritical. I had us skinny dip yesterday. But that was before we spent all night snuggling naked in each other's arms. If we fuck, I want to make sure I have a clear head. I need to make a pros and cons list. I need to talk to Oaklee. *But how do I ask Oaklee if I should fuck Sebastian without explaining everything else?* Of course, she'll say I should fuck my husband.

"Fine, I don't need you naked to have my way with you." He winks and then stretches and gets out of the bed. Then I'm staring at his naked ass, hard and muscly, until he covers it with the towel that I remember he came to bed with.

Dammit, why did I insist on wearing clothes today?

———

"ARE you trying to outdo me on being more adventurous?" I ask, panting behind Sebastian.

He laughs. "When you chose the activities, we zip-lined, jet skied, and skinny-dipped all in one day. All we're doing today is going for a hike."

"Yea, a hike across the entire island." I lift my arms over my head, trying to catch my breath. I'm wearing jean shorts and a tank top. I have a Hawaii ball cap and cheap sunglasses from the hotel gift shop, but none of it is doing much to block out the heat. Even though it's only spring, it's hot in this jungle. Sweat trickles down the back of my neck.

"We've only been hiking an hour. We have two hours left to reach the waterfall."

"Two hours! Are you serious?"

I sit down on a rock, not believing that Mr. Not Adventurous really planned this long of a hike.

He hands me a bottle of water. I take it and start chugging.

"The worst is over. It's mostly flat from here on out."

"It's not the incline that's getting to me; it's the heat. And the fact that I hardly ever work out."

Sebastian stretches his arms over his head until the T-shirt he's wearing rides up. He's not sweating at all, and I haven't heard him breathe hard once. This is a leisurely stroll for him.

"Why not?"

I shrug. "I'm not a gym rat. And I don't usually have time to explore the outdoors like this and get exercise that way."

"You should really try working out—"

I put my hand up. "I'm going to stop you right there. I agree. I don't need a lecture from a guy who has the body of Greek god."

"Actually, I prefer a Roman god; they were more ripped."

I roll my eyes.

Why can't I remember that one night? Maybe if I had the memory, I wouldn't want him so badly. Maybe he's terrible in bed. Who am I kidding? He's probably incredible in bed. If I remembered, I'd only want a repeat, which apparently the Roman god won't do.

"I thought you preferred to be called King."

"Only when I'm making you come."

I sigh. "We really shouldn't."

"Why not? It would be fun."

My heart thumps in my chest, but not because I'm out of breath from the hike. "How much fun it would or wouldn't be isn't the problem."

"Then tell me what you're worried about, and I can fix it for you."

"Just like that?"

"Just like that." His eyes twinkle with his promise. He truly thinks he can solve any of my reservations around us having sex.

"If we fuck, are you going to fall in love with me?" he asks.

"No." I'm not capable of loving anyone.

"Are you going to get emotionally attached?"

I shrug. "I don't think so."

He scrunches his mouth until it's pursed together as he thinks. "You won't."

"How do you know?"

"I'm an ass, you've said so yourself. And once we fuck, I'll pick up my asshole game so you can't possibly grow attached. Problem solved."

"I'd prefer nice, sexless Sebastian to asshole Sebastian who I get to fuck all the time."

He shakes his head. "That's the wrong choice. Being with asshole Sebastian is totally worth the mind-blowing orgasms I could give you."

I laugh. "I can give myself mind-blowing orgasms, thank you very much. I just need a friend."

His eyebrows raise. "A friend who is fake married to you to protect you from something that you won't tell me about?"

I nod. "Exactly."

"You should be glad I like you, Mills. I wouldn't be fake married with no benefits to just anyone."

"Mills? You're giving me a nickname now?"

"I could go back to calling you Mrs. King."

"Nope, I like Mills."

He holds out his hand to help me up. Reluctantly, I take it.

He pulls me up, and our bodies near.

"How about we make a deal?" he asks, his breath hot against my neck. I like this kind of hotness.

"I thought we already had a deal and a bet?"

His eyes darken. "We don't have an arrangement."

I laugh.

"You finish this hike with me, and I'll give you a kiss when we reach the top."

"I don't get anything out of that deal."

He grabs my hips and jerks me tight to him until our lips are hovering just over each other's. I stare into his deep eyes, and I've never wanted to kiss him more.

"Are you sure about that? I think you get a romantic kiss overlooking a waterfall in Hawaii on the only honeymoon you may ever take. You get to remember how it feels to be kissed by a man who truly wants you. You get to know how it feels to be desired desperately. And you'll be reminded that you are a sexual creature who deserves to have the best sex of her life. Then you'll realize that you do want to be married after all, not because you need a man, but because you deserve to be fucked like a queen every damn day. That's what you'll get."

I can't breathe. I can't respond.

Sebastian's eyes flicker over mine, and then he steps back and holds out his hand. I take it gladly. I've never wanted a kiss more than I do now. This hike just got a lot longer. Unbearably long.

"Maybe I can get that kiss now," I say.

He turns to me with serious eyes. "No. I'll kiss you when we make it to the waterfall. A woman like you deserves the best first kiss."

"But this won't be our first kiss."

He frowns. "Yes, it will. It's the only first kiss that matters."

17   SEBASTIAN

I should've kissed her. Right then and there.

We've been hiking for almost two hours since the moment she told me to kiss her, and I refused until we made it to the waterfall.

Big mistake.

I've been hiking with a hard-on the entire time, not the most comfortable thing in the world.

But I'm determined to give her the best kiss I can. I want it to be romantic and perfect and magical. I want it to make her believe in love again. Not that she should fall in love with me, but that love and magic can exist. I don't want her to turn cynical like me.

Our kiss isn't going to be magical, that is if we even make it to the waterfall. We were supposed to arrive at the waterfall twenty minutes ago. I'm pretty sure we're lost, but I won't tell Millie that.

When, or if, we ever make it, the kiss is going to be far from perfect. We are both covered in sweat from the incredible heat. Millie has about a dozen mosquito bites because I forgot to pack repellent, and I have a sunburn on my fore-head because I didn't wear a hat.

Our muscles ache, and even though I still have two bottles of water and a granola bar in my backpack, we are dehydrated and hungry. I didn't plan this well. I was just focused on getting us to the waterfall, on giving Millie a magical moment.

Millie deserves it. She deserves the perfect kiss. And dammit, we didn't come all this way to not let it happen.

All hope is lost.

Suddenly, Millie starts singing 'Heart Attack' by Demi Lovato. She's completely out of breath. Her hands rest on her hips as she tries to suck in more oxygen with each step, but it doesn't stop her from trying to belt out lyrics about not falling in love.

"For real, I think I'm going to have a heart attack." Millie folds her arms over her head, her chest rising and falling, panting. Her cheeks are red, her face is dripping sweat, and her hair is a mess, tied back behind her ball cap. There are sweat stains all over her shirt, and her freckled legs have red swollen spots from mosquitos and where she's gotten too much sun.

"Maybe you should stop singing then. You sound like a dying horse."

"I. Do. Not." She pants between each word.

"You. Do. Too." I pant just like her to prove her point.

"I think you're trying to kill me. But I hate to tell you, if you kill me I don't have any money for you to collect and I don't have a life insurance policy. So there is nothing to gain by killing me," Millie teases me.

I laugh, knowing that Millie is just kidding, but it is a thought that has crossed my mind. A strategy that she might be trying to do to me—marrying me to take half of my money. "I'm not trying to kill you, but you are trying to kill me with that voice of yours."

"Well then, you sing. I didn't bring my phone, and I need music to keep me entertained."

"I thought the very thought of kissing me was enough to keep you occupied." It sure is enough to keep my thoughts off how bad of a plan this was. All I want to do is kiss her. One kiss and I know I can convince her to repeat our one forgotten night.

"Sing, pretty boy."

"I'll sing, you drink." I toss her a water bottle. She catches it and starts drinking.

I wrack my brain, trying to think of a song. What comes out is 'Mercy' by Shawn Mendes. I sing a few bars before I hear Millie chuckling behind me.

"It wasn't as bad as your singing," I say.

She laughs. "That's not why I'm laughing."

"Why are you laughing?"

"Because the only songs you know are boy bands."

I stop, and Millie slams into my back.

"Shawn Mendes isn't a boy band. Neither is Justin Bieber," I say, remembering the earlier song I sang to her.

She laughs harder. "Stop, you're making it harder to breathe."

So then I start singing Maroon 5's 'Harder to Breathe.'

"That's a real boy band," I say.

"Oh my god, seriously stop. I can't—"

I turn, and she runs smack dab into me, chest to chest. Face to face. I'm standing downhill from her, so we are actually at eye level with each other. We breathe into each other. Our mouths are hovering over each other but not crossing the line.

Millie leans forward, her pink lips so close to mine. I

want them. It doesn't matter that we haven't found the waterfall yet. It doesn't matter that I'm not in control. What matters is that we want to kiss.

"Kiss me," she whispers.

"Are you begging, Mills?"

Her lips part, and her tongue slides through, licking her bottom lip, making it perfectly clear what she'd like me to do.

I swallow hard. This is what I wanted. I wanted her to initiate. I wanted her to beg. I wanted her to want me. To want to be kissed. To want to be fucked.

"Yes, just like your body is. Your lips have parted. Your breath has caught. You've leaned closer. Caught us both entirely out of breath so that we can't think and stop this. We are both begging—now kiss me," she says.

Suddenly, I spot the waterfall trickling behind her through the trees. I grab her hand and yank her in that direction.

"What are you doing?" she squeals. "Sebastian, I'm tired. I don't care about the damn perfect waterfall, just—"

She gasps when she sees the sight. It's the most beautiful, magical vision. I never knew things like this existed in real life. It looks completely untouched by mankind even though a trail leads right to it. Not very many people have ventured four hours through the steamy jungle to see the simple flow of water over a cliff into a small pool of water surrounded by flowers and greenery that seem to only exist in Hawaii. I've never seen anything like it.

"It's—," Millie breathes in, trying to find the right words to describe how incredible it is, but I don't give her time to think. I want to give her the perfect kiss. Partially because I want to spark her to search for her own happily ever after again, but also because I want to be her best first kiss. I want her to compare all men to me. I want to be impossible to top, so that when a man finally tops it, she can know he is the real deal.

A kiss by a man who truly loves her doesn't need to be done near a waterfall in Hawaii, the best kiss of her life just needs to be given by a man who loves her. He can kiss her by a dumpster filled with rotting fish and sewage, and it will still be the best damn kiss of her life.

I grab her neck, my thumbs caressing her jawline, and before she catches her breath, I close the gap, and our mouths meet for the first time that either of us remembers.

I forget about where we are. I forget about the waterfall. The sweet scent of the flowers. The beautiful roar of the water.

The seconds our lips touch, I'm consumed by her—her smell, her taste, her touch. It overpowers everything else. All I can feel is her.

She smells like juniper breeze. She tastes like strawberry jam. She feels like heaven in my arms.

This was supposed to be the best damn kiss of her life, but it's quickly becoming mine. I've never had a kiss like this—one that literally took my breath away, along with all of my thoughts and senses.

I don't know what is going on in Millie's head, but I hear the moans she's making, her hands digging into my chest, pulling me tighter against her, our hips slamming together. Her tongue begs for more in my mouth, and I give it to her. Our tongues glide over each other's in a teasing dance.

This kiss has to end before I yank all her clothes off and fuck her in the middle of the rain forest. That might sound romantic as hell, but I doubt when we have splinters and poison ivy and ticks, it will still feel that romantic. I want

Millie in a proper bed—my bed. I want her in that heavenly bed back at our hotel.

I pull away before she realizes the kiss is over, and I watch for a split second where her lips kiss the air between us wanting more.

Her eyes flutter open, slowly coming back to reality.

I'm still stuck in the fantasy. *What the hell was that?* There is no way that was normal. A kiss like that is a once in a lifetime kiss.

"Was that...?" I ask, even though I have no idea what I'm asking.

"Hmm," she says back, oblivious that my question made no sense.

We both take deep breaths, still pressed against each other everywhere but our lips. I'm not big on kissing. It's just a prelude to the fucking, but Jesus effing Christ—I think I've been wrong all my life. That kiss flipped my heart upside down. It wrecked my soul. It made me harder than I've ever been. It was more than just a tease—it was the whole show.

Yes, I still want to fuck her, but I'm more than satisfied just kissing her.

Millie is the first to actually articulate her thoughts into words. "If you kissed me like that back in Vegas, then it's no wonder that we ended up married. How could I let someone who kisses me like that go?"

She's so bold with her words, so Millie. I'm thankful, because it reminds me that I can't let her fall for me. I have to be a little cruel. I have to be a bit of the asshole I'm supposed to be. I have to keep her feelings out of this. Just remind her that perfect kisses exist. That love can exist if both people believe in it. I just don't.

I snicker. "Don't go getting soft on me, Mills. I made

you climb a mountain to earn that kiss. I didn't kiss you until you begged."

She steps back, and I step forward. I grab her hips, pulling her tightly against my steel cock. "And I won't fuck you until you open your pretty little mouth to me, get down on your knees to worship my cock, and plead with me to enter you."

"Asshole," she curses when I release her.

"Tease," I curse back. But Millie is anything but a tease. She's the whole package. And I think for a moment that I'm wrong in trying to push her into dating again, finding a man again. No man could be worthy of her.

She glares at me, but there is a softness to her eyes when she looks at me. She knows I'm acting mean to keep her safe, to keep her from falling for me. I look away, needing a moment to think about my next move...

"Son of a bitch," I yell as something stings my neck.

"Don't move," Millie says so calmly and sure.

I freeze. Well, everything but my heart freezes. My heart pounds a million miles a minute in my chest, still dreaming about that damn kiss. I know I'm in danger. This special moment is over, but all I can think is, *why did I stop kissing her?*

18 MILLIE

My heart teeters on the edge of so many feelings. The hurt I felt after he acted like a grade-A asshole. The fear I feel at watching what he just stumbled into. And yet the strongest emotion is still tied to that kiss.

I've been kissed before, but not like that.

That kiss was jaw-dropping, inside turning, a let's ride off into the sunset on our white horse kind of a kiss. I can't even figure out why the kiss was so incredible. He had great technique, sure. The spot he chose to kiss me was magical, the most beautiful natural place I've ever seen, and I've traveled the world. But we were also exhausted, sweaty, and sunburnt. We don't like each other, we hardly know each other, and yet...

I want a repeat. I want him to kiss me again and again.

He's kissed me before, but somehow I forgot. I don't know how that's possible when I know that I'll be thinking of this long after Sebastian and I get divorced and go our separate ways. That kiss renewed my hope in humanity, in love.

It shouldn't. Sebastian King doesn't do love. Neither do

I. Yet it felt like the universe was trying to tell us something with that kiss.

I'm horny as hell and haven't gotten laid in forever. That's it. We just need to fuck, and then we will be out of each other's systems. But no more kissing; kissing is dangerous. Kissing caused my heart to flutter—a heart I thought I'd locked away and protected with castle walls, a draw bridge, and a moat. I didn't think anyone, especially Sebastian King, had a shot at getting through, and yet, my heart did strange things during that kiss.

Focus.

"Son of a bitch, that hurt," Sebastian says, slapping his neck again.

"Don't move."

"Millie, what's going on?"

Sebastian huffed off because he was a jerk after our kiss. A kiss that affected him just like it did me. A kiss that caused him to lash out to avoid either of us getting feelings. A reaction that caused him to not realize that his foot is stuck in a fallen beehive. The bees he has thoroughly pissed off will come at him hard as soon as he removes his foot.

I have to remain calm though, I don't want him to panic and take a misstep and fall over the cliff a few feet behind him.

"Sebastian, are you allergic to bees?" I ask.

"No, I don't think so."

I nod. "Good. You're standing on a beehive, and when you lift your foot, they're all going to come after us. I'm going to count to three, and then we're going to run as fast as we can. Understand?"

His eyes are big as he nods.

I swallow down my fear. Bees are harmless; they don't

usually attack unless threatened, but we just threatened a whole bunch of them.

"One...two...three!"

We immediately sprint as fast as we can while a swarm of angry bees lurches out of the hive. We run through trees and jump over bushes to get away as fast as possible.

I know we have to get to the water. That's our best chance of avoiding more stings, but we are at the top of the waterfall. We have to climb down. We have to—

"Jump!" I shout at him.

"Are you crazy?"

"We have to."

"We could break our necks! Why are we jumping?" He slaps his legs as more bees sting him.

He's right. I shouldn't risk his life to save mine. *Think!*

The bees are getting closer. Stay calm; they won't hurt you if you stay calm.

Sebastian looks at me closer. "Millie, are you allergic?"

I don't answer. We are miles away from civilization. It doesn't matter if I'm allergic or not. What matters is that I make sure Sebastian is okay. He may not be allergic, but the number of stings he's getting can't be good for anyone.

"Millie?" he asks again.

"Let's climb down around the side and get you into the water where the bees can't get to you."

"Jesus." His eyes peer over the edge, and then before either of us can think about what he's doing, he's grabbed me by the hand, and we are both jumping over the waterfall and into the pool of water below.

I scream as our bodies fall, having no idea how deep the water is. It's thrilling and dangerous, and exactly who Sebastian thinks I am.

We hit the water, our hands coming apart on contact.

My legs hit the floor too fast, but not enough to break them or seriously hurt me. Sebastian is taller and heavier, so he hit the bottom before I did.

We both break the surface, breathing fast.

"There is never a dull moment with you, is there, Millie?"

I laugh nervously. "Nope, my life is just one crazy adventure after the next."

He laughs with me, finding my hand in the water and pulling me to him.

"Are you okay? Your foot—"

"Is fine," he finishes, taking my face in his hands as we continue to pant. Apparently, neither of us are ever able to catch our breaths around each other.

"Why did you stay when a single sting from one of those bees could have killed you?"

"You were in danger. I couldn't leave you."

"You should have run."

"You shouldn't have jumped."

I let my hands roam his face and neck where I see a few red bumps, but the bees seem to have vanished like I thought they would when we jumped into the water.

Sebastian thinks I'm wild—I am, but not in love. In love, I don't take risks, not anymore. I don't risk anything with a man. But for a second, I risk it all.

I grab Sebastian's neck and pull us together as our mouths connect. Open, raw, rough—we devour each other. Our first kiss was perfect, sweet, magical. This kiss is hungry, carnal, and intimate.

The water pushes us closer together, smashing us together until I can feel all of him. Everywhere I touch is hard—his chest, his arms, his cock. All of him is muscle and man. All of him begs me to touch him.

I forget about the consequences. I just want him. This is pretend; this isn't real. But for a moment we had a very real moment. We risked our health for the other, and that brought us closer together. It turned the tables and made me want him.

I shouldn't. This is when I should demand he be a jerk. When I should turn wild and crazy. This is when we should ensure that we are our worst because we are vulnerable. Our hearts are open after the beautiful moment we just had. And hearts are designed to fall in love and then break.

I vowed I wouldn't let that happen again.

And yet, here I am kissing Sebastian like he's my real husband. My body is sliding up and down his, humping him in the water, begging him to remove our clothes and take me right here, right now.

"Sebastian," I breathe through the sloppy kiss, one that fires through my body and practically makes me come. *Jesus, it's been too long. That's all this is. Too long since I've been fucked. I don't feel anything else.*

"Mmm," he moans back, unable to detangle his mouth from mine. His hands slide up my body under my shirt, moving so close to my breasts.

Yes.

Yes!

Just a little closer...

When suddenly, he's gone. He's no longer kissing me. He's no longer feeling me. No longer seconds away from taking me in this pool of water.

I open my eyes.

"Why did you stop?" I ask, afraid he's come to his senses and no longer finds me attractive.

"I'm not going to fuck you for the first time either of us

remembers in this freezing pool, with me covered in bee stings, and you risking your life being out here where you could get stung."

I shiver, realizing how cool the water is for the first time. He's right. We shouldn't fuck here. But hiking back four hours to get back will seem like an eternity.

I pout.

He chuckles. "We don't have to hike the four hours back. There is a thirty-minute hike to where we can have a car pick us up."

"Thank God!"

He laughs harder. He holds out his hand, and I take it as he helps me out of the pool.

He hisses when he steps out. For the first time, I see the damage of jumping into the water caused him. His ankle is swollen and bruised.

"Sebastian, your ankle, I'm so sorry. I shouldn't have made you jump."

He turns and shakes his head. "And I shouldn't have put you at risk in the first place." He tucks a strand of hair behind my ear.

"Let me help you create a makeshift brace or something to make it easier to walk."

Sebastian brushes me off. "I'm fine."

Just like that, he's back to being cold with me except when we are being intimate.

"Ouch," I wack my neck after something sharp hits me.

I don't think twice about it. I'm too busy thinking about Sebastian and how to get him to stop being so hot and cold. I know I wanted him to be a jerk to me to protect my heart, but...

"Millie." Sebastian's voice drops, and the twinkle in his eyes is now replaced with absolute fear.

I don't know what he's so afraid of.

Then the burning on my neck hits me. Already, I can feel my tongue swelling, my throat closing. I know better than to travel without my epi-pen. But when I'm around Sebastian, I forget everything but him.

"Fuck," I say, knowing that might be the last word I ever say. We are thirty minutes from a road. Thirty minutes from cell phone service. I'm about to swell up bigger than Sebastian's ankle.

I take a shaky breath. At least I'll die having had the perfect first kiss, and the dirtiest second kiss. I'll die without having my heart broken again.

19 SEBASTIAN

My nightmare happened. The thing we were trying to prevent—Millie got stung.

I realized it before she did. I tried not to react, hoping that if I kept her calm, then she wouldn't actually feel sick. But I'm not a good enough actor to hide my fear.

Now Millie is standing in front of me, gripping her neck. I know how bad her neck stings. I have small bites all over my body that all burn. But unlike her, my entire body isn't swelling up.

"What do I do?" I ask, knowing that time isn't our friend. I have to get her help.

"Get us somewhere where we can call 911," Millie says so calmly like she's just telling me directions to drive to her favorite diner—not giving me instructions that can save her life.

I nod. "The road is close from this direction." I pull out my cell. I don't have any service, but I should once we get a bit closer to the road.

Millie takes a breath, and it's already garbled. I can hear the wheezing, the struggle to breathe.

"What else?"

She shakes her head gently, giving me a fake smile that's meant to reassure me. but I see right through it. "We take our time walking toward the road together. There is nothing else we can do."

"How long do we have?"

"We'll make it," she gives me a wink.

"Yea, we will." I grab her hand and drape it over my back. "Climb on."

"Sebastian, your ankle. You can't carry me."

"Millie, climb on my back right the hell now."

She does. She may be wild, but my voice can tame her. *Good to know.*

And then I start running.

"Sebastian, slow—" Her voice catches, and she struggles to get any more words out.

"Do not tell me to slow down because I won't."

She doesn't ask me again. I run down the mountain through the trees and branches that have fallen on the path. I don't feel my ankle as I run. All I focus on is Millie, listening to her breath and hoping that I can run fast enough to save her.

I've saved people before, but never have I felt such urgency, such responsibility and need to save someone. If I fail, not only will the world lose an incredible woman, but I will never be the same. Losing Millie would be like losing a piece of me.

"You shouldn't have—" Millie takes a deep breath while I hang onto her every word.

"...stopped kissing me."

I laugh. "Are you trying to make a joke?"

She nods against my neck.

"Well, it's a horrible one."

"You," she takes a broken inhale. "Then," she exhales painfully.

"If you didn't want to fuck me, you should have just told me no. You didn't have to fake almost dying." My joke sucks worse than hers, but I hear the faintest chuckle behind me. It made her smile.

I need to keep talking. I need to distract her from whatever pain she's feeling.

"I'm going to try and guess why you wanted to stay fake married to me since you won't tell me and there is no way those Kylie Jenner sized lips are going to tell me now."

More chuckles, but these ones are softer.

Keep breathing, baby. Don't die on me.

I keep running as I think of the most ridiculous reasons I can think of.

"You have to be married to inherit an English estate."

Laugh.

"You are a princess in line to the Monaco throne and are trying to live a normal married life before being forced to marry a prince."

Laugh.

"You're secretly in love with me and think you're going to make me fall head over heels before our six months together is up."

She laughs, but it's barely audible. It deflates me. I have no jokes left in me.

You're running from something and need me to protect you.

The guess has floated through my head before, and right now, it seems like the most plausible.

Millie makes a sound, but it doesn't sound like anything I've ever heard before, and I've heard countless people on the edge of death before. Most of those people wanted to die, but the sound Millie makes is a cry to live. If she had use of her voice, it would be a warrior cry instead of the soft moan of a woman whose body is swollen and making it impossible to breathe.

The sound tells me time is up. I have to get her to a hospital as quickly as possible.

I pull out my phone—one bar.

I dial 911 and then hold it to my ear.

"What's your emergency?" I hear on the other line.

"My fr—wife was stung by a bee, and she's having an allergic reaction. We are hiking near Waimoku Falls and are headed to the road. We are less than five minutes away and need an ambulance."

"Okay, sir. I have an ambulance on its way. Is she walking on her own?"

"No, I'm carrying her."

"Is she breathing?"

I feel the heat of her breath against my neck.

"Barely."

"Okay. Keep monitoring her breathing. If she stops breathing at any point, I need you to communicate to me what is happening, and I can walk you through steps to clear her airway and give her CPR until the ambulance arrives."

"Okay," I breathe back, hating how easy it is for me to breathe and how hard it is for her to breathe. If I could give her all my breaths right now, I would.

But all I can do is keep running forward and hope I make it there in time. *So close.*

I run faster.

Then I see the road. I hear sirens in the distance.

"We made it, Millie. We made it," I say out of breath from running.

The ambulance roars to a stop in front of us, and the paramedics jump out, racing to take Millie from me and put her on a stretcher. One of them stops in front of me.

"You riding with us?"

"Yes, I'm her husband."

He nods, and I follow him into the back where they've already loaded Millie into the ambulance and begun working on her. She has an oxygen mask on and an IV in her arm.

The second the door shuts, the ambulance starts flying.

"Is she...?" I ask one of the paramedics who is administering medicine through her IV.

"My job is to get her to the hospital alive, and I will. You'll have to talk to a doctor about her long term prognosis."

I nod and don't ask any more questions as we drive. Millie's hand is within reach, so I take it and hold onto her, giving her all of my comfort and hope.

"You got this, Millie," I whisper.

We arrive at the hospital, and the doors fly open. I hop out and curse when my foot hits the pavement, but I don't give a damn about my foot. All I care about is Millie.

The paramedics pull Millie out on a gurney and then pass her off to a team at the hospital. I try to follow through the doors when a nurse stops me.

"You'll have to wait here," she says.

"But I'm her husband." I hold up my hand with my ring like I need to prove that I'm her husband or something.

She nods. "Come with me."

I follow her, and then suddenly she stops outside a door. "Sit on the exam table, and I'll have someone examine your foot."

"My foot is fine; my wife isn't. I won't leave her."

"Get your ass on the table so I can set your foot quickly while the ER docs look over your wife. They won't let you in the room anyway, and you won't be any good to her with a broken ankle."

"My ankle isn't broken."

She raises her eyebrows. "I'm fifty-three years old. I've been doing this a long time. I know a broken ankle when I see one. I know you want to be with your wife, so give me twenty minutes to set it and put it in a cast to heal it until you have an orthopedic doc take a look. Or you can be stubborn, in which case I'll make you wait for a doc to look at it, which could take hours before you see your wife. Now, which will it be?"

I frown, ready to argue.

"Twenty minutes. I promise I'll get you to your wife as soon as they will let you see her."

"Fine." I step inside the room, trying to prove to her that my ankle isn't broken, but there is no hiding it.

I sit on the table and let her quickly put my foot in a cast.

"Do you want pain meds?" she asks.

"I'm an alcoholic and drug addict. No, I don't want drugs."

She nods. "Wheelchair?"

I hop down, giving her my answer.

She smiles at me. "I'll have some crutches brought to her room. Follow me, and I'll take you to your wife."

Luckily, Millie is just in the room over. I can't breathe though when I see her hooked up to so many tubes and IVs. She even has one shoved down her throat.

My nurse takes the chart and looks it over quickly as the other nurses and docs are still working on Millie. She looks from the chart to the machine with her vitals and then squeezes my hand. "Your wife is going to be okay, thanks to you. Now, go hold her hand until we get her moved up to another room."

I nod, choking back tears and words, and then I go to Millie. When I squeeze her hand three times, I swear I feel her squeeze back three times. That's all I need to know that everything is going to be okay. We are going to make it.

I look down at her hand. I have no idea how I'm going to let go of her hand in six months.

20 MILLIE

Sebastian squeezes my hand three times. He doesn't know the meaning; at least, I don't think he does. But he saw Oaklee and me do it. He's letting me know he's here for me. He's letting me know that he cares more than any words he could ever say.

I smile inside even though I can't show him what it means to me that he's here, that he saved me. Not only that, but once he saved me, he stayed. He didn't leave. He stayed.

I try to squeeze his hand back, but I feel so weak that I barely moved my fingers at all.

"I'm here; it's going to be okay. I'm here."

Those words stayed with me while I dreamed. I wish I dreamed of my future. Instead, I dreamed of my past. Even dreaming about a future without Sebastian would have been better than reliving everything.

My dreams didn't take a different form. I didn't dream of a bright light or falling or clowns or whatever it is that people dream about that is a metaphor for their real fear. No, for every second that I was unconscious, I relived every heartbreak, every mistake, every drop of pain my life has contained.

It gives me motivation to open my eyes even faster, to get away from my past and live my present, even if my future is back to reliving my pain.

I open my eyes, afraid that Sebastian is gone. That I dreamed Sebastian King up. Or that once I open them, I'll remember he's nothing more than an egocentric ass, who is only in this relationship to get laid.

I open my eyes, and I see him. He's sitting in a chair next to my bed, slumped over face first on the edge, drooling onto my pillow, making the softest most adorable snores. He looks exhausted, even though he's sleeping. I can tell by the ways his eyes are twitching, his mouth is moving, and the adorable yet painful soft snores he exhales. What catches my breath, though, isn't the broken man, it's that he's still holding my hand.

"He hasn't let go," a woman says.

I glance away from Sebastian to the other side of my hospital room, where a nurse is pressing on the monitor next to my bed.

I'm surprised these are the first words she says after I woke up. She didn't ask me how I'm feeling or tell me a doctor will be in to check on me soon. *No—she needed to tell me about Sebastian.*

"I'm Rebecca, one of your nurses."

I smile weakly.

"You have a good hubby there. He hasn't left your side. Hasn't let go of your hand. I had to force him to get a quick cast put on his ankle. And the only reason I've been able to get food or coffee in him is if he can eat it one-handed."

I look away from her and back at Sebastian. He's too good. He shouldn't have stayed, at least, not like that. He should have gone back to the hotel to sleep and checked in on me during normal visitation hours.

I study him closer, looking at the bee stings that speckle his arms, neck, and cheeks. They're now covered in a lotion to reduce swelling and itching. I try to glance over the bed to see his ankle, but I can't with the way the bed is situated.

"I'm sorry your honeymoon was ruined, but if I can give you a piece of advice, don't let this ruin your relationship. He's a keeper." She winks at me and then leaves without checking on any of my vitals or asking me any questions. *Does that make her a terrible nurse or just skilled at sensing what people need?* Because right now, I just want a moment alone with Sebastian.

I run my hand through his fluffy hair that still is coated with saltwater and sand from our dip in the pool.

"This didn't ruin anything. If anything, it stopped me from doing something stupid that I'll end up regretting." A kiss is intense enough. If I let this go any further, there is no way I'd survive it; no way I wouldn't fall for him. And me falling for handsome men like Sebastian King would ruin me.

Sebastian's eyes open. I don't know if he heard my confession or not, but when he looks at me, really looks at me, with all the emotion in the world, my confession doesn't matter.

I want to jump his bones.

"Mills, you're awake."

I nod, realizing that I still haven't spoken out loud to him.

"Thank God." If my heart wasn't a crumbled mess before, it is now. He climbs up into the bed next to me, cradling me against his chest as we both exhale a deep breath. For a split second, this feels real. Like it would have really mattered if I had died, and wouldn't just be an inconvenience he had to deal with.

The way he presses my head against his heart, I know that he'd mourn me far longer than any other acquaintance.

What does that mean? Does he have feelings?

He can't. He's already said he doesn't feel things like that. And we haven't known each other long enough to catch feelings. Being in a hospital like this just does something to people. No matter what, it would have been traumatic watching me swell up like a balloon, about to die at any second.

But the reality hits me, and I feel tears in my eyes. Our life may only stay connected for six months, but I will forever owe my life to him. He saved me. He ran on an injured ankle to save me.

"My superman," I whisper, blinking back my tears.

He pulls away; his expression falls into one of twisted agony.

"I'm not your superman. I'm the arrogant playboy who just wants to get into your pants. Just ask the nurse, I hit on her earlier."

I take a deep breath. "Jerk." Even though he's the farthest thing from it.

"That's me, sweetheart." His knuckles brush over my cheek. "I can't wait to get you back to the hotel to play doctor and nurse." The twinkle returns to his eyes.

This is who he thinks he is. Or maybe this is what he thinks I need per our arrangement.

But something changed here in Hawaii. I saw a portal to a different side of him. I saw the man willing to go through hell to save me. No man has ever done that for me before.

Sebastian tries to pull away, to climb off the bed. I know

once he does, that he'll go back to pretending. That's all we do with each other—pretend. I just don't know when we are pretending and when we are being real.

He doesn't fight me as I pull him back. He doesn't touch me either, though. I don't need him to touch me. I need to look at him. I need to thank him.

I try to stare into his eyes when I say the words, but my eyes fall to his lips, the part of him I need connected to me.

"Thank you." I don't say what for. I don't think he would accept me getting mushy on him right now. We are both in too vulnerable a state to go expressing anything genuine right now.

I think he's going to pull away again. I think the moment is over.

Then he gives me another shock. He fills the gap between us, his lips carefully sweeping against mine. I could almost not even classify it as a kiss, that's how gentle he's being.

For a second, our lips are just brushing as we both breathe in each other's souls. Somehow this is more intimate than either of our previous kisses. We aren't touching anywhere except our lips.

And then like lightning, we both strike at the same time. We each deepen the kiss, turning it into more than just a thank you, more than just a sweet moment of understanding that we can brush off.

This kiss hints at feelings that both of us promised we would never have. It breaks all the rules we set. This kiss isn't about remembering what lead us to be married. It isn't a gut reaction after a near-death experience.

This kiss is the realest thing in our fake marriage.

We separate, at least our lips do. But I stole a part of

him with that kiss, and he stole a part of me. Which part, I'm not sure, but I'll never be fully alone again.

"Don't scare me like that again," he whispers so softly before kissing my forehead, a kiss that transfers even more of himself to me.

Then he turns and walks out the door for the first time since I arrived. The moment was too much for either of us to handle. I'm not sure what it means, but I know that whatever that was, it wasn't pretend.

And that scares the hell out me.

21 SEBASTIAN

I spin my wedding ring around on my finger. It's a type of ring I never thought I'd be wearing, and don't even remember purchasing.

It's still strange being married. And yet each time I've spoken to someone else—the nurse at the hospital, the waiter at dinner, the butler at the hotel—calling Millie my wife falls off my tongue easier and easier.

She's isn't my wife, in any sense of the word. We haven't fucked. We've barely kissed. We know nothing about each other's history. And for the past week, we've hardly talked to each other except when necessary. We know a line was crossed that day.

Our first kiss toed the line.

Our second pushed us over.

Our third sent us tumbling over a cliff.

Not to mention our experiences rescuing each other from death. There is no going back. No pretending that I can just be her asshole and her my wild plaything.

Something was stirred in both of us that day, some

emotion that neither of us thought we could feel. And yet, we did.

But over the last few days, we've squashed any feelings we've had. The day Millie was released from the hospital, we went to different sides of the hotel suite and stayed there. I didn't take care of her, and she didn't pamper me. It was an unspoken agreement. We didn't share a bed. We rarely ate dinner together. We both spent our days watching TV alone.

And it worked.

Now we can be in the same room and there are no longer any feelings, just sexual tension, exactly what I wanted.

"It's still raining. Doesn't look like we will get to enjoy the beach or go on any other adventures before we have to leave tomorrow," Millie says.

I stand from the couch on my good leg and hobble over without the help of my crutches. After Millie woke up, I eventually got my ankle x-rayed. As the nurse told me, it was broken. Several weeks in the cast and then physical therapy after is my future.

I stare, getting lost in the beautiful woman with the strawberry streaks in her hair, the freckles, and a single bee sting on her neck. I'd break my ankle all over again if it meant saving her. I'd break every bone in my body for her.

That doesn't mean I have feelings for her. It just means I don't want to see a woman like her get hurt when I can do something to fix it.

"I don't think we should go on any more adventures. The last one about killed us both," I joke.

She laughs. Apparently, no joke is too soon with her, which makes her even more intriguing to me.

"Probably not. I think Mother Nature is trying to tell us we shouldn't be together."

"Nah, it's just probably monsoon season or something."

She shakes her head slowly. "That's in the fall. It's spring. I talked with the concierge, and he said that before we came, they hadn't gotten more than a sprinkle in over a month. I think we are bad luck or something."

I take a deep breath, and all I get is Millie. I haven't been this close to her in days. I haven't gotten the honor of smelling her. Her scent is always a little different each day. Some days she smells like lavender, other days peppermint, sometimes like the ocean, and then sometimes it's sugar and spice. Today, she smells like fire, like spice, like want.

Millie is wearing jean shorts and a T-shirt, and I bet if I slipped a finger in her panties, she'd be wet. Maybe not because of me, but because sex is already on her brain.

"Actually, I think we should have one last adventure," I say.

She folds her arms in front of her chest and looks at me. "You can't be serious. It's raining. Your cast can't get wet. And I'm not taking any more chances that one of us gets hurt."

"We won't go outside. In fact, we won't leave this hotel. How much trouble can we get into if we don't even go outside?"

She raises her eyebrows as a glint of a smirk touches her lips. "This is us we are talking about. Somehow we ended up married, broke your ankle, and almost killed me. Anything is possible."

"True, but this will be worth it. We have one last night before we get back to reality. One night before we learn the truth about each other. Before we leave paradise. Before we start pretending that we're already over so people aren't shocked when we finally are. The small risk is worth one last awesome night." My chest tightens when I talk about us one day being over. We were never something to begin with, I remind myself.

"What do you have in mind?"

"We get dressed up in our finest clothes. Have a romantic dinner. See where things take us. Pretend for one day that we are a real married couple; that we are really on our honeymoon."

She opens her mouth to talk, but I press further.

"Pretend I'm not in this cast and that you didn't almost die. Pretend that we love each other because we both know love isn't actually in the cards for us. We are in the most beautiful place in the world, in one of the most expensive hotel rooms, and we are two of the hottest people in the world."

She blushes at that. "One night?" Her eyes light up, telling me she knows exactly what this means. We are using our one night, our one redo—tonight. This is it, there won't be a repeat. If we are going to live together, we need to get this out of our systems. Tonight should be the night. We won't get a better setting.

"One night," I answer her.

Her eyes rake up and down my body in heated waves, even though I'm only wearing boxers and a ratty T-shirt. Even though I smell and haven't showered in two days, I can tell she'd let me fuck her right here right now if I just said the word.

But I want tonight to be perfect. If we only get one night together, I want it to be the best fucking night. A night that we will never forget, unlike last time. And if we are really lucky, it will trigger the memories of that night too.

I flick a piece of her hair back off her shoulder, the only touch I allow myself for now. "Go shower, do your hair and makeup, wear your nicest dress and your sexiest lingerie." I wink at her when she's about to protest the lingerie part.

"Go," I push her in the direction of the shower. Luckily, there are two bathrooms, so we can both get ready at the same time. I hope she gets dressed slowly because I have an unforgettable night planned.

22 MILLIE

My hand shakes as I try to run my eyeliner over my upper lid, resulting in a wavy line.

Fuck.

I put the eyeliner tube down and pick up some Kleenex to wipe it off, but all I do is smear the black liner everywhere. I toss the Kleenex in the sink. I'm going to have to use remover to get it off.

Instead, I grip the sink, knowing the problem isn't with my makeup, it's with me. I'm so nervous.

My hair is curled, and I'm wearing a simple black dress that dips down, showing off plenty of cleavage, while also hugging the curves of my stomach, waist, and hips. I feel sexy as hell in this dress, but only a man who likes plenty of curves will find me attractive. I'm not a stick-thin model. I have breasts, a waist, an ass.

Some men think that's what they want until they see me naked, and then they change their minds. Or they talk to me after about losing some weight, going on a diet, exercising more.

Sebastian has already seen me naked, though, and his

eyes told me he had no complaints. It only strengthened his resolve to fuck me more.

He did mention me exercising more, but it had nothing to do with my weight, rather my stamina—that I can get behind.

I take a deep breath. This is about one night. He's not going to want to fuck me again after tonight. Those are his rules. He isn't trying to date me; he isn't trying to trap me permanently. It's just about one night of sex. One night where we are anything but ourselves.

One night to remember forever.

I stare at myself in the mirror. I'm a wild child. I don't do makeup or dresses. I don't usually curl my hair or wear heels. In fact, I had to call down to the gift shop to see if they had any. Luckily for me, they had one nice pair of black strappy heels.

This isn't me, I say to myself as I look at half of the makeup and curls in my hair.

Tonight it is. It only makes me want to dress up and wear more makeup. I want to impress Sebastian. I want his jaw to drop, his eyes to bulge, his heart to race frantically when he sees me. I want him to not be able to keep his hands off me. I want him to fuck me against the door because he can't wait until after dinner.

I take the makeup remover wipes and clean my face from the black smudges. Then I start again with a renewed sense of purpose. My hands don't shake this time. I'm in control. I'm going to look like a freaking goddess that he can't resist.

There is a gentle knock at the bathroom door twenty minutes later.

"There's no rush, just want to make sure you're okay," Sebastian says through the door.

I smile. It's been two hours since we decided on this plan. I've never spent this long getting ready before. I've also never looked hotter. Every inch of me has been shaved or waxed. My hair has never been this curled. My makeup is flawless. The dress is one of Oaklee's she slipped into my suitcase somehow. It fits too tightly, but that only makes it more perfect. I stand in the heels full of confidence. Tonight I won't stumble, I won't fall, I won't make a fool of myself. Tonight is going to be perfect.

I take my time walking to the door, for one to ensure that I don't stumble, and two because Sebastian's voice sounded just a little nervous, a little needy, and a little greedy. I like Sebastian King a little off-kilter.

I open the bathroom door. Sebastian is standing in the opening with a bouquet of exotic flowers in his hands. I don't notice his reaction right away because I'm too busy drooling at how well he wears a suit. I remember back to the wedding, how well his tux fit him then.

But this is one of his own suits, and it looks like it's been glued to his biceps, his stomach, his thick thighs. His hair is styled but not overly so. His beard has been shaved into perfect stubble. The only part of him that isn't completely perfect is the cast around his ankle and the crutches leaning against the wall behind him.

Finally, I notice his reaction, and it's nothing like I expected. I can't read him. It's like he's gone into shock or something. His expression is blank. His eyes are blank. His mouth doesn't drop open like I expected. He doesn't even move to hand me the flowers.

"Sebastian? Are you okay?" I try to hide my worry, but I can't. Not after everything we've gone through together. He could be having a heart attack or something for all I know.

He exhales and comes to life in a split second. "No, I'm

not okay, but it has nothing to do with a stroke or whatever you must be thinking. It has to do with how incredibly beautiful you are, Mrs. King. How hard it's going to be to sit through an entire meal with you and not be able to touch you like I want."

I grin, pulling my bottom lip into my mouth. I don't think he could have said more perfect words to me.

"We don't have to go to dinner," I say.

He steps forward, not at all hobbling on his ankle that must throb every time he puts any weight on it. But the way his eyes shine as he watches me tells me he doesn't feel any pain. The only pain he feels is in having to wait to have me.

He holds out the flowers to me, and I take them, inhaling a deep floral breath.

"Yes, we do have to go to dinner." He reaches out and strokes the side of my face with his knuckles. "You're going to need your strength for what I have planned for you."

My eyes darken, and I have an insatiable ache between my legs. "I thought you only fucked women once?"

He shakes his head. "I said one night, not one fuck."

I suck in a shaky breath. *No, I will not let him affect me. I will not let him make me nervous.*

"Are you ready, Mrs. King?"

I nod. "Yes, Mr. King. The sooner we go to dinner, the sooner we can come back..." I let my hand trail down my chest, and he watches.

"Jesus, you're mean," he growls into my ear.

"You're the one who insists on dinner."

He clears his throat and then holds out his arm like a gentleman. I hook my arm through his, thankful to have his arm keeping me on my feet as I walk in heels for the first time in years. Sebastian is steady on his feet even though one is in a cast.

"You sure you don't need your crutches?"

"I'm sure."

Sebastian deposits the flowers in a vase he's already prepared, and then we are walking out of the room toward dinner. The anticipation is killing me; I can't wait until we walk back into the room after dinner.

It's only for one night. I have to remember that, because if I don't, I'm going to let Sebastian ruin me. I'm going to let him take my heart, and that can't happen.

Maybe it will help me remember what happened that night. Sebastian seems to think us getting married was my idea, but if he knew my past at all, he'd know that is the last thing I would ever suggest to anyone.

We head into the empty elevator, and Sebastian hits the button for one floor up where the restaurant sits.

Nervous tension fills the small space as the doors close. Every nerve in my body is shooting off, begging to be touched, begging to go back to the hotel room and fuck. Dinner is going to be a struggle unless I get a little taste first.

"Kiss me," I say.

He looks at me but doesn't move.

"Please, kiss me," I beg, my voice heady and needy.

I grab his neck, not giving him a choice, but his lips were already halfway to crashing down on mine. He tastes fresh, minty, and hot. My tongue licks over his, pulling the kiss deeper. My lust demands that he doesn't stop with just this kiss, tempting him until he can't resist me.

The elevator creeps up. *Please, get stuck. Please*. I don't need a bed. I'm just as happy getting fucked against the wall of this elevator.

But the doors do open on the top floor. Sebastian grabs both of my cheeks, pulling my face away to end the heated kiss. I breathe hard and fast, while he seems barely phased.

"Not fair," I whisper.

He chuckles quietly. His eyes glance down between us, and I follow his gaze until I see his hardness straining against his zipper. "Oh, Mills, I'm definitely affected. But I still want to have dinner with you first."

I shake my head. "You're supposed to be an asshole. I might just want to keep you as my husband, otherwise."

"Trust me, Mills. When I'm through with you, you won't want to keep me. But you might want more than one night with me," he breathes on my neck before taking my arm in his and leading me off the elevator like nothing just happened.

We walk side by side to the hostess stand.

"Mr. and Mrs. King," the hostess says without asking for our names. "I have the private room all ready for you. If you will just follow me."

My eyebrows shoot up. "Private room?"

Sebastian kisses the back of my hand. "Only the best for my wife."

We follow the hostess to an outdoor patio. Turns out the private room is an outdoor terrace with a small intimate table for two overlooking the ocean, romantic lights hanging overhead, and roses everywhere.

I blink back tears. "You did all of this for me?"

"I arranged it. I didn't actually decorate the space myself. Don't give me too much credit."

Sebastian pulls out my chair for me and then sits across from me. I try to catch my breath. No man has ever done anything remotely this romantic for me.

"Stop," Sebastian says with a grin. "This is all pretend, remember? Tonight we aren't ourselves. We are pretending to be married, so go all in."

"So you won't be yourself later? You'll be pretending to

be good at sex, because if last time was any indication, it was very forgettable."

He chuckles in his deep and sexy way. The way that makes my stomach do somersaults.

I look around but don't find any menu. Our glasses are already filled with champagne.

"We're breaking our healthy vacation rule?"

"We're breaking all the rules tonight."

I blush. "And what are we eating?"

"Does it matter?" His gaze is heated and electric.

Nope, it doesn't matter at all.

My question is answered, though, as our waiter brings over some heavenly smelling bread. I don't do carbs very often, but I'm eating everything in front of me tonight.

"Welcome, Mr. and Mrs. King. Tonight, we are doing a tasting of the chef's menu created especially for you. Do you have any allergies or preferences I should be aware of?"

I shake my head, as does Sebastian.

"Excellent. Enjoy the bread and champagne. I'll have another course for you soon."

I hold up my champagne glass, and Sebastian mirrors me. "To breaking all the rules."

The corner of his mouth lifts in approval. And then we clink our glasses together before taking a sip, not breaking eye contact.

"So what are we going to talk about on this extravagant date that just prolongs what we both want?"

Sebastian's eyes light up. "We talk about who we wish we were."

"What if I'm perfectly happy with who I really am?"

"You're not. But even if you are completely content, there must be some part of you that you wish you could change. Something you've always wanted to try or do."

"Astronaut," I say immediately.

"That's hot. I'm married to a smart astronaut." He scrapes his teeth over his bottom lip and practically purrs at me.

"Yes, you are, and I'm about to leave on a mission soon, so we better make tonight a night to remember."

He laughs at my role-playing. I don't know why I said astronaut. It just sounded fun and as far away from my actual life as possible. "What about you, hubs? What's your story?"

His jaw twitches, and then he says, "Bartender."

I raise my brows up, and my grin stretches across my face. "Really? I chose something original, and you chose bartender?"

He shrugs and then sips his champagne. "Maybe I'm looking for something more ordinary. Or maybe I think bartenders are sexy, and you'll find me sexy if I'm a bartender."

"Well, you're in luck, I do find bartenders sexy."

Course after course comes out after that. I continue to pretend to be the nerdy astronaut, while he pretends to be the sexy bartender. Neither of us mention our real life. We keep that separate. He's right, it's fun to be someone else for a night under the stars with the ocean waves crashing in the distance.

But even with all the pretend, neither of us can stop thinking about what is going to happen after dessert is over. So much so, I'm starting to get second thoughts. Not about the sex, but about protecting my heart.

"I'm going to the restroom a minute," I say after I finish my dessert. Not because I have to go, but because I need some space to think.

Sebastian nods.

While I'm standing to go into the restroom, all the lights in the hotel go out. Suddenly, I'm standing in the darkness with only the moonlight lighting the small patio.

"Sebastian?" I ask. I can no longer see him, but I feel him move close.

"Don't think, just be."

Then his lips find mine in the darkness, and I forget about my doubts. I forget that I shouldn't be falling for him, and I just fall.

"Fuck me, Mr. King."

"Oh, I plan on it, Mrs. King."

The lights flicker back on at our declaration. Then we race to get back to our hotel room. As much as I'm okay with fucking him on the balcony or in the elevator, we both still prefer the bedroom.

23 SEBASTIAN

I should have had us eat dinner in our hotel room. There is no way we will make it the one floor down before I devour her. Her taste is so addicting, more addicting than any drug I've ever taken.

I know I have to be careful with her, but I crave sex, I demand all of her.

I saw the doubt in her eyes before she got up from the table, thank goodness for the darkness to give me a chance to change her mind. If she turned me down tonight, I'd go insane. I need her more than I need oxygen. She's my sole focus.

Millie slams against me while the elevator doors close. My ankle throbs as I'm putting too much weight on it, but I don't care. I'd cut off my leg if it meant fucking her.

The doors open, and we keep our mouths locked, stumbling hard into the hallway wall opposite the elevator.

"Ow," Millie groans.

I bite her bottom lip, giving her an entirely different kind of pain to complain about. I'm rewarded with the most delicious moan that runs from her lips and hits me straight in the cock. These last few days together have been torture not getting to fuck her, but now, it's finally happening.

Millie pushes me away and then jumps into my arms, wrapping her legs around me. I grab her ass in my hands, thankful to have her in my arms. This will be so much easier to get her back to the bedroom as fast as possible so that I can have my way with her.

My ankle can barely hold my own weight, though, and her's sets me off balance entirely. I slam her back into the wall, trying to keep us upright.

She pants against my lips. "I need you, now."

Her words are enough to get me to fly. I don't know if I literally fly, levitate, or teleport us to the hotel room, but somehow we make it there in record time. I rest her back against the bedroom wall, not wanting to let go of her.

"God, you are the sexiest minx I've ever seen," I kiss down her face, over every ounce of caked-on makeup, as my hand rides up her thigh to grip her ass.

Our kisses are hungry and unstoppable. I kiss down her throat, begging it to make more intoxicating dirty sounds, but somehow, that gives her a second to think—a second to realize what we are doing.

"I—I can't," she says suddenly.

I stop kissing her neck but don't remove my hand from her ass.

I stare at her in the eyes. I'll honor her wish, if this is what she really wants, but I can see it's not because she doesn't want me. She's terrified.

The entire time I've known Millie, she's been the most confident person I know. But right now, she looks timid— like she wants to crawl into a closet and lock herself away from the world.

I think I know why, and it kills me. If she ever tells me

the truth, I'm going to kill the bastard who made her feel this way.

But I'm not going to let the monster take away a moment meant to be pure ecstasy.

"Talk to me, Mills."

She bites my lip, and I know I'm not getting another word out of her.

"Do you want to fuck me?"

"Yes," she whispers.

"What's stopping you?"

Again there is a flash of doubt behind her eyes. "I won't hurt you," I whisper.

"I know, that's not it..."

She hugs her middle. She doesn't think she's enough.

Jesus, this woman is more than enough. She's more magnificent than any woman I've ever seen. She risked her life to help me. She took me on the craziest adventures. She got me to marry her somehow that night. I have no doubt that it was her that caused us to be husband and wife. At first, I wanted to yell at her for it. But now, I'm beyond thankful to her.

If she doesn't want to fuck me, then fine. But I refuse to let her think less of herself. I refuse to let whatever haunting words another man has said to her play in her head while I do nothing. If I do anything, I'm going to ensure that my words replace his.

Thunder rolls overhead, and I hear the pitter-patter of the rain pick up again. It had stopped momentarily during our dinner but must have started again. This time I don't curse the rain. I welcome it.

I tighten my grip on her ass. "Hold on."

I walk determinedly outside with her still in my arms.

"Sebastian! What are you doing?" she squeals as I

throw the door to our balcony open, the rain immediately pelting us with its heavy drops. It won't take long until we are soaked—*perfect*.

"Sebastian!" She pounds her fists against my chest, trying to get me to let her go so she can escape the drumming rain.

I'm determined, though. Nothing is going to make me let her go, not until she understands something. I'm more determined to make her see the truth than I am to fuck her, which is the absolute opposite of how I should feel. I shouldn't be emotional about my fake wife.

Another crack of thunder sparks overhead, and I push those thoughts out and focus on my goal.

"Will you stop squirming?" I say.

"Will you get us back inside before we add getting hypothermia or struck by lightning to the list of things that have gone wrong on this trip?"

I smirk. "The odds of us getting struck by lightning are like a million to one."

She shakes her head, trying harder to get out of my arms. "No, not if you are outside on a high balcony during a thunderstorm. The odds are like one in ten."

I laugh. "Stop fighting me, and I'll tell you why we are out here. Only then will I let us go back inside."

She stops squirming and hitting me. I walk us over to one of the lounge chairs. I sit down with her straddling my lap, and then I take the sleeve of my shirt and wipe over her eyes.

"Stop! You're going to get my makeup all over you."

My eyes slice through the rain to her, telling her to stop fighting me.

She does.

I keep wiping until all the makeup is gone from her

face. "You don't need this. You're the most gorgeous woman without it. You don't need to hide behind it."

I grab her ankles and remove each of her heels. "Just like you don't need these."

She sucks in a breath as I grab the back of her dress. "And you don't need this dress." I rip it open at the back but don't remove it. My point is made.

"Do you feel my cock?" I ask, knowing that she can feel how hard I am for her as she straddles my lap.

She nods her head slowly, heat flowing through her body, making her cheeks flush. I'm sure her panties are soaked, and not from the rain. But I won't push us any further than this unless she wants to, even if she gives me the biggest case of blue balls that have ever been recorded.

Her hands curl around the back of my neck, stroking my hair between her fingertips.

"You're smart and sexy and adventurous," I say.

She breathes in all of my words, considering them.

"Let go of all the words that hurt you. Let go of the past and just be present with me now."

She exhales sharply.

"You are the most confident person I've ever met. Don't let go of that version of you. That part of you isn't pretend, no matter how much you think it is. I've seen the confident, brave woman. The woman who risked getting stung by a deadly bee to help me. That woman isn't afraid of anything."

She bites her lip, and I think I've gotten through to her, even though I suspect I've ruined the mood. Fucking in the rain isn't nearly as sexy as it is in the movies. In real life, it's wet and cold and uncomfortable.

Her hands leave my body, and then she grabs the straps of her dress and slides them off her shoulders. Then her hands push the rest of the fabric down until it's bunched at her waist.

I can't breathe. My mouth falls open, and rain drips down my face blurring my view of her fucking incredible body.

"Fuck me, Sebastian."

24 MILLIE

Sebastian King is a player. I know that. I know that he knows how to feed me lines to get me into bed.

But when he spoke, it didn't feel like a line. It felt like the truth. Maybe I'm naive, but I want to fuck him. I want this. I want to feel like his queen, if only for one night. So I push all my doubts and insecurities out of my head, and I let the confident, smart-aleck Millie take over.

"Fuck me, Sebastian. And this time, make sure I remember." I nip at his earlobe as I elicit a deep throaty growl in response to my demand.

I expect that he's going to take me here in the rain. I shiver, though.

"Oh, I will. But first, I need to warm you up."

He scoops me back in his arms, somehow not missing a step even though he's walking on a cast. A cast he wasn't supposed to get wet—*oops*.

He devours my mouth again as he carries me back inside. I've never felt this beautiful, this wanted. I don't know how Sebastian was able to read between the lines. *How was he able to figure out that I'm not this confident woman when it comes to men?* Somehow, he did exactly what I needed.

He tosses me down on the bed and then walks calmly into the bathroom. I stare at his soaked ass and shirt clinging to his back as he walks. When he returns, his shirt is off. Water droplets cling to his sharp chest, and he has two towels draped over his shoulder.

I reach out to take one from him, but he shakes his head. I lay back in anticipation as he uses one of the towels to wipe the water from my face, then down my neck. I suck in a breath when he rubs the towel over my bra, my nipples hardening, wishing there was less fabric between us. I never realized that a man taking care of me like this is the sexiest thing a man has ever done for me.

I'm in heaven as he continues down my body, over my underwear, and then down my legs. My mouth runs dry as he finishes, then steps back and dries off his chest while never breaking eye contact.

I'm practically naked in front of him, in my bra and panties with my dress around my waist. I've flaunted my naked body in front of him before, but I've never felt this exposed. He sees beyond my flesh. He knows my fears and anxieties without me speaking them. I don't know how but him trying to take care of me makes this experience all the more incredible.

"Don't worry, Millie. When I fuck you, there won't be anything gentlemanly about it." He grins, and if my panties weren't already soaked, they are now.

And then he's undoing his pants and pulling them down until he's naked and glistening from the rain still against his skin. I try to keep my eyes from descending down his body, but I can't help it. And when I see his cock, I panic.

He's impressive. He's a sex god. He's charming, and I'm—

Sebastian leans down and kisses me, stopping me from finishing my thoughts. His tongue sweeps into my mouth, claiming me as his, causing my tongue to swell and my lips to tingle from his touch.

"Don't think about anything except that kiss."

My brain floods with images of that kiss. I burn the image, the taste, the touch, the feeling into my head. There is no way I'll forget this night.

I regret drinking those glasses of champagne during dinner. I don't want anything to impede my ability to remember.

"Strip," Sebastian says as he sits on the edge of the bed.

I sit up as his appreciative eyes travel down my body. I unhook my bra, immediately, letting the wet material fall to the floor. I know my boobs look good, but the rest of me has more curves than most men accept as beautiful. I let my dress and panties fall next, and then I hear Sebastian gasp.

"Come here." Sebastian hooks his finger at me as he lays back. I walk over to him, he grabs my hips, and then I'm straddling his face.

"I've wanted to eat you out since you strutted around naked after leaving the hot tub. I've been dying to know what you taste like."

I've never had a man eat me out before. I've never had a man go down on me. I've never had a man make me come from his tongue.

I should tell him. I tense. My thighs straighten, keeping his tongue from diving into my body.

His eyes flicker to mine—*he realizes the truth.*

"Tell me," he commands.

"What?"

"Tell me. Once you do, you'll be free of it. It will be just words. I'm about to devour you, and I sure as hell won't stop until you come. I don't care about the failure of men before me. I don't care if they were too dumb to taste you here. Too inexperienced to make you come. Say it so that you can be free."

"I've never had a man go down on me before."

"Good girl."

And then his tongue sweeps over my clit. It's like a shot of lightning through my entire body. I jolt at the explosive touch.

Sebastian grabs my thighs, keeping my body against his mouth as he hums lightly, adding vibration as he licks me.

I grab his hair, holding on as the pleasure intensifies. I never realized that having a man lick me like this could be so good. I lose my mind as he continues torturing me with his tongue.

My body tightens more and more with each lick, until my thighs are clenched around his head. I'm not sure he can breathe with me over him like this, but he doesn't seem to care. And I—I can barely think.

Please, remember this.

He changes everything when he pushes two fingers into my slit. I gasp as he fills me with his fingers. His tongue dances over my clit as he moans over it like it's the most delicious thing he's ever tasted.

"Sebastian," I whisper, suddenly going quiet. Everything stills for a moment, even the rain and thunder stops cracking.

I swear I can hear my own heartbeat. I can feel the blood flowing between my legs in gentle pulses. It's the quiet before the storm.

And then, the storm lets loose.

I arch my back, and my body convulses, rattling as an orgasm rolls through me like thunder. I yell out Sebastian's name as my body shudders.

"I've never felt..." I pant.

Sebastian smirks beneath me. "There is a reason they call me the king."

I laugh and blush before rolling off him. But he grabs my hip, stopping me from rolling all the way away from him.

"I'm not done with you yet, wifey."

My heart races when he calls me wifey, but I quickly shut it down. *This is just about sex, remember heart? Just sex. No feelings. Feelings lead us to get hurt.*

He rolls me onto my back as he grabs a condom and sheaths himself before settling between my legs.

"No man has ever made me come before—thank you." I like sex. I like it because it makes me feel powerful. It makes men weak. It makes men want me. But that's the only reason, not because it's ever felt this good for me.

He smiles at me with his crooked grin that makes him look like a boy instead of a man. "You're about to come twice in one night."

"Sebastian, I can't."

He growls at me. "You can—trust me."

I nod. I do trust him, and that's beginning to become a problem.

His thumb presses over my sensitive clit. There is no way I'm ready to come again. But Jesus, my body responds to that one touch. And then he's pushing inside of me.

"Holy fucking Sebastian," I say as he fills me to the brim.

He chuckles—it's deep and masculine and relaxes me.

He pushes further in, stuffing me completely, and that's when I realize he's not all the way inside me.

"Kiss me," he moans as he lowers himself over me.

I kiss him. I focus on the kiss, letting it consume me. That is until he thrusts, and my body soars.

"You're mine, Mrs. King," he growls against my ear.

I've never liked being claimed. I'm an independent, modern woman. But when he goes all caveman like this, I want him to do it again.

"Say it."

"I'm yours, Mr. King."

"And?"

"You're mine." *At least for tonight.*

And then everything changes. He's no longer the gentleman; he's the king. He pounds into me like he owns my body. His thumb plays my clit like it belongs to him. His tongue dips into my mouth like it's our millionth kiss instead of our tenth.

Our bodies are like magnets, pushing and pulling together as Sebastian thrusts harder and faster. He demands everything from my body, not letting this be anything but incredible. My body is going to remember every thrust, every look, every moan. I'll remember it all because he burned it into my memory.

My body is sizzling with need, but I'm still greedy for more. I grab his ass, sinking him deeper inside me. He responds by pushing my legs back until there is no way he can thrust any deeper, until we feel completely connected to each other.

I feel the undeniable need to speak—to explain to him what he's doing to my body. To tell him how appreciative I am. But I can't form words. All I can give him is breathy cries and moans of pleasure.

"I know," he whispers over my lips before pulling them roughly into his mouth.

And then it happens. Sebastian's body goes rigid, my body explodes, gripping him harder than a vice grip, my orgasm pulses around his cock. It's an experience I've never had before. Sebastian gave me two unforgettable experiences in one night. *How will my heart survive letting him go?*

Sebastian resumes his rocking into my body. His growl is penetrating my broken heart and fills a spot in my soul as he releases his own orgasm.

I'm used to men who pull out immediately feeding me some garbage about how good it was and then falling asleep snoring moments later. Those men meant something to me. I expect even less from Sebastian, my fake husband.

What I don't expect is for him to stay inside me far longer than necessary, like he can't bear to pull out and end the intimate side of our relationship.

"Do you remember?" he asks, referring to the first time we must have done this.

I shake my head with heavy breaths.

"Me neither," he says, stroking my face. "Which is a damn shame, if it was anything like this."

I feel the same way. I'm sure our first round of sex was good, but I didn't realize until now exactly what I was missing out by not remembering. Now I do, and it feels like an enormous loss.

Sebastian pulls out, and as he does, a loud, ominous crack of thunder booms through us like Mother Nature isn't happy with our separation either.

Join the club, I think to myself.

Sebastian gets up and goes to use the bathroom, and I wait for my turn in it. There are two bathrooms in the suite, but all my stuff is in this one. I don't want to have to walk down the hall to the other one.

Sebastian stands over me just as I'm about to roll off the bed for my turn in the bathroom.

"Where are you going?" he asks.

"Bathroom."

He shakes his head. "You're not escaping that easily."

He grabs me by the midriff and pulls me back into bed with him. He has a washcloth, and he takes his time cleaning between my legs. Then he pulls my back to his front before draping us with the covers.

He's spooning me. This was the last thing I expected him to do.

My heart hammers as he holds me—somehow, this feels more intimate than the actual sex.

"Tell me about your darkness," he says into my hair.

And for the first time in forever, I want to.

25 SEBASTIAN

I feel Millie's heart racing against my chest as I hold her. Her breathing hasn't slowed, and she's still hot. It does nothing to help me regain my composure. Even after going to the bathroom and coming back, I still haven't returned to my normal in control state.

I've never felt anything like I did when I entered Millie. It was like I was coming home, becoming grounded in a way I didn't know was possible to feel with another person. She filled some part of me that I didn't know was empty.

And now I'm spooning and snuggling with her in bed—something I never do. I'm not doing it out of obligation. I want to hold her—all night or maybe even longer than that...

I want her to talk to me. I want to know what she's thinking. What she's feeling. What she desires. What she needs.

However, I know the most important place to start is her darkest secret, the man or men who hurt her. We are in our thirties. She should have had dozens of orgasms by dozens of men by now. She should have experienced a whole world of men. Instead, she found the assholes. No wonder she calls me that—it's her defense mechanism.

"Tell me about your darkness." I choose my words carefully. She can tell me anything. My words make no assumptions that her darkness is another man, but if I had to guess, it is.

A man she dated treated her wrong.

Her father abused her.

An uncle touched her.

Something happened that caused her to not be able to experience an orgasm with a man—until now.

I feel a strange, wicked pride knowing I was the man to end her dry spell, to conquer the darkness that she has yet to share with me. But I don't focus on that. I want to hear her. I want the truth.

This is completely out of character for me. Usually, I just bang women and send them on the way, usually the same night, definitely before breakfast.

But I crave every word Millie is going to say. I want her to want me, to need me, to let me help her. I shouldn't want to. It feels too much like therapy, like work. I'm not a therapist, but I might as well be because the work I do is therapy. But I never bring my work home. Until now.

I'm not sure I've earned her words yet, so it doesn't surprise me that she doesn't immediately spill all of the dark things that have happened to her. A real husband would already know, but I'm just the fake stand-in helping her escape her past.

I hold her in my arms, hoping it brings her enough comfort to talk. I've heard enough people spill their guts to know that the most important part is just being patient, just being there for her to open up when she's ready.

My fingers wander to her spine, and I trace down it,

watching as chills roll through her body with a shudder, bringing life back into her.

"I'm here. I'll wait all night. And if that isn't long enough, I'll wait as long as it takes. Even if we aren't together anymore."

She sucks in a breath, like she's sucking in all my words and using them for strength.

I suck in a breath too because if she's about to tell me what happened, then I need to be prepared for the monster she is about to call out. And I'm going to want to kill that monster.

Millie is the most confident person I've ever met. At least, that's what she exudes. She's confident and adventurous and fun, but it's all an act. It may be who she wants to be, but it's hiding the truth. It's hiding the lack of confidence, the pain that someone caused her.

Maybe she's able to play so confidently because her darkness isn't that vast. Or maybe she's an actress in real life. Tomorrow when we head home, I'll learn who she really is—her job title, where she lives, what she does in the real world. But I don't care about any of that, because what we experienced here was the real us. The parts of us that matter, that we hide from the world. Hopefully, we can take more of these parts back to the real world instead of just having to pretend.

"I don't know if I could pin it on one moment or a series of moments," she starts.

And suddenly, I can't breathe. My mind goes to all of the darkest of places—she was raped, abused, tortured. I'm not going to survive her words.

"I've never had a particularly bad experience with men. Never had a man take things too far. Never been hurt by a man. Never been abused—nothing like that."

I exhale a breath and grip her tighter, like that will somehow protect her from ever being hurt.

I want to talk, to tell her to continue, but the silence is easier for her to fill if I don't. So I wait for her to continue. I'm patient, and eventually, she does.

"But I've never found a relationship that was particularly amazing either. Never found that once in a lifetime kind of love that people talk about."

I hang onto her every word, wanting to know more. I'm an excellent listener. I have all the patience in the world, but I've never struggled so hard to keep my mouth shut as I am right now.

"I thought I had found it. Numerous times, with numerous men. But each time, I was wrong."

I kiss her shoulder, rewarding her for talking, but she still hasn't told me anything specific. *I need details, Mills! I need to know whose ass to kick.*

"Every time I thought I'd found my happily ever after, something happened—a car accident killed the first man I thought I loved."

My heart breaks for her.

"I guess I became broken, numb to the world after that. With each man I was with after, I tried so hard to be perfect. I tried to have the perfect relationship, afraid that if I wasn't enough, it would be taken from me."

She cries, I feel her warm tears falling onto my arm wrapped around her front. Still, I don't let myself comfort her beyond holding her.

"I thought I was enough to keep them. I tried to be the perfect partner. I lost weight or gained weight to be beautiful in their eyes. I learned to cook fabulous meals and would be exactly what they wanted in bed. Sometimes I was wild; other times, I was innocent, adventurous, whatever it was they craved. But it was never enough to keep them. Eventually, they all left."

She sucks back a sob. I squeeze her as tight as I can.

Just get it all out, baby. Get it all out.

"I know I'm not good enough to be in a relationship. To get married. I would never make a good wife. And I can't handle any more heartbreak. But thank you for giving me a night where, for once, I felt worthy."

I can't take it anymore. She may not feel she was abused. But whatever these men did to her, it was borderline abuse. They wrecked her confidence. Destroyed her hope for a real relationship. And I won't have it.

I turn her toward me until we are lying on the pillow eye to eye. What I have to say is important, and I need her to start believing my words. It's the first step toward healing. I take her hands in mine.

"Millie, you weren't the one who failed in your relationships—they were. Those guys weren't worthy of you. Even the guy who died, he never even gave you an orgasm. That's not love. That's not romance. That's a man who doesn't realize your worth. Millie, you are incredible, and you would make an incredible wife someday if that's what you want. Don't let any man or any past relationship tell you differently."

My heart throbs as I speak. I could be that man. I could be the man who shows her her worth. Who values her above everything else. Who loves her.

Now that's just crazy, my mind reminds me. *You're a bachelor for life. Millie might make a great wife, but you would make a terrible real husband.*

"Do you hear me?"

She nods.

"Do you believe me?"

"Yes."

I kiss her sweetly on the forehead, but it's as much for me as it is to comfort her.

"Now, tell me about the man who keeps texting and calling you, the man you are afraid of. What of him?"

Her eyes flick to the phone on the nightstand like she just now thought of him, and I curse myself for bringing him up and ruining this moment, but I need to know. I need to know who she's running from.

"He's an ex."

"Did he hurt you?"

She shakes her head. "Trust me, it was me—not him that broke us up."

I frown. I know deep into my heart that it wasn't Millie who messed up the relationship. She's not capable of doing anything wrong, anything to make a man leave. But I know now isn't the time to argue.

"It's him you're running from, right? He's the reason we are going to be fake married for six months? So you can show him that you've moved on, and he'll leave you alone?"

"Yes," she breathes. "Will you help me?"

I pull her to my chest. "I'll do anything for you. If it means staying married for longer than six months, I'll do that too."

She shakes her head, but this time, I don't let her speak. I might just need this relationship to last longer than six months myself. Already, I can't imagine the pain at her leaving.

26 MILLIE

Last night was...it was...*holy fuck*.

I can't describe how I felt. I can't describe how I feel now. I just can't...

It was beyond incredible. No man has ever fucked me like that—in a way that was both about fucking and, dare I say it, lovemaking.

Sebastian King fucked me hard and fast, but he also made love to my body, caressing and stroking it until I bent to his will. Until I wasn't in my head anymore. Until all I could feel were the thousands of tiny explosions dancing all over my body as I came.

I came—during sex with a man.

I thought I was incapable. I thought I just couldn't. I thought...well, I thought I wasn't worthy of an orgasm. That Mother Nature decided that because of all the fucked up things I've done that I would never orgasm with a man. It was the world's way of keeping me away from men because I wasn't good for them, and they weren't good for me.

But what if I was wrong?

What if I just hadn't found the right man?

There is a loud knock at our door. I squint my eyes open. I'm exhausted after our round of fucking last night.

The pounding doesn't stop. Sebastian must be a heavy sleeper because his naked ass doesn't stir at all.

I sigh and then grab one of the hotel's white robes before slugging to the door and opening it.

"Mrs. King, I'm here to take your bags down. The car is here to take you to the airport."

"Shit!"

"Mrs. King?" the young bellhop says.

"Um...give us five minutes."

"But the car—"

"Tell the car to wait."

I close the door gently in his face and then run back to the bedroom. I stop abruptly when I see Sebastian sleeping so peacefully stretched out on his stomach, completely naked in all his glory.

I bite my nails as I smile at him, remembering everything. I may not ever remember our real first time together, but there is no way I'll ever forget last night. I'll file it away to relive over and over and over and over again.

And hopefully, Sebastian is up for breaking his little rule—it's the least I can do to thank him for staying married to me a little longer.

But that's for later, right now we have to get to the car and to the airport.

"Sebastian," I grab his ankle and shake it, but it does nothing. He doesn't move.

"Sebastian!" I holler louder as I round the bed.

"Sebastian!" I yell even louder as I shake his back.

He turns and smacks me right in the nose.

"Jesus," I curse as my eyes water, and I see stars.

"Oh my god, Millie. I'm so sorry!" Sebastian jumps out

of bed, and tries to access my nose, but I don't lower my arms.

"I'm fine. We have to go, though." My words are muffled as my hands cover my mouth and nose.

"Let me see," Sebastian says, gently touching my wrists.

Slowly, I lower my hands, and the look of concern on Sebastian's face intensifies. His eyes darken, his jaw twitches, his forehead wrinkles as his thumb traces the bridge of my nose.

"The good news is it doesn't look broken. The bad news is it's bleeding and most likely going to bruise."

"We have to pack. Our car to the airport is here," I say, sounding nasally, the taste of iron spilling onto my lip.

"First, you need to put some ice on your nose and eye." Sebastian heads to the kitchenette, hobbling on his cast, and I follow after, tilting my head back to keep the blood from dripping everywhere.

"Sit," he says.

I do, and then he hands me a bag of ice to hold against my face. I move to get up. "Stay," he says, blocking me from getting up.

"But we have to go."

"I'll take care of the packing. You take care of that nose."

I nod as a sneaking smile spreads. I don't know how Sebastian thinks he won't make a good husband someday. He's such a sweetheart.

After that moment, though, the rest of the day goes to hell. Our car leaves, assuming that we changed our flight, so we have to take a crowded bus that only had two seats left on opposite ends of the bus. We were late for our flight and had to change to a flight that flew through Seattle and then on to Los Angeles, which meant we didn't have first-class seats together anymore. Instead, we both sat in two middle economy seats on opposite sides of the plane.

By the time we landed, we had barely spoken to each other all day. We were crabby. And we hadn't talked about the future at all.

We had an agreement that we'd learn all there was to learn about each other as we flew back home. We'd tell each other the truth about ourselves.

Instead, we weren't even close enough to talk. And as we ride back in the back of a cab to Sebastian's house with his crutches between us, I feel like the high we were on before we left is gone.

The world is back to being against us.

The truths we are supposed to share, stay hidden.

I think back to the other part of the night—the part that was equally as special and memorable as the sex part. The part that was tender and kind and intimate. Sebastian looked into my soul and found the darkness.

He thinks the guys I've been with are the problems.

My phone buzzes, and I stare down at the text message from my ex.

Sebastian thinks the stalker is my problem.

"We're here," Sebastian says.

He climbs out and wheels his suitcase up to the elevator. I follow with my backpack. Once inside the elevator, there is no spark. Nothing moves us from the misery we feel. When the doors open onto the top floor and Sebastian leads me to a door, I hope everything will change once we get inside.

And it does, but not because Sebastian suddenly starts talking to me, but because I learn one truth about Sebastian. He's fucking rich. Like billionaire, I own half the town, rich. My mouth gapes as I follow him inside his apartment.

Now we are going to talk. Now is the time to discuss if we are going to have a conversation about who we are, if we are going to fuck again.

Which better be yes, because there is no way I'm going to survive living under the same roof as him if we don't.

"I'm beat, and I have a meeting at six in the morning I have to get to. There are two spare bedrooms, choose either, and if there is any food in the fridge, you're welcome to it. I'll give you the grand tour tomorrow after I get off work."

My mouth falls wider. *Is he serious? Are we seriously not going to talk? About anything?*

"Um...sure, I get it. I have to be up early, too," I lie. In fact, other than packing up a few items to bring over from my old apartment, I have nothing to do tomorrow.

"Goodnight, Millie," Sebastian says, not even looking back at me.

He's back to being the asshole that I thought was all a lie. In reality, this is who he is. The man who doesn't care once he's fucked a woman. The man who is now done with me.

I stomp down the hall to one of the spare bedrooms and collapse on the bed. My face is swollen, along with my feet from being in an airplane all day. My stomach rumbles, and my face is oily. I should shower, and eat, but the only strength I have now is barely enough to lift the comforter up and crawl under.

Sebastian's right to stay away from me, though. He thinks the men in my life were the problem in my relationships. He doesn't realize the truth—I'm the problem.

27 SEBASTIAN

My alarm wakes me up at five-thirty. Like a robot, I go through my normal routine.

I put on my workout clothes and guzzle a glass of water. I meditate for fifteen minutes on my balcony before heading to my workout room. I spend ten minutes stretching, before forty-five minutes on the bike instead of the treadmill, the only change to my routine due to my fucked up ankle, and thirty minutes lifting weights.

I grab a second glass of water.

I shower.

I get dressed.

I make a cup of coffee and a protein smoothie.

Then I head out the door, using one crutch as I hobble along.

When I park at my office, I take a deep breath. My routine is so ingrained into my life that I didn't even stop to think about Millie.

Millie—my heart lurches in my chest, begging me to turn the car around and go after her. To find out how she slept last night. To feed her breakfast. To find out everything about her.

To fuck my routine.

Blow off work and just spend every waking second with her.

I want to learn what she does for a living. I want to tell her what I do. I want to ask all the questions I've been avoiding.

For a moment, I let the desire grow. I let myself think about that night. *Was that really only two nights ago that I was fucking her in a resort suite in Hawaii?*

Why didn't I fuck her every night? Now reality is going to get in the way.

Who am I kidding? Reality already got in the way the second we left for the airport yesterday. Everything that could go wrong, did. Maybe that was for the best, because if I'd sat with her in first-class and talked all the way home, I would have fallen for her. Just a little. Just enough that I wouldn't be able to push her out my head. Just enough that I would actually turn the car around and head back to her.

Instead, I've become an asshole again. I ignored her all night and didn't even wake her before I left. She's going to hate me, but it's for the best.

Just like it's for the best that I get back into my routine and go inside my office like nothing's changed. I'm the same man. I'll go to work and continue on with my normal life. I'm just helping a friend away from her ex—that's all.

I climb out of my car and grab my crutch—cursing it to hell as I use it to walk inside. I can mostly walk without the need of the crutch the way the cast was done, but the doctor told me to keep off my foot as much as possible would help it heal, so I'm trying to behave.

I hobble on my crutch inside the healing and rehab center where my office is.

"Oh my god, Sebastian, what happened?" Shelly, the receptionist, asks as I walk inside.

"Just a small accident while I was in Hawaii. I should be able to get the cast off in a few weeks."

"That must have ruined your honeymoon."

I pause. It should have completely ruined it, but after that night, everything changed.

"How is Mrs. King doing? Are you going to have a reception or a big wedding to celebrate?"

Jesus, what's with all the questions? I run my hand through my hair, the back of my neck perspiring a little as I think about how to answer her question.

"No, we liked the spontaneousness of the wedding. I don't think we will have a big reception or anything."

Shelly pouts. "You should. I'm sure your wife would love to have a big wedding to celebrate. And I want a chance to hook up with a sexy groomsman." She bats her eyes seductively at me. I know she doesn't mean anything by it; Shelly is like another sister to me.

"We'll think about it," I say to get away.

I frown as I hobble along to my office. The rest of my day will go better. Shelly is nosy, that's all.

However, news of my wedding and ankle spreads around the office until even patients are coming up to me congratulating me and wanting to hear the story of how I broke my ankle rescuing my wife.

Eventually, Shelly got me to spill, and then she blabbed to everyone until I eventually had to lock myself in my office to get any work done. My day is usually about answering emails, taking meetings, ensuring the staff has everything they need and are up to date about the latest techniques to help our patients.

I also handle the financials. We're a non-profit that helps people. My salary barely covers my car payment, not that I need it. My family owns a restaurant chain, several bars, and a few hotels. Money isn't an issue. And money wouldn't get me out of bed every morning anyway.

But by lunch, I've had enough. When another loud knock raps my door, I decide it's time to work from home the rest of the day. I can't handle any more questions about Millie. *How did we meet? How did I propose? How did I break my ankle? What does she do for a living?*

The questions are endless.

I hop on my one good foot to the door to turn away whoever is at the door. When I throw it open, I realize that I shouldn't have opened it.

Kade and Larkyn are smiling at me with knowing expressions on their faces.

"What are you two doing here?" I ask my brother and sister-in-law. Kade works in an office building uptown, taking care of the part of the business that makes money. And although Larkyn runs the non-profit with me, she doesn't usually come into the office but a couple of times a week, usually preferring to work from home where she can be near her kids.

"Taking you out to lunch."

"I was going to skip lunch and head home."

"To Millie?" Larkyn's eyes light up.

"No, my ankle is just killing me," I lie.

Larkyn frowns. "You should invite Millie to meet us for lunch. Where does she work? We can pick a spot where she can meet us."

"No," Kade says suddenly.

Both Larkyn and I snap our heads to him.

"We need to talk with just Sebastian," Kade says.

My brother and I exchange icy glances. Of all the people that I have to convince that my marriage is real, Kade is the toughest. He knows me better than anyone. He knows that all I've talked about for years is never wanting to get married.

And then all of a sudden, bam, I'm married. I know it's going to lead to some suspicions, and I'd rather be anywhere but at lunch with them.

———

"WHEN DID you and Millie start dating?" Kade asks me.

"Six months ago," I answer, lying through my teeth.

"Oh, it's so romantic. Why didn't you tell us you were dating and getting serious?" Larkyn asks.

"Because I knew you'd do this." I stare at my brother as I pop a bite of my salad into my mouth, challenging him to be different. To not criticize me, or say that my marriage is going to fail. That I'm not cut out for marriage. I already know all of this. I don't need my brother telling me.

Larkyn looks from me to Kade, completely oblivious to our battle of wills.

"We just want to know because we love you. Now, tell us about the honeymoon and the romantic way you saved her and ended up breaking your ankle," Larkyn asks.

I sigh and then go into the story of us hiking and how I ended up hurting my ankle before carrying her to safety.

Larkyn swoons, but Kade looks at me like he isn't buying it. He's not buying that I'm spontaneous, or adventurous, or married for that matter.

"Excuse me, I need to go the bathroom before we

leave," Larkyn says, getting up from her wicker seat where we are sitting on the terrace of an upscale restaurant. She squeezes my shoulder. "You have no idea how happy I am that you found someone. I was worried about you, but you look so happy now. We need to plan a get together soon so we can get to know her better."

I nod.

"I'll meet you in the lobby in a second," Kade says to Larkyn before she leaves. And then he turns to me, and I know he's about to give me a big brother speech.

"Alright, let's hear it. I'm not cut out for marriage. I'm making a big mistake. I jumped into marriage too early."

Kade just stares at me.

"Out with it."

He reaches into the pocket of his suit and pulls out a stack of papers. His life could have been my life. If I was normal. If I wasn't addicted to drugs and alcohol. I could have worked in a big office in a suit and gone to client meetings where I drank fine whiskey and made deals like him.

Instead, I wear jeans and a company T-shirt every day. My office is surrounded by patients who are detoxing and cursing and vomiting. Trust me, detoxing isn't a pretty sight. There is nothing fancy about my life. The only part of my life that is anything like I expected as a kid is the high-rise apartment. And that is just because of my inheritance.

I may not be trusted or want to work in the family business, but that doesn't mean that I haven't earned every drop of money that I inherited. I just earn mine by staying sober and keeping out of the newspapers, while Kade earns it by working hard in a fancy office.

If Kade only knew the truth, that technically I'm not sober anymore. I broke my ten-year sobriety, and that's what led to me making a stupid decision and getting married to Millie in the first place.

Kade tosses the papers on the table without a word. I glance down.

"What's this?"

"Your prenup."

I frown as I pick up the papers that he had drawn up for me. I don't read them over, but I see mine and Millie's full name on them. Rose—her middle name is Rose. Beautiful.

"Hey," Kade snaps his fingers in front of my eyes. I dazed off thinking of Millie.

"We don't have much time to talk before Larkyn comes looking for us."

"Why are you handing me a prenup? We're already married. And what are you doing getting involved in my business anyway?"

"The prenup is to protect you. It doesn't matter that you are married, you can still sign a prenup after, especially since you got married so fast. That, or you can get it annulled now before things get messy." He tosses a second set of papers in front of me—annulment papers.

That pisses me off. "That's all Millie and I are to you, a big joke? One you can just toss some papers at and make go away?"

"No, actually. I don't think you are a big joke. That's why I want to protect you. Because when this fails, and it will because you haven't known her long enough, you will be protected."

"I don't need a prenup!" I stand up.

Kade does, too, in his incredibly calm way. "If she truly loves you, she'll sign the prenup. It's incredibly generous and just protects the family assets you wouldn't want to give up anyway."

"You mean *you* wouldn't want to give up. You're the only one who cares about the business."

"Read it. It protects the healing and recovery center too. She could get half otherwise."

I hadn't thought of that. My life's work—Millie could take part of it. She could demand it since we are legally married, even if everything else is fake.

Kade holds the paper against my chest, begging me to take it.

"And if she signs it, you'll leave us alone. You will accept our marriage. You won't secretly be betting on when it will fail. You won't tell me I told you so if it does."

Kade nods.

I snatch the papers and head home, intent on getting Millie to sign them, but end up mindlessly driving around for a while to blow off steam.

Millie will sign them because she doesn't give a fuck about my money. And this is all fake, I try to calm myself as I drive.

But Kade is right. Eventually, this marriage will end, in less than six months in fact, and whether he says it or not, he'll be thinking it.

When I get to my apartment several hours later, I have every intent on having Millie sign it. On finding a way we can stay friends and put the physical part of our relationship aside.

And then I see her, standing in my kitchen in nothing but a towel, her hair wet from a shower.

I forget about the prenup.

I forget about how weak my heart is right now.

All I want to do is fuck her.

28 MILLIE

I should have expected Sebastian to walk in. It's six in the evening. That's when most people get off work.

But for some reason, it didn't register with me. I wasn't planning on letting Sebastian see me standing in his kitchen in nothing but a towel, and yet, that's exactly what happened.

"What are you doing?" are the first words out of Sebastian's mouth.

My heart flutters because even though his words are an accusation that I shouldn't be standing here, tempting him, his eyes are filled with desire. The tightness in his body tells me he's holding back, standing in the doorway because if he comes any closer, he's going to do something he regrets.

"Am I not allowed to shower?" I ask as I feel my pulse beating in my throat.

"You're allowed to shower. Did you come home from work early?"

"No."

He blinks, not expecting that.

"Did you just finish working out?"

"No."

His eyes slide down my body, taking in the swell of my breasts over the towel, the curve around my hips, and then down my bare thighs. I relish in the feel of his heated gaze over my body, how he appreciates every bit of my body, and I remember exactly what he did to it.

Only one night.

That's all we get. Those were his words. I try to remind my body of that, but he's turned on a desire that I don't know how to turn off.

"Why are you only now showering then?" His voice is low and deep, but I think it's more out of lust than anger. He's trying to make sense of me, trying to understand why I'm standing here in a towel tempting him.

"Because night time is when my day usually starts."

His forehead wrinkles. "What do you mean your day usually starts now?"

I shrug. "I'm a night owl. I work at night, not during the day. Hawaii was the opposite of my normal life." Everything about Hawaii was out of character for me.

He nods like he understands, and I suspect everything about Hawaii for him was also out of the norm.

"We should talk," I say.

He nods again but doesn't speak. His eyes stay locked on my body. He doesn't look like he wants to talk. He looks like he wants to devour me.

Finally, he speaks. "Go get dressed. Then we can have dinner together."

I nod and hurry to my room to get dressed. Mostly so I don't do something stupid like jump into his arms and kiss him against his will. It's clear that he still finds me attractive, but is just as much of an ass as I thought.

I gathered the rest of my things from the apartment that

I shared with Oaklee, which wasn't much. I left my bed at Oaklee's, so it was mainly just a bit more clothes and toiletries. I select a pair of jeans and stretchy top and put them on before combing my wet hair, but I don't bother blow-drying it. Then I head back out to the kitchen.

I assume Sebastian will order takeout for us, or he has a chef who cooks for him, so I'm surprised to find him standing in his expansive kitchen behind his large stainless stovetop cooking.

"You cook?" I ask.

"Yes," he says, offering nothing more than a one-word answer.

"I thought we were going to talk. That means you have to say more than one-word answers."

"We will."

Great, now we are onto two-word sentences. We are never going to get through this night.

Sebastian continues to face the stovetop as he cooks. We are going to need some alcohol to get through this night. I'm going to need it to tell him about my past and keep my desire for him at bay. And he's going to need it to loosen him up and stop making him such a giant prick.

I glance around the room but don't spot a bar or place where he keeps his alcohol. I head to the fridge, hoping he has some white wine or champagne chilled as both are my favorite.

His fridge is perfectly organized. It looks like a celeb's fridge who his giving a house tour for Architecture Digest. Like it's been organized and cleaned for a special occasion. But there is no way it is; he didn't know that he'd be bringing back a wife when he went to his friend's wedding.

I easily scan the fridge filled with lean meats, vegetables, fruit, and water. There is nothing unhealthy in his fridge. But then I spot what I'm looking for. There is a single bottle of white wine chilling in the fridge. I remove it and then go in search of wine glasses. I open almost every cabinet before finding two wine glasses pushed far into the back of a cabinet.

Seems strange for a bachelor. Most men I know who live alone have their alcohol on display or in the easiest cabinet. He must just not be a wine drinker.

I pour us both a glass, and I take a sip as I watch him work at the stove in his jeans and T-shirt that says something about healing on the front. It's not what I expected. I expected him to be wearing a suit when he returned to work. Instead, he's wearing casual clothes. Not that I'm complaining, his ass looks great in his dark jeans, but it just goes to show how much we need to have a conversation. I have no idea how he made the millions he obviously has to own an apartment like this.

Sebastian plates the food he's been hard at work at and then finally turns to see what I've been doing. He frowns when he sees the wine glasses I'm holding.

"I'm sorry if you were saving this bottle for something, I'll buy you a new one," I say as a vein pops out on his forehead.

"It's fine, I just don't usually drink wine on a Monday."

"Oh, I just thought the alcohol was needed for us to get through this conversation."

I follow Sebastian to the small two-seater dining table that I doubt he ever eats at. That is until he pulls his chair back, and I see the scuff marks on the floor where he's obviously pulled out his chair on a regular basis. When I pull my chair out, I see no such marks.

"Do you usually have dinner at this table by yourself?"

"Yes."

Back to one-word answers.

I sigh, deciding we both need some food in our systems and definitely lots of wine. The food Sebastian cooked is delicious and simple—grilled chicken, asparagus, and a green salad.

"You're a good cook."

"Thank you." And then he looks up as if he knew what he was going to see when he did. "Look." He nods in the direction of the skyline behind him.

I turn, and my breath is taken away by the view of the sun setting behind the skyline.

"Wow."

"This is why I sit here to eat my dinner every night. It's peaceful and reminds me that life is precious and beautiful. That I deserve to live a life that is full of wondrous things. And I should protect my body so I'm able to enjoy such wonders."

I turn back, realizing what Sebastian just did was more incredible than the view. He let me into a part of his soul. And he did it without a drop of alcohol needed. He was brave.

Maybe this conversation will be easier than I think.

"What do you do for work?" Sebastian asks. It should be an easy question for me to answer after he bared his soul to me. And yet, it's one of the hardest. It's embarrassing for me to say.

But I need to tell him. I lift my wine glass, needing liquid courage to be brave like he was. I open my mouth to speak, when there is a knock at the door.

My eyes shift from Sebastian to the door.

"Are you expecting someone?" I ask.

He sighs and gets up, making it clear he knows who it is. I stay in my seat as he goes to open the door. It doesn't shock me when a skinny blonde looking model waltzes into the room. It doesn't take a detective to figure out who this woman is—someone who has shared a bed with Sebastian. Someone who might have shared multiple romps in his bed with him.

The woman stops dead in her high-heeled shoes and skin-tight white dress when she sees me. "Oh, did I interrupt something? I was just coming over to drink my wine and enjoy the sunset with you. I didn't mean to intrude."

Sure, you didn't.

I fidget in my seat as Sebastian wordlessly enters the room. We agreed that we wouldn't cheat while we were married to each other, but that was before we had our one night together. Before we returned to reality. Before hot neighbors showed back up in our lives.

I don't know how to introduce myself to this woman. If she is someone who Sebastian might want to see again after we get divorced, then I don't want to insert myself as his wife. So I wait for Sebastian to decide how to handle her.

"Chloe, this is Millie King," Sebastian says, stepping around the woman and helping me out of my chair.

He used his last name as mine, Chloe and I realize at the same time.

After a long pause, he puts the final nail in the coffin. "My wife."

Chloe gasps as shock rolls over her red lips, blue eyes, and curled blonde hair. She shifts her weight nervously. "I didn't realize when we were together that you were seeing someone else."

Her voice sounds hurt. She must be a recent conquest, and my heart breaks for her a little.

"I didn't cheat. Millie and I's relationship started recently, and we fell hard. I just knew I wanted to be with her forever." His fingers tangle with mine, and I feel like we are one. It's the first time I've ever had that feeling when a man holds my hand.

"I didn't realize you were looking for a wife. If I'd known, I would have wanted more than one night," Chloe says.

Sebastian shakes his head. "I wasn't looking for a wife." He turns to look at me before he says his next words that capture my heart. "I was looking for Millie."

Yep, my heart is his.

It's all an act. He's just saying this to make our marriage look more believable and get this woman to leave.

I look over at Chloe, and I see tears in her eyes. It's clear that Chloe had feelings for him, whether or not there was ever a hope of Sebastian returning her feelings.

"I'll, uh, just go then. It was nice meeting you, Millie."

"I'll walk you to the door," Sebastian says, putting his hand on the small of her back as he leads her out.

My jealousy grows, watching the small gesture. He just told her I'm his wife, that he wanted me and no one else, and yet him touching her is what is pushing me to the edge. I grab the bottle of wine and pour myself more. I look at Sebastian's still full glass.

He returns as I hold the glass to my lips.

"I met her in the elevator."

I smile. "Is that how you pick up all your women?"

He ignores me, and I swear he can see down to my anxieties about that woman. "I brought her back here and fucked her."

I wince.

"I had my one night with her, and then I was done with her."

"It didn't look like you were done with her."

209

"She lives on my floor and works similar hours to me. She comes over twice a week, and we share a meal together, nothing more. She's just a woman I can talk to, but I only fucked her the one night. I didn't change my rules for her."

He sets my wine glass down on the table and takes my wrists in his hands.

"I wasn't finished with that," I say breathlessly.

"I'm not finished with you."

29 SEBASTIAN

I grip Millie's wrists in my hands. I can feel her pulse racing. But I don't need to feel her pulse, watch her breathing, or see the way her pupils dilate to know what she's thinking—the same thing I am.

Millie wants me. Just like I want her.

But we both feel an air of apprehension. Me, because I know what having her again will do to me. And her because she sees Chloe as a threat.

I can't do anything about my own apprehension, but I can do something to fix Millie's.

"She means nothing. She was nothing but a good fuck. She meant so little to me that I didn't even remember that Monday nights are the night she usually comes over because all I was thinking about is you."

She swallows so hard that I can see her throat bob. "You're allowed to have feelings for her. This is all pretend."

Her words are a knife to the gut, but I know they aren't true. She feels something when I hold her like this, when I kissed her, fucked her. If not, she wouldn't be jealous of a woman who means nothing to me.

"I know I am, but I don't. The only woman in the world I could possibly have feelings for is you, Millie."

She sucks in the tiniest of breaths. She doesn't want me to notice her reaction, but it's there. I notice everything about her. There is no way I'd miss her reaction to me telling her that I feel more for her. What, I've yet to figure out, but definitely more.

"Me too," she says, telling me she has feelings but no way to put them into words.

I nod solemnly. This wasn't supposed to happen. We weren't supposed to feel anything. But no matter what feelings we have, it won't change the result. We will eventually get divorced. It's what's for the best, for both of us.

"Where do you work?" Millie asks as we stand inches apart, our heated breath warming each other, her wrists still in my grasp.

"I'm half owner of a non-profit that focuses on the healing and recovery of addicts."

She smiles softly. "Such a sweetheart. You really aren't an asshole at all."

I smirk and pull her tight to me. My lips hover over hers, but not giving her the kiss that she's begging for. "I can still be an asshole when I want."

Her eyes gleam.

"What do you do?"

She takes a deep, steadying breath. "A little of everything."

"What does that mean?"

"It means I'm a wanderer who hasn't found her calling yet."

I frown at her non-answer. "What was your last job?"

"Security guard."

"Security guard? And the job before that?"

"I've also been a bartender, a photographer, a driver, and an event planner."

She really is a wanderer. Full of life and adventure. She's free. I can't handle that kind of disorganization in my life. I need order.

"My last real relationship was in college. Other than that, I just fuck women once and then move on to the next," I open myself to her.

"In the past, I've only done real relationships, no one night stands, until you. But I think you've changed me on that. I want more one nights and fewer relationships. All of my relationships have ended in heartbreak." I can feel her wounds as she speaks. I may not get all the details, but I can still feel the pain.

"I'm a control freak. I need order and the same routine every day."

"I'm messy. I like the freedom of not being tied down to any one person or job."

"I can't fuck you."

Her hands drop out of mine, and she backs away. I don't know if I let go, or she pulled them out at my admission. She grabs for her wine glass, like that might dull the sting of my words.

"Ask me," I say, stepping back into her space even though she shifts, begging for me to release her from this conversation. "Ask me why."

She clears her throat, but it comes out raspy anyway. "Why can't you fuck me?"

"I'm an addict."

Her eyes widen with surprise but no judgment.

"It used to be drugs and alcohol." I step closer again, and this time she doesn't retreat.

"I've been sober for over ten years. But I'm worried I might fall back into addiction again."

She opens her mouth to speak.

"I think I'm addicted to you." With my words, I pull her into a kiss—a desperate, heart wrenching, addicting kiss. One that I know there is no stopping. One where I will kiss and kiss and kiss until I've taken everything I need from Millie, but I won't stop until I've taken more than she's willing to give. That's the life of an addict.

I used to think it was alcohol's fault. In reality, I'm just addicted to pleasure, to joy, to life. That's why my life is regimented. But once Millie entered my life, I realized all the things I was missing.

Right now, I can't think about my addiction. All I can think about is feeding it.

Millie gasps when I let her breathe again. She's the only one with the power to stop me.

"I should stop you then," she pants heavily.

I nod. She should. I will only destroy her.

She thinks for a second then grabs onto my neck with one arm as she kisses me so hard our teeth clash and our tongues battle.

She moves to set the wine glass down on the table, but that's not where I want the wine glass. It's where I want her.

I sweep our dishes onto the floor. The clatter barely registers in my brain. I'm no longer in control; that's what happens when I become addicted. And I'm about to surrender all of my control to Millie.

I grab her hips and lift her up onto the table as I spread her legs and step between them. She finally sets the glass down behind her, less destructive and more in control than I am, and then she grabs my shirt, lifting it over my head. I work the buttons on her jeans and begin to pull them off.

"You know dresses give me better access," I say.

"I hate dresses, but if you promise me more orgasms if I wear them, then maybe I'll start."

I grin and then yank her pants and panties off before kneeling between her legs. Her eyes grow big as they watch me study her so intimately and closely.

I love every inch of her body. Every curve. Every freckle. Every imperfection. She doesn't try to hide who she is; she just is.

I grab her thighs, and then I plunge my tongue between her folds. She tastes so sweet, already drenched for me. But I want to give her as many orgasms as I can tonight. I remember how she screamed my name last time, and that sound is an addicting melody to me.

I try to slow my pace as I lick between her folds and find her clit. But I can't. Every pant she makes, every moan, every cry that brings her closer to orgasm is feeding my own addiction.

And then she's gripping my hair, screaming my name, as she comes around my tongue.

One orgasm isn't enough; I want more. So immediately I start licking again.

"Sebastian, I want your cock. Please."

I grin. She's right. I need to give her more than just my tongue.

I stand and shove her shirt up, needing to taste her breasts as her fingers fumble against my zipper.

Her nipples are hard and pointed. She's not wearing a bra beneath her shirt. I'm not even sure if the woman owns a bra, which makes me happy.

"Please," Millie says again, her voice full of need as she grabs at my hips.

I lean in close to her mouth as my tongue traces her full lips. "Be careful what you ask for, Millie. Once I start again, I won't stop."

Her cheeks blush. "Good, I don't want you to stop."

I pull a condom out of my back pocket before I push my jeans down. I sheath myself and barely push at her entrance, waiting.

"Fuck me, Sebastian. Show me how good it feels to be fucked by a King. Remind me what it's like to be claimed by a man who's addicted to me."

I give her a devilish grin. "You think you know what it felt like to be fucked by me before, but you have no idea. I was holding back. This time I'll give you everything."

I slam into her body with my last word so hard that the table she's lying on shakes roughly, her arms raise over her head, pushing back against the floor to ceiling window behind her to keep from slamming her head into the glass. I might have gone too far already.

But when the seductive gleam returns to her eyes, I know that she likes this new roughness. This animalistic desire to fuck her no matter the consequences. The uncontrollable nature of not even being able to make it to the bed down the hallway before I have her.

I thrust into her again, this thrust just as punishing as the first.

"More!" Millie screams.

Again I thrust, somehow sinking deeper into her, before pulling all the way out and doing it again and again. The wine glass shakes roughly next to her on the table.

Alcohol used to be my addiction, but I beat it. I got

clean and healthy. Millie is my new one, but I'm not sure I'll ever want to beat this new addiction.

I grab the glass and lift it to my lips.

"What are you doing?" she asks, her voice more panicked now that I hold the glass in my hand than when I started fucking her.

"I'm not going to drink."

She exhales.

"Technically, I already broke my sobriety the night we got married. And then again when Oaklee forced me to drink, but I haven't since. I have no desire to drink."

I bring the glass to her lips and pour the wine over them, letting a little spill out. I trace the cool liquid down her breasts over her nipples that somehow harden even more at my touch.

Then I lean down and kiss her. "You're my new addiction."

One final thrust sends us both over the edge into our orgasms. Millie screams my name as pleasure overcomes her senses. I roar my own ecstasy. I slow my thrusts, but at the last thrust, the table creaks.

Millie grabs my arms, and I catch her hips, but it's too late, and we tumble to the floor in a pile of broken wood.

"Oh my god," we both laugh. This destruction feels as much an end as a new beginning. A table that I've sat at thousands of times is now gone. My routine and control —gone.

We keep laughing, my head resting against her chest as we lie naked in the rubble. But it won't stop me from wanting her again and again and again.

"You said you were a night owl?"

She nods.

"Do you have anywhere to be?"

"No."

"Good, because tonight I'm going to feed my addiction until you tell me to stop."

"What if I never tell you to stop?"

I shudder, because the answer scares me.

"Then, I'll never stop."

30 MILLIE

I pant hard, still not having caught my breath as I lie naked on top of the covers in Sebastian's penthouse bedroom. The sun has started peeking up over the buildings. We haven't slept one second. All we've done is fuck.

On the dining room table we broke.

The couch.

Against the wall.

In his bed.

We've fucked everywhere.

I didn't believe Sebastian at first when he said he'd get addicted, when he said that's why he only fucks women one time. He's afraid of what will happen if he has too much of a good thing.

I understand now. But there is no way I want this to stop. It's too good. I don't want to let him go.

I glance over at him. His hard chest rises and falls as he tries to catch his own breath. I let my eyes wander down his ribbed abs, down to his glorious cock. I've never been with a man who reads my body so well, who can anticipate my desires before I even realize them myself.

Sebastian starts to roll over toward me. He cups my head in his hands and presses a kiss against my lips.

I moan into the kiss. *We have to stop.*

"Sebastian, we should talk," I say. There is no way we can fuck again. It's not physically possible to go again. And yet, I feel him growing hard against my stomach, and my own wetness spills between my legs as he continues to kiss me.

He laughs when I push against his chest.

"I know, let's talk. But you're going to have to do it while we shower, I have to get to work."

I blink at him rapidly. "You're still going to work? You didn't sleep at all."

He pulls me out of bed as we walk naked toward his large shower, complete with a rain shower head and a dozen other nozzles that all point in different directions. He turns one of the knobs, and the rain shower head comes on before he turns back to me.

"If I don't go to work, I'm going to want to stay and keep fucking you. And as incredible as that sounds, I know that I've already made you sore enough. Our bodies need a break."

He steps into the shower, pulling me with him. When I step in and feel the warm water, I feel the familiar ache, and know that he's right. We need to stop, and if him going to work is the only way, then fine.

"So, I'm guessing our one night only deal went out the window?" I tease as he grabs the shampoo bottle. He squeezes some in his hand and then massages it into my scalp.

"I want to fuck you every day until we decide that our marriage is over," Sebastian says.

I exhale. Fucking Sebastian every day for the next five

in a half months seems like heaven. Until he decides the pretending is over, then it will be hell.

"And when our marriage is over, how are you going to handle your uh...addiction problem? I don't want to be responsible for you becoming an alcoholic or something again." *Maybe we can keep fucking even after we are no longer married.*

He shakes his head. "I won't go back to drinking. I'll go through my usual process when it's time to break up. I'll do the therapy and detoxing."

"You'll detox yourself of me? How will that even work?" I ask as he tilts my head back to wash the shampoo from my hair. *How does this feel more intimate than anything else we've done all night?*

"I'll get rid of everything that reminds me of you. I'll give myself some time away from any of our mutual friends. I won't look you up on social media. I'll need a full break when this is over. It should be easy for our friends to understand since they think we will be going through a real divorce."

I nod. A complete break, cold turkey. That's what he's asking for. It's probably for the best.

"Okay. I can do that," I say.

And then he's running a bar of soap over my body, and I can barely think. My body tingles everywhere he touches.

"What about you?" he asks.

But I have no idea what he's talking about as his hand runs over my breast and down the front of my stomach. I'm seeing stars, and thinking of all the times he touched me last night.

"Millie?" He chuckles at my reaction.

"Hmm?"

He laughs and removes his hands and starts washing

himself, which is just as distracting as having his hands on me.

"What about you? What do you need from me to make this work?" he asks again.

I pause. I need this to end right now before I fall head over heels in love with him.

"Just keep being an asshole when you can outside of the bedroom, so I remember that we aren't right for each other. Point out all our differences. This is just good sex, that's it."

He nods slowly. "Just good sex. Trust me, I'd make a terrible boyfriend. And an even more terrible husband. I work all day, have a rigid routine, and then would fuck you all night. You wouldn't get any sleep. It would be a horrible life."

"Horrible," I repeat his words under my breath. But it doesn't sound horrible. It sounds amazing. I've already experienced one night of his rigid routine, and it involved him cooking for me. And the lack of sleep doesn't bother me if it means I get all the orgasms. *What could be bad about this life?*

Sebastian steps under the water, washes the soap off his body, and then steps out to wrap himself in a towel while I gape.

"So what are you going to do today while I'm at work? Are you working tonight? I never got a clear answer on what job it is you are currently doing."

It's because I was fired from my last job, and I'm currently unemployed, but that's too embarrassing to talk about.

"I'm going over to Oaklee's to chat a bit. I'll convince her we're in love but are nervous we jumped in too fast, so when we get a divorce, she'll accept it. And I'll see if she'll spill any more details about how we decided to get married in the first place."

"Good idea. You can also arrange to have your stuff moved in," Sebastian says with the towel wrapped low around his hips as he walks to the closet to get dressed.

Yea, except I already moved all my stuff in, he just doesn't realize it yet. He's truly a king, and I'm a pauper. There is no way this could ever be real. I have nothing to offer him but sex. I have no career. No money. No furniture. All I come with is a lot of baggage.

I turn off the shower and am wrapping a towel around my body when Sebastian comes back into the bathroom with a scowl on his face. He thrusts my phone at me.

"We need to talk about your stalking ex."

I look down at the phone and see the text threats from an unknown number. I take the phone and hit delete, blocking yet another new number from my ex.

Sebastian tucks a strand of wet hair behind my ear. "Don't worry, we will find a way to handle him. We should go hang out with our friends tonight publicly, make a big splash so that news spreads to him, and he realizes he doesn't have a chance with you."

I nod.

"He's not dangerous, is he?"

"No, he would never hurt me. He just wants me back."

"Well, that's not going to happen. You're mine."

———

"WHAT CAN I get you two to drink?" the waitress asks.

"Two white wines," I say, looking to Oaklee for clarification. We have shared many meals at this restaurant before, and we almost always enjoy our salads while sharing a bottle of white wine.

"Actually, uh, just water for me," Oaklee says.

I stare at her like she's just grown horns. I don't ever recall Oaklee turning down wine, which only signals I'm going to need alcohol to get through this conversation.

"Just the one glass then," I say, and the waitress leaves. I lean in across the booth. "Spill."

"What? You know I'm pregnant, I want to hear about how your honeymoon went. And how you're living with a gazillionaire in his incredible penthouse."

I did not know she was pregnant. She must have told me the night of our wedding. I attempt to wipe the shock off my face and distract her with an innocuous question.

"How do you know Sebastian is a gazillionaire?

Oaklee rolls her eyes. "Everyone knows."

I sigh. "Stop trying to distract me. You already know how the honeymoon went and living together is great, but we are so different, and everything moved so fast. I'm not sure it's going to work out. Just look at you and Boden. You've been together forever, and it didn't work out."

Oaklee turns somber.

"Are you two back together?"

"No."

"The baby is his, right?"

"Yes."

I nod, assuming already that it was. There is no way she could have fucked another man and found out she was pregnant by him after the wedding. And she's not a cheater.

"I know it would be better if we had gotten married, but I just couldn't..." She stares down at the glass of water in front of her, and I notice the tears watering her eyes.

"Oh, Oaklee." I run around to her side and hold her

again, holding her head against my chest. "It's going to be alright. It's going to be better than alright. You are going to have a baby. You've always wanted a baby, and you're going to make a great mom."

I stroke her back as she sobs a little. "It wasn't supposed to be this way. He wasn't supposed to cheat. He wasn't supposed to hurt me. After I saw them together, I just couldn't go through with the wedding. I can't be married to a cheater."

I nod. "Of course, you can't."

Oaklee sits up slowly, and I wipe the tears from her eyes.

"Don't," she says.

I frown and pull my hands into my lap. "Why not?"

"Because I have more to say." She doesn't have to finish her sentence for me to know the rest of her sentence is going to hurt me. She has the same expression she did when she told me in the fifth grade that she accidentally killed my fish she was watching for me while I was on vacation.

"Sebastian was the one who set Boden up. He got him drunk. He found the women. He bought the hotel rooms. He's the reason Boden cheated."

I suck in a breath—*asshole*. But then, I already knew that. I know that Sebastian helped his friend cheat. And yet, it seems so out of character for Sebastian. It seems strange he would throw away ten years of sobriety on one night that led to his friend cheating.

I wish more than anything I could remember that night. I wish I could remember the events that led to Sebastian and I getting drunk, getting married, fucking in our hotel room. I wish I could remember it all because I know that there has to be an explanation for it all.

As much as I want to pretend that Sebastian is a pretentious jerk, deep down I don't think that's who he really is. *But maybe I'm wrong? Maybe he can hide his true self when his cock is deep inside me, and his thumb is playing with my clit?*

"I just think you should be careful where Sebastian is concerned."

"I get it. I'll be careful." I look away from Oaklee as I try to remember what happened. I try to reconcile the man who saved me and shares a bed with me with the man who would get drunk and help his friend cheat.

"Wait..." I say, as I realize something. "How long have you known you were pregnant?"

"Since two weeks before the wedding."

"So, at the bachelorette party and after the wedding, you weren't drinking?"

She shakes her head. "No, I replaced a lot of the wine and champagne with sparkling apple juice."

"So, the alcohol you made us drink in the limo wasn't really alcohol?"

"Correct."

"How drunk were Sebastian and I the night we got married?" I ask, hopeful that maybe Sebastian didn't actually drink. Maybe it was all a false assumption, and there is another reason we don't remember.

Oaklee shrugs. "You seemed pretty drunk."

I sigh. Nothing about that night makes sense to me. I stare down at my wedding ring. But it led me to an incredible guy. One I would have never spent time with if it wasn't for our mistakes that night. So I don't regret it, even if I have to give him up eventually.

Still, I should tell Sebastian what I know about that night, about not drinking in the limo. At least that will make him feel better and might trigger something about that night for him.

Right now, though, I have to be a friend. Sebastian may not be in my life for much longer, but Oaklee will be in my life forever.

I hug her again. "Come out with us tonight."

She smiles. "I'd love to. I want to see and hear all the stories about how you and Mr. Filthy Rich ended up together."

I lean my head against hers. *You and I both.*

My phone buzzes, and I don't have to look at it to know who it is.

"Is Trevor still trying to find you?" Oaklee says, her voice shaking a little.

"Yes."

Oaklee hugs me tighter.

"Don't worry, Sebastian will protect you. He has more than enough money and resources to protect you. Tell him to hire a bodyguard, though. You know Trevor, and he won't stop."

I nod, agreeing. But I'm afraid as soon as Trevor is no longer a threat, that will be the end of Sebastian and me. There will be no reason to stay together. So getting Trevor out of my life as quickly as possible no longer seems like the best idea.

31 SEBASTIAN

I have everything arranged. I was supposed to pick Millie up at the condo at seven, and then we were going to meet everyone at the club for dancing and drinking. Well, everyone but me will drink. I'll focus on my new obsession —Millie.

I pick up my phone to text Millie. I smile when I see her programmed into my phone as 'Wifey.'

ME: Hey, wifey. I had a problem come up at work. I'll be twenty or thirty minutes late to pick you up. Looking forward to tonight.

WIFEY: Hey, Hubby. I'm actually on my way back from Oaklee's. I'll just Uber to you, and then we can drive together. That way we aren't late.

ME: Perfect. See you soon.

. . .

AND YET, I feel a tightening in my chest at the thought of Millie coming here. This is my baby. This is the best of me. I don't want her to see the best of me. I promised her she'd see me as nothing but a jerk outside of the bedroom. Tonight was supposed to be the start of showing our friends how incompatible we are.

"Sebastian, you're needed in room eleven," Shelly pokes her head in.

"Can't Jade handle it?"

"She went home for the day."

I sigh. So much for wrapping up my day before Millie gets here.

———

"IT'S OKAY, get out the anger if you need. Destroy the furniture. Rip apart your pillow. Do what you need to do, but don't give up. Your life depends on it. Don't you dare give up," I say to Zach, one of our newest patients.

He's nineteen—an adult by most people's standards. But I was younger than him when I started drinking, when I got addicted. And I can tell you, there is nothing about being a nineteen-year-old addict that makes you an adult. He needs help, and that's why we are here—to get him help. Without us, he'll be thrown in jail or end up dead if he keeps using like he is.

He grabs his chair and throws it against his bedroom window. It doesn't break, though. He isn't the first who has tried to break a window while staying at the rehab center.

"You're angry. I can understand that. Get your anger out; you'll feel better."

He glares at me, and I know he's about to turn his anger on me. He doesn't want to be here. He doesn't realize he has a problem, and we can't hold him here. I just hope he'll realize that he needs to be here.

He starts toward me, ready to bulldoze me over to escape. I stand firm, balancing on my good foot, and when he gets close, I wrap my arms around him and hold on for dear life.

At first, he fights, hitting me hard in the mouth, and I know he's knocked a tooth hard enough that it's bleeding.

"Shhh, it will be okay. It sucks, but it gets better. I just want to hug you, not restrain you." I soften my hold, showing that he can go if he wants, I won't physically stop him.

He hesitates. And then he collapses into my arms, a ball of emotions and tears and apologies and curses.

Zach grew up in a group home. He's been on his own since he aged out last year and most likely hasn't been hugged much in his life. That's all he's looking for—human connection.

We stand like that for a while. And after a bit longer, I get him to agree to go to a therapy session and to take our boxing class to get his anger out. Only when he's finally settled down, do I leave him with one of our therapists.

I have no idea how long I was in that room, but I suspect that Millie has been waiting for me for a while.

I sigh, hobbling out of the room, knowing I look like a mess. I see her standing in the hallway staring at me with big eyes.

"I'm sorry I'm so late," I say.

Her eyes seem watery, and she bites her bottom lip as she comes up to me.

"Hey, are you okay?" I ask, lifting her chin to meet my gaze as she walks up to me.

"Mmmhmmm," she says, dabbing at my bloodied lip with a Kleenex.

I search her eyes and see the want as she stares at me.

"You heard?" my shoulders drop.

She nods. "I didn't mean to. Shelly sent me down the hallway to your office. I heard your voice. I didn't realize it was a therapy session. I shouldn't have overheard."

"No, you shouldn't have." It goes against patient confidentiality. And also because of the way she's looking at me now, like I'm a good person. She's seen behind the mask that I put up to keep people out. Now there is no way to put the mask back on.

"This doesn't change anything. You're still an asshole to me," Millie smiles as she speaks.

"Good," I say, even though I know she doesn't mean it. She saw the best of me, the kindness and tenderness I have when I'm working with patients.

"Does that happen a lot?"

"Yes. We have therapists and doctors who are better at helping people. But sometimes my job is convincing people they should be here in the first place. And to deal with them when they get physical. I don't want my staff to be in danger, and I don't like drugging patients to calm them down. I must look like a mess, and I'm really sorry we are going to be late."

"You look like my Sebastian. And I think everyone will understand why we are late."

"Nope, they won't understand because everyone outside these walls only sees the asshole, the playboy, the jerk. They don't get to see this side of me."

Millie links her fingers through mine, startling me, but

damn does it feel good to be connected like this. "Got it. Back to being your usual controlling mean self once we leave."

I nod as we walk outside, taking in her appearance for the first time. She's wearing jeans, a black V-neck shirt, and flats. She's not extremely girly, and she's not wearing a dress, but it doesn't stop me from wanting to jump her in the back of my Porsche before we go.

No, control yourself. We are already late.

———

WE PULL up in front of the club where we are meeting our friends, and we're over an hour late. Millie leans over to me. "Just so you know, I like you when you're caring and also when you are a prick. It makes no difference to me." And then she kisses my cheek.

I grab her wrist and pull her back to me. "Oh, yea?" I kiss her hard, yanking her bottom lip into my mouth as I nip until her lip is swollen. I drive my hand into my hair, fussing it up so everyone assumes why we were late. "I think you like it when I'm an asshole more than when I'm being sweet."

"Maybe I do." And then we both step out of the car and enter the club hand in hand. I use Millie as a crutch instead of using my actual crutches I hate.

Our friends holler at us from a circle of couches in the corner of the room as we arrive. It's mostly everyone who was at Oaklee's wedding with a few more of my co-workers I usually hang out with.

"You finally made it! Now, you can cover our drinks, you asshole," Boden shouts at me as he raises a glass from his seat.

I feel Millie glare at me. "You invited Boden?"

"Yes? He's my friend, and I thought we were trying to get Oaklee and him back together."

She shakes her head. "You're an idiot." She pulls away and goes to talk with Oaklee.

I run my hand through my hair, messing it up even more. My shirt is wrinkled and stained with a drop of my blood, and I haven't slept in twenty-four hours. I look like hell. I guess we are going to show our friends how incompatible Millie and I are tonight.

Millie and Oaklee head out onto the dance floor, while I walk over to Boden and take a seat.

"Be nice to Oaklee and Millie tonight," I say as I sit.

Boden rolls his eyes. "When am I anything but nice? And Oaklee's my ex. I'll be nice but not friendly. We're over. There is nothing that will cause us to get back together."

"Why? What happened?" I don't understand how you go from wanting to marry someone to not wanting to be in the same room with them.

Boden takes a swig of his beer. "Really? The king of one night stands is asking me why I don't want to give my ex a second chance."

"I'm not that guy anymore. I'm married now, remember?"

Boden laughs. "Okay, right."

"What is that supposed to mean?"

"It means marriage doesn't change anything. One woman, especially a woman like Millie, won't keep you satisfied for long. You'll be looking for something new and exciting in a matter of weeks if you haven't already."

I stand up and knock his beer from his hands.

"Hey, what was that?" Boden asks, bewildered.

"That was me holding back from kicking your ass. Don't you dare talk like that about my wife ever again. I'm not going to punch you because you're my friend, and it would ruin everyone's night, but keep your mouth shut if you don't want a black eye and a fat lip. Also, I won't be paying for your drinks tonight, so don't you dare start a tab under my name. And if you knew what was good for you, you'd leave now and apologize tomorrow if you want to remain friends."

I storm off. My rage is flowing through me. And for the first time in years, I want to drink. I want to pick a fight. I want—

My eyes catch Millie out of the corner of my eye, dancing, swaying her hips to the music. And then she sees me. And her body changes. Her eyes tell me to come to her. She'll fix it.

I want her. More than alcohol or fighting or fucking one night stands. I want her. This doesn't feel like any other addiction I've had. This doesn't feel shaky or reckless or controlling. This feels warm and welcoming and calming.

I head to where she's dancing with Oaklee. Millie whispers something in Oaklee's ear, and Oaklee walks away so it's just Millie and me.

We don't speak. Millie just leans into my chest, resting her head there as her arms go around my neck, and we slow dance together even though this song is fast. For a moment, the world stops, and it's just her and me.

Our hearts beat together, our hips sway in unison, our bodies become one. Too many feelings flood through me, feelings that I can't name. Feelings I shouldn't feel for a woman who I was only supposed to stay married to for six months. We are still at the beginning of our time together, but when you have such a short amount of time with someone, every moment feels too short.

I know that time is going to move too quickly, so I try to soak up every second I can with Millie. I try to remember it all. No matter how my heart is shifting, I know I'm not husband material. I'm too broken. One slip would destroy us.

"I'm scared," Millie whispers into my chest.

Her words hit me like a punch to the gut. She can't say what she's feeling either, but her words tell me she's scared of what we are feeling—scared of the pain that we could inflict upon each other.

"Me too." I kiss her hair, wishing I had the words to comfort her. I do work healing people, helping them recover from their addictions, but I don't have any words that can comfort her.

"Sorry to interrupt, but I need Millie a second," Oaklee says, tapping me on the shoulder.

Every muscle in my body is screaming to hold onto Millie and never let her go, but reluctantly, I run my hands down her arms until only our fingertips are touching, and then I let her go.

I watch as Millie and Oaklee head toward the bathroom until they are out of sight. Then I head back to where our group is, but Kade corners me before I make it back.

"Did she sign the prenup yet?" Kade asks.

"I don't give a damn about the prenup. I don't need her to sign it. We aren't getting divorced, so it doesn't matter anyway." My words aren't true, but what I mean is that Millie won't take half my money. She doesn't care about my money.

"Sebastian, I'm just trying to protect you. She needs to sign the prenup. I saw your little spat earlier. You may not plan on getting divorced, but it could still happen. Even the best of marriages, couples who are deeply in love still end up divorced. Love isn't always enough."

I push past him, the anxious desire to quell my anger returning. I head toward the bar as old habits take over and sit down at the bar. I won't actually order any alcohol, but I think this was a mistake—all of it.

I can't pretend we're together.

I can't pretend we're fighting.

I can't pretend anything with Millie.

But what can I offer her?

"What can I get you?" the man behind the bar asks me.

"Club soda."

He nods and then returns a moment later with my drink. When I grab the glass, I realize how much I feel like smashing the glass. I have pent up anger about Boden. About Kade. And even Millie. I don't know how I'm going to survive five more months. Five more months when I know this is all going to end.

I glance over my shoulder, hoping that Oaklee is no longer in need of Millie so we can get out of here. But I spot Oaklee talking with Larkyn.

I stand from the bar, leaving my drink on the counter, and head toward Oaklee.

"Where's Millie?" I ask her.

She frowns. "She said she was coming to find you."

"We'll help you find her," Larkyn says, being able to read the tinge of electric fear zipping through me. I can't explain the feeling, just that something doesn't seem right.

I nod and start walking through the crowded night club. Every woman with blonde colored hair I think is her, but each face I search ends up not being her.

Did she leave without telling me?

I pull my phone out of my pocket and dial her number. It rings and rings, but no answer.

I text her, but I don't get a response. No little dots form, letting me know she's texting me back.

And then, I panic. After the connection Millie and I shared, there is no way she'd just leave. She's not with any of our friends.

Something's wrong. She wanted to stay fake married to me because she was running from her ex. All the little hairs on my body stand up, and I know she's in danger. I had one job—to protect her. And I failed.

32 MILLIE

I should have never left Sebastian.

That's the thought that keeps playing in my head as I follow Trevor into a corner of the club so we can talk.

I was safe in Sebastian's arms. And then I followed Oaklee to the bathroom so she could vent about Boden and ask for advice on how to tell him she's pregnant.

When I came out to find Sebastian, Trevor met me instead.

"What do you want, Trevor?"

"You're a hard woman to get ahold of."

I cross my arms and puff my chest, trying to act like I'm not intimidated by him. I won't let him bully me. I won't let him have any control over me. Even though we are in a dark corner of the club, we are still in public. Surely he's not going to do anything to harm me here.

"We're over, Trevor. I don't think there is any reason for us to talk or be in each other's lives. I've changed my number for a reason."

Trevor puts his forearm over my head and leans in until I'm trapped between him and the wall. Sweat forms on the back of my neck, my pulse jumps, and my breath hitches. My muscles stiffen, and my eyes dilate. My entire body goes into fight or flight mode.

I want to fly, but there is nowhere to run. All I have left to do is fight.

"We have a lot to talk about, actually," Trevor breathes over me.

"No, we have nothing to talk about. We are over." I try to push past him, ducking under his arm, but he lowers his arm at the last second, and my neck collides with his thick muscle.

Trevor grabs my left hand and jerks it up so he can inspect my ring. "This is some ring."

Chills run down my spine. I've never truly been afraid of Trevor until this moment.

"Let me go," I say calmly, hoping that if I stay calm, he'll release me.

"Not until we talk."

"You're done talking," Sebastian says, standing over Trevor. He doesn't move in. He doesn't charge. Three little words hang in the air, exuding control and power. Sebastian may not be in a suit. He may not rule a courtroom or board-room, but he demands to be listened to when he speaks.

Trevor, though, isn't phased. He continues to grip my hand, holding my fingers so tightly that I can feel the blood struggling to get through my veins to the tips of my fingers.

"Let her go, now." Sebastian's voice is deeper, gruffer, and full of threats without using violent words.

"You must be her new husband. I'll let her go. I don't want anything to do with the whore. You'll soon learn that she makes a terrible wife. I just want—"

He doesn't get the rest of his words out. Instead, Sebastian's fist hits Trevor square in the jaw.

I stand frozen as I watch my fake husband pummel my ex's face—a man I once loved.

"Don't ever talk about my wife that way again. You're going to stop texting her. Stop calling her. Stop stalking her. First thing in the morning, we will be filing a restraining order against you. Trust me, we will get it. If you so much as come into the same room as us again, you'll be arrested," Sebastian says, before taking my hand and pulling me away from Trevor.

"You're shaking," Sebastian says as he pulls me tight against his body.

I look down at my hands and realize that I am.

"Come on, we're going," Sebastian continues to drape his arm around my body, holding me tightly to him as we make our way through the bar. I can't think. I can't focus on anything.

When we get to his car, Sebastian doesn't separate from me until he has me tucked into the passenger seat. Once in the driver's seat, he takes my hand again, holding it tightly as we drive back to his condo.

"Are you really going to file a restraining order?" I ask, surprising myself when those are the first words I speak.

Sebastian parks the car in his private spot below his penthouse and then looks at me, really looks at me, like he can understand everything I'm thinking from my eyes.

I wish he could. It would be easier than having to tell him everything. I have so much to say. About the events that led to us getting married. About Oaklee. About my past.

And yet, I have no idea where to start.

Sebastian unbuckles both of our seatbelts, still not speaking. "You're incredibly brave, you know that?"

"What?" I ask, breathlessly.

"You. Are. Brave."

He kisses the back of my hand.

"You. Are. Strong."

He lifts my chin and kisses one cheek.

"You. Are. Fierce."

He kisses my other cheek.

"You. Are. An. Incredible. Wife."

He kisses me on the lips like this is the last kiss he'll ever get. It's full of desperation. Or desire. Or longing for something he knows won't last.

"Yes, I'm going to file a restraining order. I'm going to make it clear to the fucking world that you are mine. And I'll make sure that you never have to be afraid of Trevor again."

He doesn't give me a chance to respond. Trevor left me speechless by getting physical. Sebastian is leaving me speechless because I didn't realize a man could be so kind, so loving.

He grabs ahold of my hand as he pulls me into the elevator. When the doors close, I wait for him to kiss me. For his hands to roam over my body. For him to show me exactly what he has planned once we reach his condo.

"Don't look so disappointed," he says.

I look up at him.

"I'm planning on fucking you, dirty girl. But both of us are already on edge. I don't want to spark any more anxiety or fear. I want to fuck you long and slow. I want to cherish you. Take my time with you. Remind you of how incredible I think you are."

Make love to you, my mind fills in what he's not saying.

And God, do I want that. We've fucked a lot in our time together, but he's never been gentle and sweet when he's inside me. I get the sense he wants to slow time down. He wants to worship my body. And I can't think of a better way to spend the evening.

When the elevator opens, he lifts me up, cradling me in his arms as he kisses me so gently that if my eyes weren't open, I wouldn't be sure he actually kissed me. Once inside, he kicks off his shoe before carrying me straight to his bedroom, hobbling on his cast.

He lays me down on the bed. His body hovers over mine.

"You okay?" he asks, his eyes burning into my body, looking for any clue of pain that Trevor might have caused.

"He didn't hurt me."

Sebastian shakes his head. "The fact that you don't realize he did hurt you means he hurt you."

I frown but don't have time to think before he's kissing me. His tongue is darting into my mouth, possessing me, and controlling me.

I grab onto the neck of his shirt, holding him close to me, gripping it so tightly, afraid that he's going to pull away. If he stops kissing me, I might speak. I might tell him about my past, about everything. And if I speak, he won't want to keep kissing me. He'll think the worst of me.

Sebastian lifts his head from my lips.

"Don't stop," I beg.

His smile shines down on me, warming me and helping me to forget the pain. He lifts his shirt off over his head, and I no longer have anything to hold onto to keep him close except his skin. So my fingers claw at his chest, begging him to keep kissing me.

He starts his kisses again, but he doesn't kiss my lips. He kisses everywhere else, worshipping my body as he works his way down my body. He pushes my shirt up so he can access my skin.

"How did I get so lucky to have a woman like you even for a short while?" His tongue licks over the bottom of my breast and up to my nipple.

I moan in delight as he licks over my pointed tip.

"I'm not as nice and perfect as you think I am."

"No, you're messy as fuck," he grins with my nipple in his mouth before biting down. "My bathroom looks like makeup and hair products have exploded everywhere."

I open my mouth to protest and say that's not what I meant about not being nice or perfect, but Sebastian shoves his fingers in my mouth, silencing me as his tongue lingers then traces down my stomach to just over where my jeans rest.

"Suck," Sebastian demands.

I suck his fingers.

"You're also a blanket hog. I never wake up with any blankets anymore. You have all of them, hiding your naked body from me."

He removes his fingers from my mouth, and I open to tell him to give me a real critique when his fingers slip under my jeans and find my clit. His fingers swirl around, and I know I won't be able to talk except in moans and groans until he stops.

His eyes light up; his smirk grows as he watches me be teased by his fingers.

"You're also spontaneous to a fault—too trusting, stubborn, secretive, bold, merciless, forgiving." He stops teasing me and grips my jeans, yanking them down before he delivers his final blow. "And none of that makes you anything but the perfect wife."

Our eyes hold each other as I search for any part of him that doesn't believe his statement. He believes I'm the perfect wife. *Maybe because I've been so different than I was in other relationships? Maybe he hasn't dealt with me long enough to realize that my spontaneous, fun, flirtatious manner can cause problems? Or maybe he truly believes it?*

I look down and realize he's naked as he settles between us. "You're perfect, Millie. Believe that, no matter what I or any other man says."

His words hammer through me, making me chill.

He reaches back to grab a condom, but I stop him with my hand. I'm on birth control. I don't say it with my words, but he knows. There is a trust between us. I guess that's what happens when you save each other's lives. When you care about each other more than anything else.

He spreads my legs and enters slowly, like he needs to move slowly so he can remember every inch as he slides inside me. When he's filled me, he grabs my hips and holds me close before his lips land on mine again, kissing me tenderly as he rocks into me.

Every thrust, kiss, touch is all saying the same thing. The one thing we are both too scared to say—I love you.

Those are words we will never say. Because if we do, we'd have to stop pretending. Those words would make this real. And despite the feeling being true, love isn't enough. It's not enough for him to no longer be an addict, or to become spontaneous enough for a life with me.

And I'm too out of control, too purposeless, too me to ever be with him for real. Not to mention my past or how we came together.

So I cherish every moment as he thrusts in and out, knowing it might be the only time I'm ever truly loved like this.

Our orgasms come too fast. We explode, our love dancing around the room, but still never spoken.

Sebastian pulls out and then wraps his arms and legs

around me, holding me tight against his chest, not even giving me a moment to clean myself off.

"I'm not good for you, Millie. You deserve better," Sebastian whispers, telling me why he can't be with me.

"I'm no good for you either," I whisper back.

33 SEBASTIAN

That night changed things.

I no longer struggle to remember to call Millie my wife. I think about her constantly—at work, at home, in the shower—everywhere.

And my most important task has been protecting her.

I got the restraining order against her ex filed the next day. Because of who I know and how much money I have, that was easy.

I hired a private investigator to keep an eye on him and make sure he wouldn't be coming for Millie.

And I hired a security guard to protect her whenever she leaves the condo. Not that she's super happy with that or finds it necessary, but my private investigator found a prior domestic abuse call on Trevor's record. A fact that I'll keep to myself. I don't want to worry her more than necessary. She said he never hurt her, but that doesn't mean he won't to get her back.

I lean down and kiss Millie on the cheek. She rolls over and groans. "I should get up."

I laugh. "It's seven in the morning. You went to sleep

246

like two hours ago. You should sleep, I'll see you when I get off work."

She grabs my shirt and pulls me back to her. "Or you could stay." She kisses me with everything she has, which is surprisingly a lot for being completely asleep.

I laugh and pull myself away from her. "I have to go to work. And you need your sleep so I can enjoy you when I get back."

"You can enjoy me now."

So tempting.

"I can't. I have to go to work. Are you working tonight?" I ask. Millie got a job at an emergency response call center this week, which has severely reduced our time together. It only makes every moment that much more fleeting. And her security guard that much more important.

She sighs. "Yes."

"See you for dinner before you go?"

"Am I dinner?" She bats her eyelashes at me.

"Definitely." I pull her bottom lip into my mouth and kiss her harder than I intended to. Now she's starting to wake up fully.

"Go back to sleep, my beautiful wife."

She smiles with her eyes closed, pulling her sheets up higher around her neck. It takes everything I have to walk away from her and go to work—*five more months*. I have five more months to enjoy every second with her.

I need to find a way to convince her to quit her job, and I need to cut back at work so we can spend all of that time together. Because I don't have the strength to keep walking away from her like this.

34 MILLIE

"Sebastian?" I ask as I creek the door open to his condo.

No answer.

I exhale a breath as I push the door all the way open. We have three months left until we decided to stop pretending we are married and file for divorce. But if Sebastian sees what I'm carrying in this box, he might decide to call it quits early.

A small whimper comes from the box as I flip the lid up. A ball of brown fluff jumps up and licks me in the face.

"You're lucky Sebastian isn't here, or we might already be kicked to the curb." I bob the first of the five puppies on the nose as I carry them into the kitchen.

"Where should I put the dog supplies?" Andrew, my security guard asks.

"In the kitchen. Thanks, Andrew."

He puts the bag of supplies on the counter. "Are you all set for the rest of the day?"

"Yep."

"See you tomorrow, then."

I nod with a small sigh. Trevor hasn't bothered, texted,

or called in two months. I don't know why I still need a security guard to follow me around everywhere.

I set the box of puppies down the floor, and they all start crying, trying to get out of the box. I tilt it and let them out and do my best to corral them in the tiled kitchen by moving some dining chairs and the trash can.

"Stay in the kitchen, guys. I know you're hungry. I'll feed you." I start digging through the bag of dog food and bowls I got from the shelter. I mix the food with some supplemental formula the volunteers gave me. They said the puppies could eat solid food now, but that it might help to give them some formula since they don't know their exact age or how long they've gone without their mother's milk.

"Alright, everyone, dinner's ready." I set the bowl down and wait...

One, two, three...I'm missing two.

"Looking for this?" Sebastian asks, holding up one of the puppies with a stern look on his face.

I wince and try my best cute guilty face as I reach out for the puppy in his arms.

"I didn't realize you were home," I say as the puppy nibbles on my chin.

He looks to the furball in my arms. "Obviously."

"So, you aren't a fan of dogs?"

"It's not that I don't like dogs. I have enough people to take care of in my life; I don't need more to take care of. And I particularly don't care for untrained little beasts that will pee on everything and destroy my furniture."

I hold up the puppy. "This little guy won't destroy your furniture, will you?" He licks my nose, and I smile before turning to Sebastian. "See? He agrees."

Sebastian shakes his head. "Where did you get the puppies?"

"A volunteer at the shelter called me."

"And why would a volunteer from a shelter call you?"

"Because I've fostered stray dogs and cats before, so when they can't find a home for them, they call me. The puppies will get adopted easily, but they need a little special care until they fatten up a little. They are malnourished after being away from their mother and need to be eating solid food before they can be adopted."

"How long?" His voice is stern, but he's not that pissed at me. He's just trying to hold onto his control. This isn't the first time in the last three months that I've pushed him out of his comfort zone.

"Two weeks."

He sighs. "Just keep them in the kitchen, that way we can minimize the damage."

"Um...about that..." I spot the last missing puppy peeing on the rug behind him in the living room.

Sebastian follows my gaze to catch the puppy in the act. He goes to pick up the runt. I expect Sebastian to scold him, but instead, he lets the pup lick his face before lowering him over the temporary barrier I set up to keep them in the kitchen. Then Sebastian digs into my bag of supplies, which mostly just consists of dog food, formula, and bowls.

"There's a pet store two blocks from here. I'll walk there and see if they have some puppy gates and pee pads."

"You're the best, hubby." I smile brightly, hoping it will earn me a smile before he leaves. Instead, I get a grumpy grimace.

"You're lucky I like you, wifey."

I smile at his comment before going back to taking care of the puppies. "You guys better behave, so he doesn't try to kick you out."

When Sebastian returns thirty minutes later with not

only a gate and pee pads but dog toys and adorable little collars, he obviously isn't upset they are here. He looks at them the same way he looks at me—with adoration and love. *Maybe my spontaneousness is rubbing off on him after all?*

That is until the next morning when we wake up to five very naughty puppies. But even then, he helped clean up the mess and snuggled with me and one of the pups on the couch afterward. And as I lie resting my head on his chest, I have to remember—this isn't real, and I only have three more months left.

35 SEBASTIAN

"It must feel good to have the cast off. I know you weren't expecting to have it on this long, but I'm glad we waited the extra time to ensure it healed properly," the doctor says as he removes my cast.

"Uh, yea, feels great," I say because that's what I'm supposed to say. But in fact, it feels horrible. Of course, I want the cast off, but it means I only have weeks left until the six-month time limit is up. Until we are to stage a fight. Until we are supposed to file for divorce.

Trevor hasn't been bothering Millie. In fact, he seems to have moved on and is dating another woman in his office. Millie is safe.

We've been married long enough that it won't be embarrassing when we break it off, but not too long that our friends won't encourage us to fight to stay together.

Oaklee probably already knows the truth about our relationship.

Larkyn suspects.

Kade thinks I should have already divorced her.

Boden is an idiot who I haven't spoken to in months.

There is no reason we need to keep the act up. No outside reason to stay together.

Except, my own heart. My own addiction to her.

I thought these six-months would move slowly. I thought her spontaneous and adventurous spirit would drive me mad with the need to control everything. Instead, it's brought me new life and focus on only controlling the important things in my life that keep me from turning back to drugs or alcohol.

"So you're a newlywed. That's exciting. How is married life?"

I should say it's horrible. She's controlling or she's messy or we bicker a lot, something to start the process of acting like there is trouble in our marriage. The last few weeks I've been trying to drop hints at work. Trying to say little things that bug me to Larkyn.

But every time I start to complain, somehow it comes out as a compliment. Somehow it makes it seem like we are more in love than ever. Every time I try to say how awful it is, it backfires. In the five months we've been together, we haven't had one real fight.

So instead of pretending our marriage is horrible, I just say, "It's great."

"Good, you're all set," the doctor says.

I hop off the table and put weight on my ankle for the first time now free of a cast. I'm thankful to have complete freedom during my last few weeks left with Millie.

When I get back to my penthouse, I don't expect Millie to be here. She's been working a lot in the evenings, and my appointment wasn't until after I got off work.

Shadow, the puppy that Millie ended up keeping, comes bouncing down the hallway to me when I enter. He's peed almost everywhere, ripped up carpet, chewed the legs off of two chairs, and destroyed all of my shoes, but he still makes me smile every time I see him. Another thing I'm going to miss when we get divorced and Millie takes him with her.

"Come on, buddy. Let's go get you fed."

I carry him to the kitchen when all of a sudden, Millie pops the cork on a bottle and yells, "Congrats!"

I startle, and Shadow barks happily at her as champagne spills everywhere.

"I thought you had to work?" I say with a large grin as I grab her and pull me to her as Shadow wiggles between us.

"I changed my days. I couldn't miss celebrating that you got your cast off."

"With champagne?" I raise an eyebrow.

"Non-alcoholic champagne."

"What's the point then?"

"It's fun to drink out of the flutes, that's the point. I also ordered in dinner since you know I can't cook and maca-roons, your favorite, for dessert."

"How do you know my favorite dessert?"

"I asked Larkyn."

"You've been hanging out with Larkyn?"

She kisses me, playfully. "Yea, I can see why you two are such good friends. And I get the best dirt on you."

"I don't like you hanging out with her," I say, pulling her lip into my mouth.

"Too bad. I learned your guilty pleasure is watching Keeping Up with the Kardashians."

"Stop," I say, kissing her again. And then I spot the food behind her. "Sushi? Really? You know I hate sushi."

She bites her lip to try to hold back her huge smile, but she can't. In fact, her entire body screams light, bright, and happy. She's wearing a bright blue sundress making her eyes sparkle. Her hair is loose in messy waves, and she's painted her nails a bright pink color.

"I want you to give sushi a second chance. And if you hate it, that's what the macaroons and fake champagne are for." She's so excited to have me try the new sushi that there is no way I can turn her down.

I put Shadow down, and he goes to work chewing on my shoelaces.

"I'll try, but only because I plan on eating you for dessert."

She blushes with a twinkle in her eye as she looks at my healed ankle. "I can't wait to see what you can do now that you're completely healed."

I laugh and dip her before kissing her again. "Oh, my dirty girl. I think we should skip dinner."

She pushes me back. "Nope, you just don't want to try any of the sushi I got. There is no getting out of this. Put your charming grin and lustful words away. We are eating and celebrating first."

"But my way is celebrating."

Her cheeks puff out from grinning so much as she shakes her head.

"Sit." She points to the new table we bought together after we broke the last one.

I sit, and she carries over a large assortment of sushi before sitting down across from me. I focus on looking at how beautiful and incredible she is instead of on the gross raw fish in front of me.

She pours the bubbly sugar water into two glasses and hands one to me. "To finally getting your cast off."

I clink my glass with hers.

"Now, what is it that you don't like about sushi?"

"It's undercooked and cold, and the texture and smell is..." I shiver at the thought.

She laughs. "Try this one." She picks up a piece with her chopsticks and holds it up to my mouth. She waits patiently for me to open. I would do anything she asked. All I want to do is make her happy. Maybe it's my addiction to her talking. Or maybe...

I open my mouth, and she puts the sushi into my mouth before I can finish my thought. I start chewing, surprised that it's warm, has a tough texture instead of the chewiness I'm used to, and doesn't have a strong fish smell or taste.

I swallow.

Millie claps excitedly like I just won a race or something.

"What do you think?"

"Not bad."

"Yes!" She makes a pumping gesture with her hands. "I knew I'd get you to like it."

I stare at the plate of 'sushi,' but most of it is cooked, not raw, so no wonder I like it.

"I'm not sure you can call this sushi."

"We have to start with baby steps. I'll get you to be more adventurous eventually."

I scourer over the sushi pieces. "Where are the raw ones?"

She points to the corner closest to her. I pick up my chopsticks and get one of the pieces.

"You're going to try one?"

I nod.

"Close your eyes when you do."

I scrunch my nose in confusion but do as she says, not sure how this will help. I pop the bite into my mouth, feeling the cool, salty, fishiness of the bite. At the same time, I feel her lips come down on my throat as I swallow.

I moan as the bite goes down.

I open my eyes and find Millie straddling my lap.

"What are you doing?"

"Making sure you have a good experience with sushi. Did you like it?"

"I'll eat sushi all day if it means you'll kiss my throat like that."

Her eyes darken. "I changed my mind."

"About what?"

"I can't wait until after dinner." She grabs my neck as her lips land on my mouth harshly, like there is no possible way she can get enough of my lips and tongue.

I grab onto her hips, yanking her body tight against mine as I kiss her back. I love that she's always pushing me to try new things, but right now, all I want is her—just her.

I wish I could say the words, but for now, my kisses will have to do. Kisses that I'm addicted to. These kisses are the only thing keeping me sane right now.

Her hips start moving, grinding over my lap as her body craves more.

I lift my hips, pushing my erection into her, wanting her to feel as good as she possibly can. The moment is full of frenzy and lust. This moment very much feels like before, when we broke the table.

"Don't break the table," Millie says with heavy breaths as she keeps kissing me as I lift her up.

"We won't." But I also know there is no way I'll make it to the bedroom either. I need inside her.

Thank God she's wearing a dress. And when I slide my hand up her inner thigh, I realize she has no panties either.

I spread her wetness around as I lift her up, trying to find a place to fuck her without having to wait.

Her fingers are already fumbling at my zipper, trying to get my pants down. And then she's reaching into my pants and grabs my cock.

I growl as she takes hold of me. There is no way we are making it to the bedroom.

I press her back against the wall as I push my pants down with a gleam in my eye. "Good thing my ankle is all better, so I can do this."

My cock pushes at her entrance as she holds on tightly to my body. She arches her back and moans as I push deeper.

Then our mouths are locked together again. Her hands fist my hair, and I pound into her, pushing her closer and closer to her orgasm while chasing my own. I can't get enough of this woman.

I've fucked dozens of women over the years to the point that my friends and family have thought of me as a manwhore. But none of the women I've been with come close to making me feel the way I do when I'm with Millie.

I thrust harder into her, until I'm sure we are making a dent in the wall. Her moans only grow louder, more desperate. I know her body well. I know what to do to prolong her orgasm and what to do to make her come immediately. I know how to tease her and how to please her. I know how to make her screaming angry and how to worship her. And there hasn't been one moment where I haven't loved everything about her.

I love her.

I've never said those words to a woman before. Never even thought them. But I think them now. And for the first time, I want to say them. I want to shout them from the rooftops.

I don't think while I'm thrusting inside her is the best time to say those words for the first time. So I stay silent, vowing to find the perfect way to say the words.

But I have to say something.

I wait until we've both come. Until we are both floating high and then I mutter the closest thing I've ever said to 'I love you.'

"I don't want to pretend anymore."

36 MILLIE

I don't want to pretend anymore.

Those words. He's said them before.

He's said them before...

Suddenly, it all comes flooding back.

How we ended up together.

Why we ended up together.

What the plan was.

I go white. My heart jumps to my throat. My hand trembles, still grasping onto Sebastian's neck.

"Baby, are you okay?" Sebastian asks still inside me, able to sense everything about me without saying a word.

I kiss him softly, not able to speak. Sebastian just told me that he wants more than just pretend. He just fucked me like he didn't want this to end. And I can't even speak because my thoughts are racing a million miles a minute trying to process how I remember, how I forgot.

I was drunk, so drunk. That's how I forgot.

And now I remember everything.

"Shower with me?" Sebastian asks, as he sets me on my feet.

I nod, still speechless.

He doesn't speak either as we walk toward his bathroom—both of us shedding the rest of our clothes as we walk. Sebastian turns the water on, and I get us fresh towels, needing a moment alone to compose myself.

Oaklee led me to believe that what Sebastian did that night was the problem. And at the time, I thought he was the problem. But I ruin everything. I ruin every relationship I've ever been in. Turns out, I ruined any chance Sebastian or I ever had before our relationship even started.

I hang the towels next to the shower and then step under the water, where Sebastian is already waiting for me. He wordlessly starts washing me, but I know he's studying me. I'm not usually this quiet. He knows something is wrong.

I should say something—anything. But I can't. Because I can't believe what I've done.

And I don't know how to fix it. Or if it can be fixed. I don't know...

No, I can fix it. It will be a process, but I can fix it.

But Sebastian will never forgive me. It's too much to forgive. There is no chance at more. In less than two weeks, this ends as planned. The most I can hope for is that he never finds out the truth and that he can think back to our time together with some small joy. Despite how we got together, he has become more than that. He has become my everything.

"I'm sorry—I shouldn't have said that," Sebastian finally says, and he pulls me into his bare chest.

"No, you shouldn't have."

"I'm sorry."

"Me too. If I were looking for a husband, I would choose you. I'm just not looking. That's not what I want."

"I understand." His voice is firm and strong, but there is an undertone of confusion beneath his strength. Inside, he wants more. So much more.

After we speak, everything shifts once again. Gone is the lust and charge between us. Now we are just two empty vessels headed toward the end. And our end was never supposed to end in happily ever after. Our end is just that —an end.

I can't think about what that will mean, though. Hopefully, tomorrow we can go back to some level of normalcy so that we can enjoy our final two weeks. But if not, then I'll remember tonight forever.

We both get dressed and climb into the bed.

"I don't want this to change, yet," I say.

"It won't." Sebastian pulls me onto his chest as he snuggles with me.

He says things won't change, but it has. Usually, he would have fucked me again, feeding his addiction of me, but it seems he's trying to wean off me already.

It's for the best.

Twenty minutes later, Sebastian is snoring, and I'm still wide awake, thinking about all the things I have to do. All the things I have to fix before our time is up so Sebastian doesn't get hurt.

But all I can think about is how badly my heart is breaking. *Is his breaking too?*

I know my eyes aren't going to close. I want to remember every moment of our time together. I'll sleep when he's at work tomorrow.

I run my hand through his gorgeous thick hair. "I'm so sorry, Sebastian. So sorry...I ruined everything."

A tear spills from my eye and lands on his cheek.

"I love you. And in a different world, I would stay married to you, and it would be more real than any other love in the world. But I fucked up, and now I'm just going to have to love you from afar."

37   SEBASTIAN

I hold Millie's wedding ring as I sit on the couch. She's currently in the shower getting ready to go to over to Kade and Larkyn's tonight. It's Larkyn's birthday, and Kade is throwing her a big party.

It's supposed to be the night where we fake a fight and tell everyone how miserable we are together. Then Millie will ask Oaklee if she can stay with her tonight. They will have a pity party and talk about how horrible their men are, and then eventually, one of us will file for divorce, and that will be that.

That's how everything is supposed to go. That's been the plan all this time—for six months now.

And yet, these last two weeks have been the hardest of my life. Every moment has been moving toward today. And as much as I applied the breaks, swerved, done everything I could to stop us, to slow down time, nothing has worked.

To make matters worse, Millie won't talk to me at all about us except to plan today.

She's afraid—and I can understand why. Her ex is a piece of work. The more my private investigator looked into him, the more criminal charges he dug up. I can understand why she's afraid to enter a real relationship again.

But that's what we've been doing for months now. I can't remember the last time I did pretend with her. I can't remember ever pretending. Every moment with Millie has felt real.

I twist Millie's ring around on my pinky finger, examining it. I wish it would jog my memory. I wish I would remember where I got the ring. I wish I could remember our wedding night. Maybe it's for the best, though. Because if I remembered that night, things might not have led me here.

I'm supposed to pretend we are bickering and fighting. But I can't, no matter how hard I try. Millie doesn't want to talk to me. She doesn't trust me. She doesn't trust that I love her. She doesn't trust that this is real. So I'll just have to show her how real we really are.

"Sebastian?" Millie says as she pads down the hallway. I tuck her ring into my pocket. "Have you seen my wedding ring?"

I shake my head. "Nope, I haven't seen it."

"Huh. I took it off to shower and put it on the bathroom counter, but it's not there anymore."

"I can help you look for it. But if we are supposed to be fighting, maybe it's best that you're not wearing it."

She rubs her bare finger. It doesn't look right without her wedding ring on her finger. And the way her face falls, I know she'd rather be wearing it. But I have something special planned for tonight that involves it.

"Yea, I guess you're right."

"You look beautiful, by the way." I stand and take her hands in mine, trying to get her to stop thinking about her missing ring. I kiss her cheek, careful not to mess up her hair or makeup.

"Thanks, I feel weird wearing a dress. It's not usually my style, but I know how much you like me in a dress."

"I like you in anything. Dresses are my favorite because I can do this." I lift her dress and find her cunt bare. Once again, she's not wearing panties or a bra.

She gasps as I touch her. "Sebastian, don't. I can't—"

But then she's coming. It's not a full explosion, but enough to take the edge off and give her a beautiful glow.

She blushes when I remove my hand. "You ready to go?"

She nods, her pink lips gaping, still in shock of what I just did to her. I take her hand in mine, and then we head to the suburbs where Kade and Larkyn live.

I park on the street outside the house. Millie and I haven't spoken much on the drive over. We just held hands in comforting silence. These could be our last moments together as a couple. Tonight, Millie could end up sleeping at Oaklee's, or I could end up sleeping here at Kade's.

I can't let that happen. I'll do everything I can to change her mind. It might not be fair to do this publicly, but I think it's the only way she'll listen to me—the only way we have a shot at a future. And right now, I'm not ready to give up.

"You ready?" she asks. It's a loaded question. She doesn't know the thoughts racing through my head. She doesn't know how far I'll fight to keep her, but she's about to.

I grip her hand tighter. "Yes."

Her eyes shake back and forth like she's reading my thoughts running across my forehead, but of course, she can't.

"We'll stay friends after this? Maybe meet up on some

island somewhere for a weekend or something every couple of years and just hang out? No matter what happens after tonight," she says suddenly.

I do my best to hold back my grin, but I feel it all the way in my toes. She still wants more. Whether she says it or not, she wants more. That is all I need—hope.

"Yes, no matter what, we will still be in each other's lives."

Her lips pull back into a thin smile, and then she bites her bottom lip like she isn't sure that's enough.

It's nowhere near enough, baby. Soon you'll realize you can have everything you never knew you wanted.

Once out of the car, though, I try to take Millie's hand back in mine, but she pulls away. *And so it begins.*

Larkyn and Kade's house is a nice suburban home with a large garage, plenty of space, four bedrooms, three baths. It's beautiful and homey, but not too big. It doesn't show off the true wealth that Kade has. Larkyn didn't want her kids growing up in something too grand.

There was a time when I thought a house like this would be the last thing I want. But when the kids come running at me, and I scoop each of them up, my heart all of a sudden feels empty. I've never wanted kids, never thought I'd be a good father, but I want to learn to be one. Millie would help me become a good father. And she'd make a great mother. I want everything with her.

"Millie, Sebastian, I'm so glad you could make it," Larkyn walks over and gives each of us a hug.

I watch Millie closely. I don't touch her. I don't put my hands on her. But I also won't be the one to start a fight.

"Happy birthday, sis," I say.

"Thank you!"

"Is my big brother treating you well?"

"Of course, he went all out for the party. He's out back arranging a band for dancing later."

I smile. I love that my brother takes such good care of Larkyn.

"He's spoiling me," she says.

"No, he's loving you. And you deserve every bit of it."

She lights up. "Enough about me, I want to hear about how you two are doing! It's been weeks since I've seen you together."

I keep my mouth shut, waiting for Millie to speak first. If she wants to fake a fight, here is her chance. An awkward silence spreads between us.

"Picture! I take picture," Iris says.

"Oh goodness, yes, you should get a pic of us," Larkyn says to her child.

Larkyn stands next to me, leaving Millie no choice but to stand closer to me. I put my arms around her as the squirt takes our picture.

But as soon as she's finished, Millie runs off, with some mumbled excuse about finding Oaklee.

"What's going on?" Larkyn asks, as soon as Millie is out of earshot.

I flash her a wicked grin. "I'm proposing to Millie tonight."

"I'm confused since I thought you already did that."

"If I did, I don't remember."

Larkyn's eyes widen. "I knew it! I knew you weren't together the night you got married. We weren't there, but I knew you couldn't have been hiding a woman like Millie from us. So why did you get married? Why pretend?"

I shake my head. "It's a long story, but I want to make it real."

She claps her hands together, excitedly. "Oh my god. You fell in love. I never thought I'd see the day."

"You thought I had married Millie but didn't love her?"

"Well, I thought there was some reason you weren't telling me at first. But lately, every time I've seen you two together, you are all over each other. So if you are going to propose tonight, why does Millie look like she's about to explode into a million tears?"

"Because tonight was the night we were supposed to end it."

"Oh."

"Yea, oh. Instead..." I pull out the ring. "I'm going to propose."

She looks at it closer with recognition in her gaze.

"You know where the ring came from," I say.

She frowns. "Maybe."

"Where?"

Her eyes flicker up at me. "You don't remember that night?"

"No."

She smiles. "Let's just say it's the perfect ring for you two."

"Tell me."

"Nope. Now, go win your girl. But be careful with big gestures, and don't take her first reaction as her truthful reaction. Give her time to realize that you love her for real. That will take time."

"I will."

I turn and start to head off to look for Millie and avoid Kade. I don't want to hear him yell at me for not getting her to sign the damn prenup again.

I bump into a caterer. I get tackled by Henry, one of Larkyn and Kade's kids. But I don't find Millie.

I head out back to where the band is setting up, and then I see her in a heated discussion with the guitarist.

I run over, afraid that the man will hurt her when I hear him speak. "You took half my fucking money! That makes you a gold digger!"

I step between the man and Millie. "Sir, step back."

He growls, looking from Millie to me. "You, her new husband?"

"Yes, and if you speak to my wife again, I'm going to punch you."

He laughs. "I'm done with her. Tell the Kings I'm sorry, but I can't play tonight, not with her here."

"And you are?"

"Her ex-husband, Noah. And a piece of advice from one ex-husband to you, her next victim—make sure yet get a good lawyer when she files for divorce. Which will be about six months after the wedding. That's when she knows she's been married long enough to ask for half of everything. She has an excellent lawyer."

He stomps off, and I can't process what he said.

"Let me explain, please," Millie says quietly from behind me.

I turn slowly. I notice others in the backyard, watching us closely, but I no longer care what anyone thinks. I just want the truth. I want to know my future with her isn't at risk.

"Is what he said true? Were you married before?"

She sucks in a breath and then nods. "Yes."

"And the rest?"

"True," she says without hesitation.

I look at her through a new light. *Do I even know her at all?*

Millie has her arms wrapped around her chest, and she looks like she's about to be sick.

"What else? What else haven't you told me?" My voice is angry. I can't hide it, and I can't keep everyone in the yard from noticing our fight either.

"I've been married three times," she says softly.

Three.

Fucking.

Times.

Holy shit. She's thirty. How does someone get married three times? Unless the bastard was telling the truth. Unless she really is a gold digger. Spots rich men to marry and then fucks them over with a divorce settlement. That's why she never works a real job. It all makes sense.

I take a step back when she reaches her hand out to touch me. I can't handle her touch right now. I need to get out of here. I need...

"That's what you get, you asshole," Oaklee says, coming up to support her friend. Her pregnant belly is round beneath her black maxi dress.

"That's what I get?"

"You hurt us, so we found your weakness. We got you drunk and then tricked you into marrying her so she could take half your money and pay you back for what you did. You'll lose half of everything," Oaklee continues.

I look at Millie dead in the eyes, and I know without her reacting that it's all true.

"How long have you remembered? This entire time?"

Millie swallows hard, and I realize I don't want to hear the answer.

I hold up my hand, stopping her from speaking as I feel all eyes on me. I feel the ring in my pocket—a ring of unknown origin. But one I plan on throwing into the ocean as soon as possible.

My heart has never beat faster, never been more panicked, more pained, more broken. I look at the only woman I ever imagined as my wife. A wife that will be able to take half of everything I own. She said it was pretend, but it wasn't, it was real. The marriage certificate was real. Legally, we existed. And emotionally, I fell for her. This is as real as it gets.

I thought I'd make it real tonight. I thought I'd cement us together forever.

It became real, but we won't be locked together forever.

And then I say the words that I thought I'd only say under false pretenses, but they have never been truer.

"We're over."

We're over.

I thought I was prepared to hear him say those words. But hearing them with all of the pain in his voice rips through me like an ax.

Our fight was supposed to be pretend, but there was nothing fake about our fight. It was completely real.

The crowd is quiet as we stand. They part when Sebastian heads back into the house.

I close my eyes, needing some strength before I chase after him.

"It's for the best," Oaklee says next to me.

I open my eyes, sending her a glare. "You have no idea what you've done."

"That was the plan all along, though."

"I didn't remember the plan until the other night. And he didn't deserve that."

"But—"

"We were wrong. It was a mistake. Boden did what he did on his own."

"Are you sure?"

I nod.

"Shit."

I don't have time to explain everything to Oaklee. I start running, even though I'm wearing uncomfortable wedge heels that I struggle to run in, I run.

I was prepared to say goodbye tonight, but only on good terms. Only if we parted as friends. I can't part Sebastian like this.

I see Larkyn in the house, who gives me a puzzled look then points to the front door. I'll have to thank her later. I run out the front door and see Sebastian about ten feet from his car.

I open my mouth, but if he hears me coming, he might get in the car and take off before I get to him. So I run, flying as fast as I can and I fling myself in front of him just as he reaches his car.

"Listen. Please."

"I don't need to hear any more. Not from a liar like you."

"Sebastian, just listen. It's not what you think."

"There isn't any possible explanation you could give me for not telling me you were married three times, stole money from unsuspecting men like a leech, and then are trying to pull the same thing on me. You're a con-woman."

I wince at his harsh words. I deserve that, but it doesn't help the situation. He doesn't understand why.

"And you were an asshole when I first met you!"

"I called you fat. I didn't try to steal half your wealth."

"I thought you had been helping Boden cheat on Oaklee. I thought you were a monster."

"And I thought I loved you. I guess we were both wrong."

There is a crack of lighting when he says his final sentence, followed by the rain pouring down in sheets.

Just like that, the world declares us over. *We're over*.

It's for the best.

"I'll see you in court," Sebastian says, pulling his door open to escape the rain.

"I don't want your money."

"And I don't want you."

His door slams shut, and then he's driving off.

Leaving me breathless as I stand in the rain.

I don't know how long I stand there in the pouring rain. Eventually, Larkyn finds me and brings me inside, wrapping me in a blanket.

"I'm sorry, I'll call an Uber and get out of your way."

"No, you're staying here tonight. I know Sebastian needs his space. And Oaklee doesn't seem like the best friend of yours to be around."

"But you're Sebastian's family. I shouldn't be here. Not when I hurt him."

She smiles as she hugs me. "That's exactly why you should be here. Now tell me everything."

So I do.

39 SEBASTIAN

I drove until I could find the shittiest, ugliest bar in town. The kind with cockroaches and everything is sticky where you walk. The kind that only serves one brand of beer and two brands of whiskey.

That's where I'm sitting, holding a whiskey glass in my hand filled with some cheap shot.

I haven't taken a sip, and yet, I still feel drunk.

The bartender walks back to me. There are only three other people in the bar. It's a slow night.

"Want to try the other whiskey? Or I can mix some fruity shit in it if that's what you need to get it down."

I glare up at the rude man. "I'm good."

He chuckles and then walks away.

I go back to staring at my glass, feeling the effects without drinking. I'm drunk not on the liquor, but on Millie. I'm drunk on the pain, the misery.

I realize there is no going back to my life before. Not after I've realized what I'm missing. Even if Millie faked everything, for me, it was real. And I want it. I just can't have it with Millie.

She's a liar.

A fraud.

A mistake.

A mistake that's going to take half my money. Not that I give a damn really. I don't need my wealth. I don't need any of it.

Millie was married three times.

She's a gold digger.

She remembered that night.

I wish I could remember. I wish I could understand what really happened. If I could rewind and remember, maybe I wouldn't be sitting here like a chump who just got his heart ripped out.

I can't shoot the whiskey. I can't drink. I won't do drugs. But I can find a woman to drown my misery in, not that I'll find one in this bar. It's probably why I chose it, so I wouldn't be tempted to do something that stupid.

"King?" A man says from behind me.

I turn, not in the mood to talk to anyone tonight. And when I see him, I'm really not in the mood.

"I wouldn't come any closer, not unless you want to get your ass beat again."

Trevor doesn't hesitate. He takes a seat at the bar next to me.

"I don't want to cause a fight. I'm here to apologize. I shouldn't have laid a finger on Millie."

"No, you shouldn't have." I grip the drink tighter, wishing I could drink it and not lose myself. "What do you want?"

He studies me a moment. "I'm here to talk about Millie."

"You want her, you can have her. We're through."

There's a pause and then a soft chuckle. "So she told you."

"Yea, she told me she's a fucking gold digger who has been married three times before me."

"Wait...you think Millie is a gold digger?"

"Yes. I met Noah. She took half his money. And that's the only reason she's married to me."

Trevor hangs his head low, and he shakes it. "Oh man, I'm going to regret this. I'm really enjoying watching you hang out your misery, but you don't have a damn clue what you're talking about."

"What?"

"You heard me. You don't have a clue. Millie is a lot of things. She's all over the place, wild, carefree, but she is not a gold digger. The one thing in the world Millie could care less about is money. Trust me, I was married to her for two years."

He might as well have punched me. The bastard was married to her longer than I will be.

"And why should I listen to a criminal like you?"

He laughs hard at that. "I'm not a criminal; I'm a lawyer. Your investigator must have spelled my name wrong, too. Trevor with an 'o' is me, a lawyer, but Trever with an 'e' has a nasty rap sheet. We share the same last name. I found out about it when I got mistaken for him during my bar exam, so don't kick yourself for screwing it up.

"In regards to Millie, I never hurt her physically. I would never lay a hand on a woman. We just didn't belong together, and I'm afraid I hurt her in more ways than I realized at the time. I know that, now that I'm in a good relationship, which is why I'm here."

"I'm confused. If you are in a good relationship, why did you stalk Millie?"

"Because I needed to give her this." He lays a stack of papers in front of me. "Make sure she gets them. And if I were you, I would listen to her before you throw away what you have. Millie and I didn't work out, but that doesn't mean I don't know what a catch she is. I saw the two of you together. You fit. We didn't. She was looking for a man who could tame her. But she doesn't need to be tamed, you know that."

I narrow my eyes and watch as he leaves. "And don't worry, she can't get half your money. But if you aren't careful, she'll get away with half of your heart."

40 MILLIE

I need to get up off the couch I've been sleeping on all night in Larkyn and Kade's home. I need to pick myself up. I need to start over. And I need to explain and apologize to Sebastian.

Not because I deserve forgiveness, but because he deserves to hear the truth. He deserves to know what happened. He deserves to understand the pain that led to me hurting him.

I can't sit here on this couch, and yet, I'm putting off seing Sebastian because the next time I see him could be the last time. Having Sebastian in my life, even when he's upset with me, seems better than not having him in my life at all.

And then I feel him. Without looking up, I know he's here. Apparently, today is going to be the last day I see him.

"Can we talk?" I ask as I look up at him. I should be the one to speak.

"No."

His word cuts through me. But he continues toward me even though he said no. *Does he want me to leave?* I can understand since this is his brother and sister in law's house.

He sits down on the couch next to me silently before finally saying, "We can't talk. You should talk, and I can listen."

He leans back, not giving me a clue to how he's feeling. To what he's thinking. But it's clear he won't be talking. This is my chance to come clean about everything. To tell him everything.

"His name was Gavin. We grew up together. Had that epic kind of love that you just know is going to last forever. Except it didn't." I swallow, it's been a long time since I talked about Gavin. But it's where my story starts—the first man who ever destroyed me.

"We were twenty when he proposed. We were poor. Neither of us went to college. We both worked three jobs a piece just to survive, but we were happy. We were going to have forever." My voice cracks, reliving the pain.

"I said yes immediately. We got married in the court-house that weekend. It wasn't much, but it was enough for us. But then things changed.

"Small things at first. He wanted more. More money, more stability. He tried to tame me. To convince me that we shouldn't live so spontaneously. I needed to focus on one career instead of twenty. I needed to lose weight so I was more appealing. I needed to...the needs just kept continuing, and I tried so hard to be what he wanted. I loved him, of course. I wanted to make him happy."

I stare at my hands as I talk. I'm not telling Sebastian this so he'll give me sympathy. I'm telling him so he can understand. No, I'm telling him so I can let the past go. So I can realize that although I loved him, he wasn't right for me. No man has been, except maybe Sebastian.

"Our relationship was chaos, a complete storm. I didn't realize the signs, I didn't realize I was drowning. We never got the chance to fix it, before he suddenly died. A fluke seizure while he was driving, and then he was just gone."

I close my eyes feeling the pain of the hole he left in my heart. "I struggled with him gone. I thought I needed a man to make me whole. I didn't realize that what Gavin had done to me did lasting damage. I didn't realize that what he did was abuse. I just thought I needed a man because that had been my entire life, and it was gone. Something was missing, so I tried to fill it."

I take a deep breath. "So I married Noah. But he was worse. I barely got out with the money I brought in. And I vowed after him to stay away from men. But then Trevor entered. He was actually a good man. He was smart and intelligent and settled. He worked as a lawyer and helped me focus my passions into one. He got me to work as a photographer. And as much as I loved the work, it wasn't who I was. I like to bounce around. I don't need money or status to make me happy."

I look at Sebastian for the first time. "That wasn't what this was about. I never wanted your money; I still don't."

Sebastian sits still as a statue, unmoving. He doesn't say anything. He's just listening.

So I continue.

"At first, I couldn't remember that night. I couldn't remember what happened or why, same as you. That wasn't a lie. I never meant to lie to you; I just didn't think my past mattered. I didn't want you to try to convince me that I was abused in any way. I'm not a victim. I don't need help.

"That's what I thought. I didn't realize that my first love really messed me up, that the abuse wasn't physical, it wasn't in my face every day, but it was there. It's going to take a lot more healing, but I realize that now. When we got together, we were never supposed to last, and I didn't want to heal."

I look at Sebastian again. "You were the one who helped me heal. You helped me realize that I was hurt. That my past relationships weren't healthy. And I've been getting help. That's why I've been talking with Larkyn. She's been getting me counseling."

I exhale another breath. "Here is what I remember of that night."

———

I ORDER a drink at the hotel bar next to Sebastian while we wait, hoping that soon we will hear from Oaklee or Boden to let us know they want to head to chapel to get married still. Or at least to tell us something.

Just as I get my drink, though, I see Oaklee in her wedding dress with mascara stained tears running down her eyes.

I exchange a glance with Sebastian.

"Go, I'll pay for your drink and then find Boden. Here's my number." He takes my phone and programs his number into it. "Text me and keep me in the loop, and I'll do the same."

I nod and then run to her, pulling her back into my arms. I had hoped they would work it out. They needed to work it out. They love each other. They seemed to be working it out in the elevator.

"Talk to me, Oaklee. Tell me what happened."

"I can't. I just can't."

"Shh, it's okay. What can I do to help? Do you want me

to get you a different room? Do you want to change out of your dress? Get a drink?"

"I don't know," she sobs.

I take a deep breath and walk us over the hotel desk clerk. "Can you get us a room with a double bed and have her bags brought from the honeymoon suite?"

An hour later, Oaklee and I have both changed clothes and are settled into a new hotel room. But she still hasn't talked to me.

"Where is Boden?" she asks.

"Let me find out."

I pull up my phone to text Sebastian. He types back the name of a club.

I show Oaklee against my better judgment.

"Let's go," she says.

"Why are we going to the club? Oaklee, you need to tell me what happened. Why didn't you get married? Why did you break up?"

"I'm pregnant. I told him, and he ran. He said he didn't believe it was his, and that he never wanted kids."

"Oh, sweetie." I hold her as we both cry and cry and cry.

Finally, she pulls away. "Let's go."

"I don't think that's a good idea."

She flashes me a look that says she's going, whether I'm coming or not. Boden is about to get his balls chopped off by one angry woman. I can't stop her, but I can join her. That's what best friends do.

"Let's go." I grab my purse, and then we head to the club to go chew Boden out.

The club isn't just any club. It's a strip club, which I guess shouldn't surprise me. What does surprise me is what we see. Boden and Sebastian with two women dancing over them. Both seem to be making out with the women, and Sebastian seems to be encouraging Boden to go further.

The scene stops me in my tracks, but it doesn't stop Oaklee. She marches over to Boden and slaps him square in the face and yells something at him before I can stop her.

Sebastian realizes what's happening and stands before she slaps him too.

I walk over to her and give them both a stern look. "Come on, Oaklee, they aren't worth it."

I lead her to the bar and order us both two drinks before I realize what I'm doing.

Sebastian comes up and sits next to us. "Boden's gone. You don't have to worry about him anymore." There's a pause. "I'm sorry."

Oaklee and I ignore him as I drink down my drink. Oaklee eventually pushes her drink in front of Sebastian.

"Drink this. You're a fucking asshole, and I'm not going to let you go enjoy yourself. Tonight, you are going to drink because I'm pregnant and can't drink. So you're going to. Both of you. We are going to drown in my sorrows and come up with a plan that doesn't leave me completely embarrassed to face all of my friends and family tomorrow."

"You could tell them that Boden is a cheating bastard who is skirting his responsibility to his kid?" I say. "There is no shame in that."

"I can't," Oaklee breaks. "We need something else to focus on."

Sebastian starts to open his mouth, but I give him a threatening look. *If you do anything, and I mean anything, that will hurt my friend, I will castrate you right now.*

He gives me a nod. "Boden is an asshole. I'll do whatever I can to help you, Oaklee. Just tell me how to fix this."

She glares at him. "For now, drink."

I down mine and order another. I assume Sebastian does as well because when Oaklee waves the bartender down, he brings us two more shots. That's how we continue —drinking shot after shot while we listen to Oaklee's pain.

"We need a diversion—something to draw attention away from what happened. We will say I was sick, and there will be redo at some point. But we need a different focus, something big," Oaklee says.

"Like what?" I ask.

She glances between the two of us. "Like you two eloping."

I gasp.

"Um, what now? How is that going to help anything? Or be remotely believable?"

"You two are the most unlikely people to get married. Everyone knows that. But if you got married, no one would care that I didn't."

I'm too stunned to process her words. She has to be kidding.

Oaklee ignores my response and gives Sebastian a smug expression. "You said you would do anything to help me. This is what I want."

"Okay," Sebastian says.

"Okay? What are you crazy?"

Oaklee grabs my arm. "Excuse us for just a moment." She pulls me into the bathroom, and I shake her off.

"Have you gone insane? Why do you want us to get married? How will that solve anything? I don't want to marry the guy who helped your almost-husband cheat."

She smiles. "Marry him. Save me from complete embarrassment. And then take half his money."

"What? I don't want his money."

"Okay, fine, just make him think you are going to. Get

him to sign a prenup to give you half by sneaking it in the marriage license. The man is filthy rich and a jerk. You don't have to actually take half but just put that fear into him. Show him that no man messes with us."

"Shouldn't we be hurting Boden right now, not Sebastian?"

"Are you my best friend or not?"

"I am."

"Then help me mess with him. We will find a way to make Boden pay too."

"Fine. If Sebastian agrees to it, then okay."

"Eek! This is just what I need tonight, a distraction!" She pulls out her phone to arrange a marriage license and prenup on short notice. Then she starts calling chapels and then her friend, Val, who will make sure everyone else shows up.

Meanwhile, I panic. Full-blown panic. "He's never going to fall for this. He will never sign the prenup. He will never get married. He'll get it annulled tomorrow."

"Then, we will mess with him until tomorrow."

I sigh and leave Oaklee alone in the bathroom and am immediately met with Sebastian.

"She's lost it. We aren't getting married."

He frowns. "Why not?"

"Because it's crazy! It won't fix anything."

"Maybe, maybe not. I never thought I'd get married."

"Well, I've been married three times. I think that's enough. I don't want to get married again."

He chuckles. "Perfect. Neither of us believes in the institution of marriage. So it will mean nothing, and we can just help out our friend. I fucked up, and I feel bad. And you want to help her. She's a mess. She needs this. We can get it annulled or get a divorce in a few months. But tonight, I think it would help."

"You're mad."

"I know." He leans in close. "Plus, I think it will be really fun to be married to you."

His lips brush my skin and tease me with want and desire. "I'm not fucking you just because we're married."

"Oh, but I think you will. It will be fun to play our own little game between just us."

His eyes are playful and light. He has no idea I plan to destroy him—that that's what Oaklee really wants.

I fold my arms over my chest. "You haven't proposed, and I don't see a ring, so until that happens, I won't give you my answer."

He smirks as he kneels down before me and produces a ring.

I'm stunned. *How did he come up with a ring so suddenly?*

"Millie Raine, will you marry me?"

"Yes." *Wait, yes? Did I just say yes?*

He grins and puts the ring on my finger.

"I'm going to need another shot," I say.

———

I LOOK up at Sebastian again. "We got married in front of everyone. And then you signed the prenup papers giving me half. You were too drunk to notice them in with the marriage license."

His jaw twitches, but he still doesn't say anything.

"After that, we passed out drunk in the honeymoon suite, and you know the rest. The only other part you don't know is why I kept it from you when I remembered. That was selfish. I knew I'd never be with you for real, what I had done was too terrible.

"But I was hoping to still have a tiny piece of you in my life. So I tried to change the prenup so you wouldn't have to give me anything. I tried to keep what happened hidden, hoping we could part friends. I know it was wrong, but I just couldn't bear to live a life without you in it. I'm sorry."

A long silence stretches. I said what I needed to say. There is nothing left for me to say, and when it's clear that Sebastian isn't going to speak, I say, "I should go."

"No."

I fall back into my seat like the full weight of the world just crashed down on me.

"It's my turn to talk and your turn to listen."

I bite my trembling lip and fist my hands, trying to keep my anxiety in.

"You should have told me that you'd been married before."

I wince.

"But I understand why you didn't."

He takes a deep breath. "I was wrong to not have stopped Boden. I didn't even realize what was happening, and then the next thing I knew half-naked women were dancing on us. He was kissing them and telling me about how he had cheated over the course of months. When you came to the club, I was chewing him out, not encouraging him.

"But I'm not upset with you for thinking I was. I should have never been friends with someone like Boden. And I understand why you did what you thought you did."

I feel tears wallowing in my eyes. This is the part where he says we're over again—that we can't even be friends.

"But I wasn't drunk that night."

I tilt my head, unsure of what he said.

"I knew that Oaklee and you were trying to get me to drink, so I pretended too. I was completely sober walking down the aisle, and you know why? Because when you followed Oaklee into that bathroom, a woman came up to me. She had overheard our conversation and said she had just lost her husband of over forty years. She saw the way I looked at you and said it was the same way her husband looked at her. And then she handed me her and her husband's wedding rings. Told me to marry you, that it would change my life. That it would be the best decision I ever made, and it was."

Tears are flowing now because I don't understand, and all I feel is a million emotions.

"Her words hit me like I was wasting my life. I didn't know if we would work out or stay married, but I planned to try. I vowed to live a real life, one where I might get hurt instead of playing it safe so that I wouldn't. I wanted real, not pretend. And that's what I vowed to do."

He scoots closer to me but doesn't touch me yet.

"When I signed that prenup, I knew what I was signing, and I didn't care. If you wanted my money, then you could've taken it. But I didn't think that was who you were. I saw you as someone who deeply cared about her friend, that's it."

I nod. "I'm sorry."

He lifts my chin. "I'm not. Because I fell in love with the most beautiful woman with a huge heart. A woman who pushes me out of my comfort zone. A woman who fights for justice for her friend. A woman who loves me so much that she spent all the money she had on lawyers trying to get the prenup we signed changed."

"How do you know about that?"

"I have friends who would do anything for me too."

"You mean Larkyn?"

He nods.

"So you've known this whole time? How could you forget if you weren't drunk?"

"After you passed out in our suite, Boden came back to get his things. We got into a fight. He knocked me out when he pushed me into the bedpost. My huge headache when I woke up was from our fight."

The pieces all start making sense. "And the condom?"

"Boden fucked a random woman in there while we were getting married."

"What a giant fucking cunt."

"He's no longer my friend. And if I meet him again, I'll kick his ass."

"I couldn't get the prenup changed. I'm sorry. I don't want your money, though. I'll sign the divorce papers, and I don't want your money." *I just want you.*

"About that." Sebastian pulls a small stack of papers out and lays them in front of me.

"My divorce papers with Trevor? Why do you have them?" I flip through them, not understanding, and then I get to the final page.

"Oh my god. I didn't sign the last page. What does this mean?" I'm so confused.

"It means, technically, you are still married to him. And both he and I would really like you to sign them. He would like to get married soon, and so would I."

I frown. Sebastian wants to get married. *So quickly?*

I swallow down my pain. "Do you have a pen?"

He holds one out, and I sign quickly. "I'll make sure he gets these, and we file again as soon as possible."

"Good."

"I'll have my things moved out of your condo today. But this means that our marriage was never real? The prenup never real?"

His face falls apart. "Legally, no. But us being together was the most real thing I've ever experienced. I love you, Millie. I. Love. You. I don't care how we started. I don't care about the lies or manipulation. And I don't want a fresh start. I just want us together, for real."

"I love you too, Sebastian King. I've loved you since you saved me in Hawaii. And it's been real for me this whole time too. I have some more healing to do personally, and I know we have wounds we've caused each other that need time to mend, but I want to be with you. However you'll have me."

He leans down and kisses me. It's full of everything— hope, love, a future. I could get lost in it forever.

"Well, Millie Raine, I want you as my wife. I've never known you as anything except my wife, and I'm not about to change that now." He holds out the ring that the old woman from the bar gave to him. "Millie, will you spend the rest of your life with me and one day marry me for real?"

"This is already real, but yes, I'll marry you." And then he slips the ring on my finger. A ring I never plan on taking off.

I never thought I'd get my happily ever after. I know I'm strong enough to live a happy life without it, but I'm glad that Sebastian King gets to be part of my happily ever after.

EPILOGUE

SEBASTIAN

I comb my hair one more time in the hotel suite mirror before I prepare to walk out onto the beautiful beach in Santa Barbara to get married. We considered getting married in Las Vegas, where this all started, but we chose the beach. We wanted to keep it simple, and this made the most sense.

The wedding will be small. Only Larkyn, Kade, and their kids on my side. Oaklee and her newborn baby on Millie's.

After I proposed, we agreed to live together a year. Millie didn't want to get married again until she had finished her therapy and was sure this marriage would last. I agreed that I would wait.

We waited three months. That's all the waiting either of us could stand. Millie's past no longer haunts her. And I couldn't wait to be tied to her forever.

There is a knock on the door. I look over at Kade, who is getting ready in the suite with me. The women and kids are getting ready in Millie's suite.

I glance at the clock; I have twenty minutes until the wedding still, so I don't know who would be knocking.

Kade opens the door, and Oaklee is standing in the hall-way. "Can I talk to Sebastian alone for a moment?"

Kade looks to me, waiting for my response. For a while, Kade was the only one not sure about Millie and I's rela-tionship. He wanted us to slow down. He still wanted a prenup to protect us both, but he's come around. He hasn't pushed the prenup topic in the last month.

Oaklee and I's relationship still needs more work. I was in the waiting room while Millie was in the delivery room when Eddie was born. Oaklee hasn't forgiven me for my part with Boden, and I haven't forgiven her for her plan to ruin me.

I nod at Kade, though. I know Oaklee won't ruin my wedding day.

Kade brushes past Oaklee, giving her a warning glance before leaving. Then Oaklee steps inside.

"Is something wrong with Millie?" I ask, suddenly worried that's why Oaklee is here. Did Millie get cold feet? Is she sick?

Oaklee smiles at my worried expression. "Millie is head over heels in love with you. She can't wait to marry you. She's been ready for over an hour and has almost stormed over and demanded the wedding get moved up an hour so she can see you again. There is nothing wrong with Millie."

I exhale a deep breath, relief flooding me. "Then, why are you here?"

"To apologize." Oaklee sits down on the couch in the small living area.

I sit down on the loveseat opposite her.

"There is no need to apologize. We both did what we did."

She shakes her head. "I'm going to be standing beside your wife when you get married. I need to apologize. I need you to know I have no ill will toward you. That I'm sorry for blaming you for Boden's actions. I don't want you to worry that I'm secretly trying to sabotage you."

"Thank you for apologizing. It really wasn't necessary. I know why you did what you did. And I'm sorry I couldn't stop Boden from cheating and hurting you."

She looks off in the distance, like I brought up painful memories for her.

"I'm sorry. But for what it's worth, you are a great mother and don't need that jerk in your life."

She smiles. "Thank you. And I know. So we're good?"

"We're good."

She exhales an anxious breath and then bites her lip as she stands. "I do have one surprise though planned for the wedding."

"Which is?"

"You'll see."

"Oaklee, I don't like surprises."

She opens the door of the suite to the hallway. "I know, but Millie loves surprises. Now, let's get you two married for real."

I follow Oaklee into the hallway, where Kade, Larkyn, and their kids are waiting.

"Ready?" Kade asks.

I nod.

Together we walk out of the hotel and down to the beach where a small arch sits near the ocean. That's when I realize my surprise.

The woman from the club in Las Vegas is standing under the arch. The woman who gave me the wedding rings and told me to be brave. The woman who told me to get married. The woman who changed my life.

My mouth falls open as I walk to her. "What are you doing here?"

She smiles at my shock. "Your friend Oaklee got my number at the club. She thought I might want the rings back when the marriage failed, but I knew it wouldn't. When she called to ask if I wanted to marry you, I couldn't pass up the opportunity. I'm Grace, by the way."

I pull the woman into a hug. "Thank you, Grace. You have no idea how thankful I am."

"I'm thankful the rings now belong to two people who will also be married until their dying breath."

A roll of thunder jolts us apart. I look up at the storm clouds brewing in the distance. "Not today, clouds."

But I don't have time to focus on the weather because Kade and Larkyn's kids start walking down the beach, dropping rose petals as they walk. Larkyn walks down after in a pale pink dress and bouquet of exotic-looking flowers.

She winks at me before gathering the kids to stand next to Kade.

Next come Oaklee and baby Eddie with a large flower tied around his head. She reaches me and then says, "If you hurt her, we will hurt you."

I smile. "I'm glad Millie has a friend like you."

Then I turn back toward the hotel stairs that lead down to the beach, and I get my first glimpse of Millie in her white dress, holding a bouquet of exotic flowers that matches Larkyn's.

Kade, Larkyn, and Oaklee all offered to walk her down the aisle, but Millie wouldn't have it. She said she wanted to walk herself down the aisle.

Tears water in my eyes as she walks toward me. I'm impatient, though, and meet her halfway down the beach and walk her the rest of the way.

"You look beautiful."

"So do you."

Those are the only words we can get out through the tears threatening both of our eyes as Grace starts the ceremony. She keeps it short and sweet, knowing the weather could ruin it any minute. When it starts sprinkling, she says, "Rain is good luck on your wedding day. Not that you two need it. You're going to love each other forever."

"Yes, we are," I say, looking into Millie's eyes.

"And with that, I pronounce you husband and wife."

I grip Millie, vowing to never let her go as I kiss her deeply and passionately. As soon as we kiss, the rain stops, the clouds part, and the sun finally comes out.

"Seems like the weather is happy you two finally said 'I do,'" Grace says.

Millie and I exchange loving glances. I grab Millie's hand, and we lead the charge, jumping into the ocean to celebrate getting married with everyone following us.

"So are you going to tell me where we are going on our honeymoon, yet? I've been thinking we should go back to Hawaii," Millie says.

"Nope, not telling you. I thought you were Mrs. Adventurous. You don't need to know until we get there." Although, she's already guessed the plan. We are going back to Hawaii and then New Zealand and then Australia. We are taking two weeks off, so we have time for a repeat in Hawaii and a little new adventure.

"No, now I'm Mrs. King. I can't believe how lucky I am to have fallen in love with a King."

"Not as lucky as I am that I'm married to you." I kiss her hard in the ocean, our hands find each other and intertwine, and I feel for her ring on her left finger. A ring that gave me the final push to start living my life instead of hiding in fear.

I'm about to start the adventure of a lifetime being married to Millie—an adventure that I know will never end.

———

THANK you so much for reading Pretend We're Over! If you haven't read Larkyn & Kade's story, grab PRETEND I'M YOURS HERE! Looking for a new contemporary read, check out my boxset HATE ME OR LOVE ME.

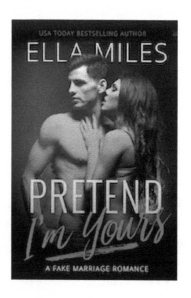

Grab Pretend I'm Yours Here!

JOIN ELLA'S NEWSLETTER & NEVER MISS A SALE OR NEW RELEASE → ellamiles.com/freebooks

Love swag boxes & signed books?
SHOP MY STORE → store.ellamiles.com

ALSO BY ELLA MILES

Dirty Addiction

Dirty Revenge

Dirty: The Complete Series

ALIGNED SERIES:

Aligned: Volume 1 (Free Series Starter)

Aligned: Volume 2

Aligned: Volume 3

Aligned: Volume 4

Aligned: The Complete Series Boxset

UNFORGIVABLE SERIES:

Heart of a Thief

Heart of a Liar

Heart of a Prick

Unforgivable: The Complete Series Boxset

MAYBE, DEFINITELY SERIES:

Maybe Yes

Maybe Never

Maybe Always

Definitely Yes

Definitely No

Definitely Forever

STANDALONES:

Pretend I'm Yours

Finding Perfect

Savage Love

Too Much

Not Sorry

ABOUT THE AUTHOR

Ella Miles writes steamy romance, including everything from dark suspense romance that will leave you on the edge of your seat to contemporary romance that will leave you laughing out loud or crying. Most importantly, she wants you to feel everything her characters feel as you read.

Ella is currently living her own happily ever after near the Rocky Mountains with her high school sweetheart husband. Her heart is also taken by her goofy five year old black lab who is scared of everything, including her own shadow.

Ella is a USA Today Bestselling Author & Top 50 Bestselling Author.

Stalk Ella at:
www.ellamiles.com
ella@ellamiles.com

Ingram Content Group UK Ltd.
Milton Keynes UK
UKHW010130060623
422929UK00003B/48

9 781951 114671